The Bones in the Pit

A Brian Sadler Archaeological Mystery

by
Bill Thompson

Published by
Ascendente Books

Books by Bill Thompson

ACKNOWLEDGEMENTS

Thanks to three people who always proof my work and offer significant comments and feedback. I appreciate my sons Jeff and Ryan for taking time from busy schedules to dive into my stories. Your help is invaluable.

Marjorie, thanks for listening during a critical important step for me: reading the entire book aloud. Thanks for tolerating the many hours when I'm writing, and thanks for your opinions and suggestions to make my books better.

I love you all.

HISTORICAL PRELUDE

Oak Island is a strange, mysterious place. It's been that way for a very long time. On the surface there isn't much to see. The 150-acre island forty miles southwest of Halifax, Nova Scotia, is covered with the oak trees that gave the place its name. Less than a thousand feet from the mainland, it's just like three hundred other tiny islands that lie in Mahone Bay. Except for one significant difference. The Money Pit.

The following information is true. In the summer of 1795 a teenager named Daniel McGinnis took a rowboat to the uninhabited island, wandered around and saw a depression in the ground. A huge oak tree with an outstretched limb stood in a clearing. Hanging from the limb was an ancient block and tackle, some people say, the kind used on sailing ships. Directly below the end of the limb was the depression. The place looked to the boy as though someone had purposely cleared some trees and dug a hole, probably a long, long time ago.

Locals frequently told stories of pirates and the area is well known to have been visited by buccaneers. Captain William Kidd was rumored to have buried a fortune in treasure somewhere in the area. People also talked of strange lights seen on uninhabited Oak Island over the years. Maybe it was a crew of pirates swinging lanterns as they hauled a chest to be hidden. Maybe they were lights caused by someone, or something, else. It is likely young Daniel McGinnis thought of those stories as he returned home, very excited at the possibilities of what he had seen.

The teenager brought two friends back the next day along with some tools. They began to dig in the middle of the saucer-like depression. The digging wasn't difficult; the ground was loosely packed, indicating someone had filled it in at a time in the past. As they dug the boys discovered other evidence that men had been here. Two feet down there was a layer of flat stones not indigenous to Oak Island. It soon became obvious they were clearing a round hole about twelve or thirteen feet in diameter. Pickaxes had been used to build it; their marks clearly became visible as the boys removed the fill dirt.

At around ten feet the boys hit logs that formed a floor. They were firmly inserted into the surrounding wall to create a platform. At this point they must have rushed to remove the logs, thinking they were close to recovering a treasure hidden below. Instead they found more loose dirt and, ten feet further down, another platform of logs.

The job was too big for three teenagers. They left the island, returned home and told a few people about their discovery, hoping to enlist help. For whatever reason they got nowhere. The townspeople weren't interested, or perhaps they feared the ghost stories and the mysterious lights on Oak Island. For years nothing further happened to the mysterious pit.

Many fascinating books have been written about what became known as the Money Pit. Between 1800 and today several syndicates were formed to excavate the hole.

At ninety feet workmen discovered a two-hundred pound flat stone with mysterious symbols carved into it. It's enticing – the code is a straightforward one and the translation is generally considered to say "Forty feet below two million pounds are buried."

Most researchers believe it to be a hoax, probably put at the ninety-foot level in the mid-1800s by men seeking to raise money for yet another treasure syndicate. Regardless of its authenticity it can play no part in answering the riddle of Oak Island – it disappeared around 1920 and no one knows where it is today.

Through boring, some reported finding evidence of a "chest" containing metal at a level around 100 feet below the surface. There also appears to be a concrete vault of some type, lined with wood or filled with wooden chests, below 150 feet.

The hole was expertly engineered to keep would-be treasure hunters confused. Much earlier than 1795, whoever built the Money Pit engineered sophisticated booby-traps in the form of at least two tunnels running into the pit from the nearby shoreline. These tunnels cause the pit to flood to sea level, around thirty feet below the surface of the island. Even in recent times when modern, expensive techniques have been employed to drain the pit, close off the flood tunnels or pump it out, nothing has worked. Lives have been lost and millions of dollars spent. So far all the work that's been done has generated no answers. Even today nobody knows anything more than the teenaged Daniel McGinnis did about what exists deep in the Money Pit. All people know is that someone went to an incredible amount of time and expense to create an engineering enigma. What does the Money Pit on Oak Island hide? No one knows.

This book builds on one of the many theories that have been postulated over the centuries since this mysterious pit was discovered.

BOOK ONE

CHAPTER ONE
New York City

The Ford pickup easily made its way down Fifth Avenue, weaving in and out of traffic as New Yorkers habitually do. Hassan Palavi knew the route well – he had practiced it every day since he received this assignment. Hassan was a descendant of a long-ago shah of Iran but he was one hundred eighty degrees opposed to the pro-USA ideals that regime had embraced. He had aligned himself politically, religiously and in every other respect with whichever terror group was in power at the moment. He was a dedicated, committed, well-trained American terrorist.

Hassan's dream was to see America crushed, on its knees and begging Muslims everywhere for forgiveness. He was willing to give anything to further that dream. And today he would be called upon to make the ultimate sacrifice. Hassan couldn't have been happier.

During a carefully timed visit that had been arranged by his Al Qaeda handlers, Hassan had been born in the United States to Iranian parents who were in America supposedly visiting relatives. He was therefore a U.S. citizen and carried an American passport. Young men this dedicated to jihad who also were full-fledged Yankees were rare – almost nonexistent. His handlers had cultivated Hassan carefully as he grew from childhood, preparing him for some critical mission down the road. Today had become the time for this American-born terrorist to perform.

Although a rarity such as Hassan was worth his weight in gold to the terrorists who had carefully molded him, his destiny today wouldn't further the cause of jihad. He had been sold like a prized stallion. Two million dollars had changed hands. The Al Qaeda group now had money to buy weapons and foment hatred and one man, in exchange, had the talents of a suicide bomber.

Without a care in the world, twenty-three year old Hassan listened to music on the radio of the stolen pickup, smoked one cigarette after another and enjoyed the breeze coming through the open window as he maneuvered down the crowded avenue. He didn't speed. With the mission he had been given it would be foolish beyond belief to be stopped by the police. Hassan was on a strict timeframe. He had places to be and timing was everything. This job had been planned down to the last second.

He stopped for a red light at 59th Street and checked his watch. He had eleven minutes to go and only five blocks left. He wanted to get past the busy two-way cross street at 57th before stopping. He pulled the pickup all the way to the left lane, passed 57th Street then pulled over to the curb. He had three blocks to go and needed to kill a little time. Hassan glanced in his mirrors and out his front windshield. There were no policemen walking on the sidewalk to create a problem for him – only the hustle and bustle of pedestrian traffic like always during the noon hour in New York City.

In the bed of the pickup truck sat ten ten-gallon canisters filled with gasoline. They were securely tethered to the wall of the truck and wired together, ready for the job ahead. Hassan gave them a quick glance probably for the fiftieth time today, making sure everything was still good to go. And it was.

Hassan lit another cigarette, idly contemplating that this would be his last one. In a very short time this street would be a mass of confusion, drama and tears. Another strike at the mighty Americans. He smiled as he inhaled a deep puff. He didn't know why he was doing this mission. He didn't care. He only knew it was going to be a big deal. A very big deal indeed. Hassan would have been saddened to know his death wouldn't promote jihad at all. He'd been bought and paid for to do a job for a very wealthy man.

He saw the infidel church, St. Patrick's Cathedral, a few blocks down the street in front of him. As the church bells began to peal the hour, Hassan looked at his watch. An alarm sounded – it was one pm. Shutting off the alarm he thanked Allah one last time for the rewards in heaven that lay in store for him only a few moments from now. Then he smiled, tossed the cigarette out the window and put the pickup into gear. Showtime.

A priest stood at a counter in Bijan Rarities, New York's most famous antiquities gallery. Dressed in a black cassock and an old-fashioned padre's hat, he resembled the character Father Guido Sarducci who had appeared regularly on *Saturday Night Live* years before. He wore sunglasses even though he was indoors but none of the staff at the gallery considered it unusual. Everyone in New York was a little different. Even the clergy.

The priest had rung the front buzzer at 12:45 pm. The security guard on duty glanced at a sheet and noted that the Archdiocese was sending a representative to the store. Without a second thought the guard opened the door to admit him. The priest thanked the guard, who pointed to the back of the showroom where Collette

Conning, the second-in-command to Brian Sadler, waited to meet with him.

They sat at her desk and the priest explained the reason for his visit. He produced a letter with the signature and seal of the Archbishop of New York at the bottom. Collette looked it over then rose and pointed. "I'll meet you at the counter over there. I have to get the manuscript from Mr. Sadler's office."

Standing at the counter, the cleric glanced around the showroom as he waited for her return. There was only one other customer in the store. He was in a small room examining some old vases. There were also Collette and the guard. He didn't see anyone who might have been Brian Sadler but he knew the owner could be in the back somewhere. It made no difference how many people were there. Everything would happen in a matter of minutes. He glanced at his watch. Exactly on schedule.

Collette brought a tray from the rear of the gallery. It was about the size of a large cookie sheet and on it sat a very old book. When she first had seen the manuscript she noticed it vaguely resembled medieval bibles she had seen. But it was old, ratty and torn. The other seven books that had been dropped off with it were beautiful, almost majestic. They were valuable. Like her boss, she had immediately dismissed this one as junk.

But one never knew. And now the Church was interested in it. So maybe there was more to this book after all. It wasn't every day the Archbishop sent a representative to look at one of their consignments.

Collette set the tray on the counter in front of the priest. "You'll need gloves to examine it yourself," she said, putting on a pair. He declined and asked her to turn to the title page.

She opened the book. *Opus Militum Xpisti*, the title dimly read on the ragged page. *The Work of the Soldiers of Christ.*

Collette thought it was strange that he really didn't seem to care what the page said. He barely looked at it. They both heard a muffled ding and the priest glanced at his watch. "One pm," he said absently as he hit a button to silence the alarm.

Nicole Farber had been preparing for trial for three days. If she weren't ready now she'd never be. Criminal law was a strange animal – many times the jury made its decision based on the characters in the play – the prosecutor, the defense attorney, even the defendant – rather than on the law itself. Many times those jurors - the human beings who held the futures of others in their hands - became captivated with good-looking attorneys, likeable murderers, people who could twist the truth until you hardly believed it yourself even though irrefutable facts were laid out right in front of you.

She was one of those good-looking attorneys. The youngest partner at Carter and Wells, one of Dallas' largest and most prestigious law firms, Nicole had made a name for herself defending those accused of white-collar crimes. She'd met her boyfriend Brian Sadler through her work. She had represented him years ago when he was a stockbroker embroiled in a massive fraud that took down the Dallas investment bank where he worked. What started as an attorney-client relationship blossomed into much more. Now that Brian lived in New York she saw much less of him but they managed to spend as much time together as they could.

She stopped working, swung her chair around and looked out the floor-to-ceiling windows at the skyline of downtown Dallas. The city's architecture was striking and she never tired of the view. As she took a moment to relax, her iPhone dinged a quiet reminder. It was 11:55 a.m. and a special program on Fox News Network would be broadcast in five minutes. She took a remote from her desk and turned on the TV on the wall in the opposite end of her expansive office. She didn't want to miss this.

A panel wrapped up a heated discussion about the continuing Congressional deadlock over spending and then the moderator said, "Stay tuned for a real treat. Brian Sadler, owner of the well-known New York antiquities gallery Bijan Rarities, will be on hand for a look at the most exciting discoveries around the world over the past few months. That's right after the break – at one pm here in Manhattan."

Nicole grabbed a bottle of water from the fridge in a corner of her office and sat on her couch. Kicking off her shoes, she sat back to watch her boyfriend do his thing. As the Fox interviewer introduced Brian she looked closely at what he was wearing. *Good for you, Brian. You're wearing that tie I gave you for Christmas. I never knew if you liked it that much or not but I'm glad you do.*

The reporter led Sadler into the topic as the screen flashed pictures from remote areas worldwide. There were shots of ancient temples in jungles, ruined pyramids in a desert, building facades built into walls in the ancient city of Petra. Brian's voiceover explained one by one the new things archaeological teams were working on. Even knowing as much as she did because of her relationship with him, she found his information interesting and was watching closely. The cameras turned back to Brian from time to time as he smoothly and effortlessly guided the television audience through the film clips that were being displayed.

About ten minutes into the program it was suddenly interrupted. On the screen flashed three words – Fox News Alert. One of the Fox regulars appeared behind the news desk and said, "We interrupt this program to bring you a special report from Manhattan. A truck has jumped the curb on Fifth Avenue in midtown and crashed into a building. This happened less than ten minutes ago only a few blocks from our studios. Our crew is en route to the scene and we'll be bringing you live footage momentarily."

The man stopped talking and put his hand to his ear. Nicole watched him listen into his earphone. "This situation has apparently escalated. Reports indicate a massive explosion has occurred. There appear to be fatalities and the scene is chaotic."

The news crew arrived and suddenly a camera was capturing the scene live for viewers to see. "Oh my God," Nicole yelled, tears running down her face as she watched her television. "Oh my God."

Inside the Fox studios on 47th Street and Sixth Avenue Brian watched the scene on a large monitor as he waited to return to his segment. When the live shot was displayed Brian looked closely. His face turned from interest to astonishment, then horror as he screamed at the top of his lungs.

"That's my gallery!"

The Jesuit priest walked briskly away from the carnage and destruction on Fifth Avenue. He turned east at the intersection and made his way through throngs of pedestrians. Many of them were hurrying the other direction to see what was going on. Everyone on the midtown streets had heard the massive thump of an explosion a couple of minutes ago. No one gave the priest a second glance as he crossed Madison, then Park and turned left on Lexington.

He popped into a McDonald's restaurant a couple of blocks up and went directly to the men's room. There was only one other person in the bathroom and he was using the urinal. The priest entered the first stall, locked the door and looked around. On the floor behind the toilet was a Macy's shopping bag. The priest pulled out shoes, a blond wig, a baseball cap and a pair of sunglasses. He put the manuscript, the detonating device he had used, his hat, black cassock and shoes in the bag and put it back behind the toilet. He now wore the blue jeans and Yankees t-shirt that had been under the priest's garb. With different shoes, the wig, hat and glasses he looked nothing like the cleric he had been only one minute ago.

As the perpetrator left, the person standing at the urinal entered the stall, retrieved the shopping bag and checked its contents. He saw the manuscript and the small detonator device. He sent a one-word text on his phone. "Go." He nonchalantly walked out of the restaurant to the bus stop a block away. Within an hour he and the manuscript would be safely at a house in Brooklyn. The Macy's shopping bag with the rest of its contents lay at the bottom of a curbside trash bin miles from midtown.

The priest, transformed into a tourist wearing a ball cap, looked exactly like a thousand others on the teeming Manhattan streets. As he walked toward the subway station at 53rd and Lexington a pedestrian jostled him and he felt a little sting on his arm. As he reached to rub it, he stumbled and fell to the pavement. He began convulsing as people moved aside. One yelled, "I think he's having a seizure!"

One concerned passerby dialed 911. But it was too late. The perpetrator of the Fifth Avenue bombing was dead.

Later that day a continent away, a man watched the news report and smiled. One score settled, two to go.

CHAPTER TWO

Rome, two years ago

It is well known that the Vatican has what is termed the "Secret Archives," an area where Popes over hundreds of years have deposited written material of interest to the Church or otherwise historically significant. Today there are over 35,000 such documents of various types including correspondence between pontiffs and ruling monarchs of England and France. Properly vetted researchers are occasionally allowed to visit the Secret Archives to study the material.

Few are aware there is another archive, this one truly secret and accessible solely by the Pope. In the depths of the Vatican several floors below the Sistine Chapel, there is a vault. Its existence is known to only a few people – as a new Pope is elected he is told about it. Aside from His Holiness there are generally four others alive who are aware of the place. But only one of those knows the combination to the door behind which lies more than a millennium of secrets – the Pope himself.

For fifteen hundred years, only the Pope has accessed the vault, never anyone else. Many of the pontiffs had no interest in visiting the repository. In fact in the past fifty years only one Pope, Benedict XVI, had decided to go there. His first visit was to place the Bethlehem Scroll in the vault's secure shelves in 2009 and he had been back a number of times since.

In his position as head of the Knights Templars and a confidant of the Pope, Dominic Cardinal Conti was one of only five people on Earth who knew the vault existed. Among hundreds of other things, many relics and documents relating to the Knights Templars had been placed there over hundreds of years. Even as head of the Templars Conti was not allowed to enter the area but Pope Benedict had one day taken an ancient book out of the vault, brought it to his office and showed it to the Cardinal. It was bound in leather and its pages were chipped and yellowed with age.

Benedict told Conti that this large old musty book was the key to all the artifacts that were secured in the papal vault. It was a register. Line by line a Pope would enter an item's title or description as he put it there for safekeeping. This book was the master list of everything in the vault.

The Pope commented on the register's remarkably good condition after fifteen hundred years. He told Cardinal Conti he was going to have the register photocopied so he could refer to the vault's contents prior to going there, saving time when he was looking for something in particular. The original would of course remain in the vault.

The first entry in that master record was dated 606 AD during the reign of Pope Boniface III. Into the newly constructed underground vault Boniface had placed a decree from Byzantine Emperor Phocas declaring Rome head of all the churches and putting rest to all conflicting claims, especially from Constantinople. In a flourishing hand, Boniface had recorded the document - the first line in a record book that by now ran to over a hundred pages and several thousand entries.

The Pope showed Conti four interesting entries in the register – four manuscripts that were the eyewitness journals of the Knights Templars. These four volumes were in fact diaries, each written at the time the events described in them occurred. They were exciting to the Cardinal. The first book encompassed the years from the Templars beginning in 1118 to the tumultuous time in the early 1300s when the group ostensibly was disbanded.

The pontiff explained to Cardinal Conti that the books were part of a private collection until around 1875 when they were donated by a wealthy Italian family to the papal collection. Pius IX, the Pope at the time, considered them so revealing and so potentially inflammatory that he locked them in the secret vault.

Since he was head of the Templars today, Conti requested to read the manuscripts. The Pope agreed to remove them, one at a time, so Conti could peruse the ancient books. Conti's excitement grew the day he held the beautifully bound first volume in his hands and read the words on its title page. *Opus Militum Xpisti.* Translated from Latin, "The work of the soldiers of Christ."

In this first volume the Cardinal read the fascinating eyewitness account of the Templars' activities from their very beginning. It was written entirely in Latin, a language well understood by Conti.

The group had been founded on the basest Christian principle – to defend the kingdom of Christ at whatever cost. What started so nobly eventually became the subject of controversy from powerful factions within the Church. Property owned by the Templars was not subject to taxation and they accumulated substantial wealth while conquering infidels across Europe. Much of this booty was handed over to the Pope but some of it inevitably remained with the Templars themselves. They began to receive criticism from high levels.

Without a doubt the Templars accumulated many treasures. Legends grew over the centuries about the relics the Knights Templars found when they occupied the Temple Mount in Jerusalem. From pieces of the cross to skulls of saints, from clothing worn by the Apostles to the Holy Grail, many tales surrounded these crusading warriors for Christ. Dozens of books speculated on the Templar treasure horde while movies such as *National Treasure* and the *Indiana Jones* series keep the exploits of the legendary group alive. No one knows for sure what the Templars had, what they delivered to the Church and what they might have kept and hidden.

Eventually all the favors and praise lavished by the Popes on the Templars stirred jealousy and hatred among others in the Church who didn't receive such attention. High-ranking officials worked behind the scenes to bring down the crusaders who previously had enjoyed the protection and favors of the Papacy. In the early 1300s the Templars were finally defeated, not by enemies without but by those within.

These honorable men were rounded up, horribly tortured and forced to confess to all sorts of vile criminal behavior such as idol worship and sodomy. Over fifty leaders of the Knights Templars were burned to death in 1310 while a weak, spineless Pope stood by doing nothing to stop it. To the world this signaled the end of the Knights Templars. But that was incorrect. The Order continued, secretly carrying on the work of its original members.

Thusly, the first volume of the Templar history ended with the apparent destruction of the ancient Order. Cardinal Conti returned it and received the next one from Pope Benedict. It was interesting, Conti thought, that although the Templars were "destroyed" in the first book, three more manuscripts relating to their history were extant. Since Dominic Conti was now head of the Knights Templars, he knew that they had carried on throughout the centuries. But he had never read the group's history written by Templars scribes on the scene. It was fascinating.

The fact that Conti was a linguist came in handy as he read page after page. The subsequent manuscripts were written mostly in Latin but also in French or medieval English. In the first book and now in the second, every so often there appeared a page of curious symbols, a coded message of unknown significance. Conti asked the Pope about what these pages might mean.

"Finish the manuscripts," Pope Benedict had said. "Then I have something else to show you that may explain your question."

Although the Cardinal devoted much of every day to reading the manuscripts, the laborious translations required six weeks before he was finished with the third volume. He made arrangements to see the Pope and exchange the book for the fourth and last one.

In his office he opened the final volume and began to read. It was quickly obvious that something was wrong. He left a message with the Pope's secretary and soon received a call from the pontiff.

"Your Holiness, could there possibly be another volume? The one I just received from you doesn't chronologically follow the third volume. It begins in the eighteenth century, whereas the last volume stopped around the mid 1400s. There's a time gap of over two hundred years."

"I wasn't aware of that, but also I must admit I've never looked at those books. Could it be that some pages are missing from one volume or another?"

"That's not the answer, Holiness. The books are intact and bound. I'm missing the years between about 1475 and 1700. I think there's a missing manuscript and I'd like your permission to use the papal resources to look for it."

"By all means. You have my permission to seek it."

It seemed unusual to Conti that there would be a missing volume in the middle. He wondered if it had been removed because there was something there so important it had to be hidden even from the Pope. Hopeful that it was still in the Church family somewhere, the Cardinal sent out an inquiry to the Catholic churches worldwide. Although unlikely, it was possible that the manuscript could be resting as a relic in one of the far-flung churches. In these times of electronic mail things were far simpler and faster than the old days when a letter to say Africa might take six weeks to arrive and that much longer for a response. Since all the volumes so far looked similar on the outside, Conti included a picture in his email to make it easier for clerics to identify what he was looking for.

Within fifteen days he had heard from all the churches, large and small. None possessed the missing volume.

Back in Vatican City a group of twenty young Jesuit priests was assigned to scour the Vatican itself. This was a daunting task – the palace had at least ten thousand rooms and bookshelves lined the walls of hundreds of them. Although Conti doubted the priests visited every single potential resting place, after two weeks they reported the manuscript had not been found. Reluctantly the Cardinal suspended the hunt for the missing book and resumed the pressing duties of his office.

In January 2013 Conti finished reading the fourth volume. It was easier than the others because it was both in French and more modern English, covering the period from 1700 until 1950. There was nothing of significance in it. The Cardinal returned the volume to the Papal Secretary but was told His Holiness could not see him today. That had been the case for a while, Conti reflected. Benedict seemed to be removing himself from those who had surrounded him.

Pope Benedict had promised the Cardinal he had something else to show him once he finished reading the last volume – something that might shed light on the mysterious coded pages that appeared occasionally throughout the Knights Templars books. Conti tried for a week to arrange a meeting with the Pope, something that would have been simple a month ago, but was denied.

He had almost forgotten about it when in February he received an email from the Archdiocese of New York. When Conti's original request went out to churches worldwide, the Archbishop had asked his staff to look closely at the books in his Manhattan residence. He wanted to ensure the volume wasn't among over a thousand other old and musty books that had accumulated over the years. It wasn't, but one of those who searched for it had come to the Archbishop recently with a newspaper article. The Archbishop read the clipping then told the young staffer to reply to Cardinal Conti's email.

"Your Eminence," the email read, "I am writing at the suggestion of the Archbishop. I participated in a search of the residence here in New York in an attempt to locate your missing manuscript. Your email contained a picture of another volume in the series of books, and I believe the enclosed article may refer to the book you're seeking."

Cardinal Conti opened the attachment to the staffer's email and saw an article from an issue of the New York Times a few days ago.

Trove of Ancient Books
Found in Nova Scotia Basement

Halifax, Nova Scotia (AP) A collection of eight books, the earliest dating to the fourteenth century, has been found in a house in Halifax, Nova Scotia, Canada. Some of the books are bound in animal skins, others in leather, and all appear to be printed on parchment. Dr. Ralph Painter, an expert in antiquarian books at Halifax's St. Mary's University, examined the items. He explained that the use of parchment is an important indicator that the volumes were created for persons of wealth or social standing, even perhaps for use in churches. Dr. Painter estimated the combined value of seven of the tomes at more than US$1,000,000. He added that their remarkably good condition, extreme rarity and collector interest worldwide could cause them to bring even more at auction. He declined to give an estimate on the eighth book, a volume about the exploits of the Knights Templars that was in very worn condition and appeared to be one of a set, the rest of which are missing. Both those factors detract from its value, the expert added.

An invoice found with the volumes shows Antoine Crane, the home's owner who died in 2000, purchased seven of the books from an antiquarian bookshop in Rome, Italy in 1921 for the equivalent of around US$5,000 in today's dollars. There was nothing indicating the source of the worn Templar manuscript or how it ended up in Nova Scotia.

The eight volumes consist of three lavishly illustrated bibles from the Middle Ages, the Knights Templars book written mostly in Latin, and four works of literature dating from the 1600s and 1700s.

Brothers Robert and Sidney Crane, the heirs of Antoine Crane, discovered the books three months ago. Both are physicians. They reside in Los Angeles, California and Athens, Georgia respectively. The men visited their father's house once after his funeral and then left it in the care of a local property manager. The house has been unoccupied from the senior Crane's death until today.

The Crane brothers said they decided to put the house on the market, which necessitated a thorough cleaning. "Dad was a bit of a packrat so the place was crammed with boxes and file cabinets," Robert Crane said in an exclusive interview with the Times. "Sid and I would open a box, glance at what was inside and put it either in a 'keep' or 'toss' pile." The books, which were in a cardboard box, aroused the immediate attention of the men due to their obvious age.

Antoine Crane was a collector of many things ranging from clocks to music boxes, according to Robert Crane. A recluse in his later years, he had over a thousand books in his home but none was of much value, the sons said. Robert and Sidney Crane are "considering our options on the sale or donation of the volumes," Sidney Crane said.

Conti's hands shook as he read and reread the end of the first paragraph. " . . . a volume about the exploits of the Knights Templars . . . one of a set . . ." Could it be? He picked up the phone on his desk and made a call. Within minutes one of his assistants was researching the Internet to find the contact information for one or both of the Crane brothers. Los Angeles was difficult – there were twelve physicians in the metropolitan area who had both "Robert" and "Crane" in their names – but Athens, Georgia proved much more fruitful. The staffer found Dr. Sidney Crane, a neurosurgeon, and handed the doctor's contact information to Cardinal Conti.

Thanking the young man, Conti reminded him that this job, along with everything else he did every day, was completely confidential. The work of the Church could not be discussed with anyone. Especially the information this young man had given the Cardinal.

CHAPTER THREE

Rome

Tucked away in a side street a couple of blocks from the Spanish Steps is a tiny outdoor trattoria, one of perhaps thousands in the Eternal City. A trim bearded man around seventy years old sipped his second espresso and read the Italian-language newspaper *la Repubblica*, enjoying the cool morning air and the sunshine. Giovanni Moretti enjoyed his morning paper and appreciated living in one of the world's great cities. And this café was only two blocks from his apartment on one of Rome's beautiful avenues. Moretti had selected a table at the edge of the patio and requested no one be seated nearby. As a frequent patron and on a quiet morning, his wishes were easily accommodated.

He waited for the man who had arranged this meeting. They had met many times over the years but lately Moretti always wondered if the next meeting would be *the* meeting. The one that would end the waiting.

Precisely at ten am Moretti saw a priest wearing the cassock and familiar red zucchetto, or skullcap, of a Cardinal stride briskly toward him. The man was tall and younger than Moretti by perhaps twenty years.

Moretti rose and bowed slightly. "Your Eminence." He gestured to the empty chair beside his.

"Good morning, Giovanni. It's good to see you again." The Cardinal sat as a waiter rushed to his side.

Bowing, the server said, "Eminence, may I get you a cup of coffee?"

"Molto bene, grazie. A double espresso for me, please. Nothing else."

The few other guests on the patio sneaked surreptitious glances at the prominent figure. Even in Rome where officials of the Roman Catholic Church were common sights, a Cardinal was accorded respect and reverence.

The two men leaned closer to each other and conversed quietly in Italian.

"How are things with you and with the bank?" Moretti made small talk as he waited for the priest to eventually raise the subject of their meeting. They chatted, as old friends do who haven't seen each other in awhile.

As far as most people knew, Dominic Conti's job was to run the Institute for the Works of Religion, commonly known as the Vatican Bank. It was an important part of the Catholic Church. Although the bank was publicly "founded" in 1942, its roots as the financial arm of the Church dated back hundreds of years, maybe more. Cloaked in secrecy, the bank had only recently begun to issue annual reports of its operations and even then there were always questions about its activities.

And in fact that was the Cardinal's job. But he held another position within the Church as well. A secret one. Dominic Conti was also the leader of a shadowy group that operated under the auspices of the Church but far behind the scenes. He was head of the Poor Soldiers of Christ and the Temple of Solomon. The Knights Templars.

The men continued their conversation until the cleric's coffee arrived. He took a sip and quietly said, "We need your help."

Moretti had often wondered when this day would come. He owed the Church a tremendous personal debt. Even as powerful as Moretti once had been, he had found himself unable to control his own fate at a crucial time. Cardinal Conti had arranged for the Church to willingly lend a hand and easily solve a problem. In exchange for a favor to be redeemed in the future. Perhaps. Or perhaps not. One never knew when dealing with people like this if they would ever call, or if the Church's favor would forever go unrepaid. But now the day of reckoning had arrived for Giovanni Moretti. This *was* the day.

"I'm at your service."

After spending an hour with Cardinal Conti, Giovanni Moretti left the trattoria. He fully understood his mission although he had not been told why the job had to be done. For now that was fine. Moretti didn't care. He wanted to repay the debt he owed this man and move on. It was the final impediment in the new life he had chosen and he had lived with the shadow for some time now. He was glad the repayment would come soon and had no concern he would be able to perform the tasks the Cardinal asked of him.

Moretti's previous work had left him with a wide network of contacts. And he could accomplish his goals for this project without having to reveal who he was. That was important.

When he arrived in Italy a few months back Moretti had set up a shell corporation in Turkey. Its owners were two trust companies in Liechtenstein. A corporation in Libya in turn owned those trusts. There would be no tracing ownership in Moretti's companies.

Today, using an email account set up through his front company, he emailed a private investigator in New York he had used for years. Moretti had never spoken with the PI or given the man his name. His identification was a string of numbers – a password – that identified him to the detective. Moretti gave the PI the name of a doctor in Georgia that Conti had provided – the doctor who owned the manuscript. The investigator accepted the job and Moretti wired $20,000 to an account he provided. Now Moretti waited.

In three days Giovanni Moretti knew exactly where the missing Knights Templar volume was. And it was in a place that he hadn't expected, one that excited Moretti.

Locating the site satisfied only one part of the payback he owed Dominic Cardinal Conti. He knew what would come next.

Moretti made a call. From his desk in the Vatican, Cardinal Conti answered on the first ring. "What have you found?"

"It's at an antiquities gallery. Bijan Rarities in New York."

"Get it. Discreetly."

The call ended, the cleric having given the response Moretti anticipated. This project was perfect. He could kill two birds with one stone, paying off one debt while collecting on another.

Now that Moretti had been given instructions, the Cardinal was determined to push for a meeting with Pope Benedict. He wanted to know what the Pope had promised to show him – the key, perhaps, to the coded pages in the manuscripts. Dominic Conti pushed his chair back from his desk, laced his fingers behind his head and thought how to do it. As his mind considered various options a ding on his computer indicated he had incoming mail. He glanced at the screen and gasped as he opened and read an email from the Pope's secretary.

This is virtually unprecedented. Now I understand what's been going on. And now I'll never find out what the Pope was going to show me.

On February 11, 2013 Benedict XVI became the first Pope in six hundred years to announce he was resigning. A month later he was out of office, his access to the secret vault in the Vatican now ended forever.

In his spacious apartment Giovanni Moretti laid out his plan on a legal pad. The more he thought, the more elaborate his ideas became until he had designed a scheme.   It was monumental and would completely mask the reasons behind it. The idea would take resources and effort, both of which Moretti could easily muster.   He wouldn't call upon the Church for help of any kind.   Cardinal Conti would have the plausible deniability he required. All Conti wanted was the manuscript.   All Moretti wanted, on the other hand, was revenge.

He placed several telephone calls. The plan would take time to execute but the project was underway.

CHAPTER FOUR

New York City

A month ago Brian Sadler had received a phone call from Dr. Sidney Crane of Athens, Georgia. The neurologist told him about the eight ancient books from his father's collection. Brian agreed to take the manuscripts, estimate their worth and provide a proposal for disposition.

Like most Americans, the Crane brothers had heard of Bijan Rarities. Brian Sadler was a frequent guest on news networks as a recognized authority on antiquities. The History and Discovery networks had produced several shows in which either he or the gallery were prominently featured. His discoveries in Mexico and Central America had made headlines worldwide and Sadler's name was well known to those who collected or had an interest in ancient things and peoples. He had been involved with some of the world's strangest and rarest things, including the Bethlehem Scroll and the discovery of ancient gold of the Maya kings deep in the Guatemalan rain forest.

When Robert and Sidney Crane found the manuscripts in the old box they discussed what to do next. The find might be something really valuable but then again it might be eight old books that should be listed on eBay. Only an expert would know and they both came up with Bijan to fill their need.

Dr. Sidney Crane emailed Brian photos of the book covers and the first couple of pages of each. Brian was immediately captivated by the beauty and condition of seven of the volumes. They had weathered time well. He called the physician and said that seeing them in person and spending some research time in the office with them would be necessary to determine their value.

Brian agreed with Dr. Crane that the Knights Templars volume was very likely one of a set and no one had any idea where the others were or even if they existed. Its content guaranteed it had been written hundreds of years ago and the book's cover looked as though it was from the early eighteenth century. It made the book interesting as an old tome but not particularly valuable standing alone, apart from the others in its set. There was also the matter of condition. The book was in poor shape at best – torn pages and a worn cover that was barely attached to the spine. Of the eight books it held the least possibility of any real value to Brian.

Two weeks later the eight volumes were at Bijan Rarities. Dr. Sidney Crane had brought them personally to New York, unwilling to trust them to a delivery service or courier. He spent only an hour with Brian, got a receipt for the books and left.

Brian laid the volumes on a side table in his office. The pictures hardly did justice to the beauty of the three bibles. And the four volumes of literature were clearly ancient and first editions, but they were by little-known writers. They had value not from their content but more for the age and beauty of the bindings, Brian mused.

He looked at the worst book first, to get it over with. As he'd suspected from the picture, this book was no different than hundreds of others he'd seen at antiquarian booksellers worldwide. It was old, for sure. Brian carefully opened the torn, moth-eaten cover and looked at the first page. Opus Militum Xpisti. Latin. It was one volume of a set, for sure. Who knew where the others were? Who cared, for that matter? The set had probably been separated long ago. If the others were in as bad shape as this one, Brian figured they'd been tossed in the trash.

The Templars manuscript was written in a combination of Latin, ancient French and English between the 1400s and 1700s, according to the diary entries in it. There were no redeeming factors on this one – no beautiful binding, no exquisite colored drawings, nothing to make this one worthwhile. Brian wasn't going to spend any time on it. This one looked like something for a garage sale, not a rarities gallery. He put it at the back of his work table.

Now the other seven books – these had possibilities. After a brief look he locked them in the vault for safekeeping.

CHAPTER FIVE

There were a dozen important projects on Brian's plate so he delegated the valuation of the seven volumes to his assistant Collette Conning. Brian felt fortunate to have her – she had been with the gallery when its previous owner, Darius Nazir, first invited Brian to Manhattan. At that time Brian was a Dallas stockbroker responding to a proposal that been sent to his firm. Nazir was seeking to raise money through a public offering of stock. That New York meeting led to an unusual set of events, the mysterious death of Darius Nazir and a fortuitous bequest that caused Brian to become owner of Bijan Rarities.

Much had happened in Brian's five years at the helm and Collette had been a big part of it all. She was like a rock, steady and strong even when she was seriously injured in an attempted robbery at the gallery just over a year ago. As soon as she recovered, she was back at her job. Brian Sadler had depended on Collette even more when he had opened the London branch of Bijan. It was due entirely to Collette's presence that he was able to be out of the office more often, either at the London gallery or in the field looking for artifacts.

It was Collette who took the phone call late the afternoon before that fateful event.

The caller asked for the senior person present, confirmed who she was then said, "This is the Archdiocese of New York. Please hold for the Archbishop."

As a practicing Catholic, Collette involuntarily straightened in her chair and fixed her hair as she waited for New York's senior cleric to come on the line.

"Good afternoon, Miss Conning. I have an inquiry to make, about a particular item I think is in the possession of your gallery. I read with interest the article in the Times about the ancient manuscripts that were found in Nova Scotia a few months back. Does Bijan Rarities have them now?"

She confirmed they were in the gallery. Seven of them were locked safely in the vault and the eighth, the scrappy book about the Templars, was tossed aside on Brian's office worktable. She told the Archbishop all this without thinking. Then she paused. *I'm acting like a schoolgirl. He doesn't want to know all this information. He just wants to know about the bibles, I bet.*

"Very good. I'll send a representative from the Church to take a look at the Templar manuscript. He'll be a Jesuit – I'm not certain which one I'm sending yet so I can't give you a name. Would tomorrow around 12:45 be a good time? He won't be long – he just wants to see the condition of the volume and look at the title page. He's doing research for me and this volume might help us. If it's what it purports to be we may be interested in making an offer."

"Of course, Your Excellency. Tell him to ask for me please."

"God bless you, Miss Conning. Thanks for your help."

Her heart was pounding as the call ended. This was the most important person she had ever spoken with, and she would remember this call for the rest of her life.

Sadly on both counts, the caller *wasn't* the most important person she had ever spoken with. And *the rest of her life* turned out to be very short indeed for Collette Conning.

CHAPTER SIX

After the explosion Brian rushed out of the Fox studios and gave a fleeting thought to hailing a cab. He had less than eight blocks to go and quickly determined walking, running actually, was fastest. It was much faster this time of day in midtown Manhattan.

He dodged traffic as he jaywalked across 47th Street and ran east toward Fifth Avenue. Turning north on the famous street and looking ahead, Brian saw emergency lights flashing from a dozen vehicles – police cars, fire trucks and a couple of ambulances. Policemen were setting up barricades a few blocks in front of him. He ran east across Fifth then north past Saks Fifth Avenue. All of Saks' massive front windows were blown out from the blast's concussion. Glass shards littered the sidewalk and he crunched over them. He passed St. Patrick's Cathedral and glanced at a priest standing on the front steps looking north.

The devastation ahead of him was mind-boggling. Where his gallery had been there was a gaping black hole. The façade of his building had been blown away at ground level and two stories above. Above street level, jagged girders and the interiors of offices were exposed to the elements. Bodies lay strewn on the streets. A half dozen cars and trucks that had been passing in front of the gallery were tossed like toys to the other side of the avenue, stacked on their sides against buildings as though a tornado had blown through. The smell of gasoline and a nasty stench carried south on the breeze to where Brian stood. He knew what the steely odor was but his mind went into shutdown mode. It didn't let him deal with that reality.

How could anyone have survived this? How could Collette . . . could she be alive?

In shock and lightheaded, Brian kept walking north, closer and closer to the massive, almost unbelievable destruction. By the time he reached 54th Street, not far from what had been Bijan Rarities, there was so much debris on the sidewalk that he was forced to stop. Traffic was still crawling along on 54th and he absently walked directly in front of a cab, oblivious to its presence. In typical fashion the cabbie honked and waved a derogatory finger at him. "What the hell you doing?" he screamed in broken English at Brian as the taxi snaked its way through.

Brian ignored him, looking only ahead at the devastation.

Hands roughly grabbed his arms from behind. "Hey, buddy. Where do you think you're going?"

Brian turned and looked blankly at one of New York's finest. Absently he said, "That's my gallery. I own that place. People in there work for me. That's where I work too."

The policeman immediately sensed that Brian was in shock. "Okay. You need to let me take you over here where you won't get hurt. We don't know what else may happen here and there's a lot of stuff on the street." The cop took Brian's arm and guided him to the west side of Fifth Avenue where a group of men were standing on the curb talking. One of them, dressed in a dark suit and tie, saw the cop approaching.

"Detective, this guy says he owns the place that was bombed."

Brian muttered quietly to himself. "Bombed. Bombed. That's just crazy." His words were slurred and suddenly his head lolled back. He began to fall to the pavement.

"Hold on! Hold on, buddy," the policeman shouted, glad he still had a grip on Brian's arm. He lowered Brian to the sidewalk and leaned him against a pole. "I think he's in shock, Detective. Not too surprising, I guess. I figure I would be too."

When Brian awoke a few minutes later a paramedic was kneeling in front of him holding an ampule of ammonia under Brian's nose. The pungent odor jolted him back into reality.

"What . . . what happened?"

"Just take it easy, sir. You're in shock and you passed out. The officer had your arm or you'd have fallen."

It took a moment for Brian to recall what was going on around him. Sirens wailed in the distance as additional help headed toward the site. Across the street and up a block he saw the huge hole that now occupied the place where his entire storefront had been. Everything was destroyed. He had no idea how anyone or anything inside the gallery could have survived. And although he knew vaguely he should be more attuned to what was going on, he couldn't pull thoughts together in his head.

"What happened?" Brian made an effort to stand up.

The detective gave Brian a hand. "Let's get some ID, sir, and confirm who you are before we talk. Sorry to put you through this right now but in this situation we have to be sure everything is what it appears to be."

Within minutes Brian had produced his driver license and a business card identifying him as the CEO of Bijan Rarities with his Fifth Avenue address a block away. His mind was beginning to clear and he said, "Was this a terrorist bombing?"

Immediately wary, the detective shot back, "Why would you say that?"

"Because the first thing I thought of when I saw the destruction was 9/11."

"That's a fair statement. I'll admit I thought of 9/11 too." The detective glanced up Fifth Avenue and watched a forklift unloading large concrete barricades off a semi-trailer. Until they knew more about what had happened today and why, Fifth Avenue would be blocked, ensuring a second truck bomber wouldn't be successful, at least in the same place.

"OK. Let me get a few basics from you. Where were you at one pm?"

After Brian's response the detective made one quick call and confirmed Brian's airtight alibi. He had been on live television at the time of the bombing. Next he asked Brian who likely was inside the gallery and took notes as Brian talked.

Other than Collette, Brian hadn't thought about who might be inside. The shock he experienced had dulled his mind and kept him from considering the terrible possibilities.

"Uh, at the very least my assistant Collette Conning and our security guard were there. There could have been others." Suddenly he felt panic overcoming him. He began to shout to workers across the street. "Have you found anyone? Is Collette OK? Help her! God, help her!" He grabbed the pole next to him, suddenly lightheaded again.

The detective grabbed his arm to steady him. "Try to stay calm. The FBI is doing the initial check and with the extent of the damage it may be awhile. There's no need to panic until we know something more. I promise I'll let you know as soon as I find out anything about your staff. Now let's think about something else. What kind of security systems do you have in place?"

"I have cameras! We can check the cameras!" Brian hadn't thought of that either but it could be the key to finding out what had happened just prior to the bombing.

The detective looked up, speaking calmly in order to soothe Sadler. "I was betting you had security cameras. Now I hope you're going to tell me the data's stored offsite. If your server's in there" - he pointed at the gallery – "we probably won't have anything to look at."

"No, it's offsite. Everything feeds to a server housed at 41st and Lex."

"That may be the only good news today. Can you call the service and get the ball rolling on producing those videos?"

By seven pm, when the full effect of what had happened hit Brian Sadler, he was at home in his apartment. Nicole had checked on him several times during the day. His parents had too.

Around three pm the Special Agent-in-Charge of the FBI in New York had called Brian's cellphone, giving him a grim report - there were no survivors in the wreckage that had been Bijan Rarities. The remains of eleven people had been removed from the smoking rubble on Fifth Avenue. Seven people had died in the second and third floor offices above Bijan. The other four were in the gallery itself. Only three were intact. The fourth was the driver – parts of his body had been recovered from the truck's cab. Although none of the deceased had yet been identified, Brian counted in his mind. Collette. The guard. The driver. One more, probably a customer. He dropped his head into his hands and sobbed uncontrollably. *What the hell is going on? Why did they target me?*

Brian talked to Nicole as a news report, broadcast from the same Fox studio where he himself sat only six hours earlier, flickered on the screen in the background.

Tears flowed as he talked to his girlfriend. "It's all gone. It's all gone. My people, my customers, my gallery. It's all gone. For what? What's this all about?"

Brian had asked the same questions all afternoon, first to himself, then the authorities, now to Nicole when they finally had gotten time to talk.

"Sweetie, they'll figure it out. I know you've been through a lot. Did you hear from Harry?" She tried to get his mind off the stark reality of the loss of two employees. She knew how much he would miss Collette, a trusted friend and valuable asset to the business.

"Yes, he called earlier." William Henry Harrison IV, the President of the United States, had been Brian's college roommate. Harry had called to offer his condolences; he told Brian he had spoken personally to the FBI director to ensure expeditious handling of this case.

CHAPTER SEVEN

Despite the urgency of the situation it took over twenty-four hours for the security monitoring service to retrieve all the footage, edit it into readable format and courier a CD to the FBI. Once it was ready the Special Agent-in-Charge asked Brian to come downtown and view the footage.

The agency sent a car to bring Brian to 26 Federal Plaza in lower Manhattan. The loss Brian had suffered was beginning to take its toll; he was staying mostly in his apartment on the Upper West Side and found himself weeping profusely without warning on a regular basis. He figured he shouldn't be surprised – Nicole had warned him yesterday that healing could take months – maybe years.

In a small conference room at FBI headquarters the Special Agent-in-Charge, Jack Underwood, and another agent were waiting. A laptop sat on the table, ready to display onto a large wall-mounted screen.

Agent Underwood began. "We have the data from all your cameras from the time the store opened at 10 am to the minute they stopped recording, which of course includes the blast. Have you viewed data from your cameras before? Are you familiar with how to navigate the data?"

Brian confirmed he was so he took the chair in front of the laptop. Accessing the CD the security company had provided, he scrolled through the cameras by number. There were six - he knew their numbers from memory.

"I think we should look at the primary camera in the showroom first," Brian said. "It's motion-activated and has about a 200 degree panorama. Three other cameras are fixed on various parts of the gallery and two are outside. After this one we can go wherever you want." He felt reasonably good at this point. He was interested to see what happened but knew the footage could hit him hard, depending on what had gone on at the gallery.

They watched Brian enter the showroom at 8:37 am followed by Collette Conning at 9:31 and the guard promptly at ten. No customers arrived until 11:31 am when a man dressed in a suit and tie was admitted. The guard dutifully checked his name off a sheet on a clipboard.

"Pause for a sec," Underwood said. "The guard was expecting your customer, from what I see here. Is that normal?"

"Yes. Our front door is always locked. Given the rarity and value of our items, walk-in traffic is discouraged. A sign on our door says, well I guess I should say *said*, that we operate by appointment only. People make appointments and Collette gives the information to the guard. He knows who to expect and marks their names off a sheet when they arrive."

Underwood turned to the other agent. "Make a note. See if we can retrieve any information off the backup of Bijan's computer system about the appointments the customers made for the day of the bombing."

"We back up automatically every night," Brian commented. "I think we can get access to Collette's information. Presuming the customers made appointments the day before, that is. If it was the same day as the bombing then it won't work unless by some miracle her hard drive still exists."

Brian restarted the video. Collette situated the customer in a small consultation room and brought in two old vases for his examination. Then she went to her desk at the rear of the showroom.

At 12:45 pm the guard admitted a priest dressed in the black robes and hat of a

Jesuit. He dutifully made a mark on his clipboard. Obviously the priest also was expected.

The cleric walked to Collette's desk. She stood and greeted him and he sat. They spoke for a moment then she gestured to a display counter to her left. He walked to the counter and Collette went down a hall that was out of range for the camera they were viewing.

"I think she's going to the vault," Brian said as the footage continued to run. "We can look at another camera to figure that out."

In a moment Collette reappeared carrying a manuscript on a tray. As she walked almost directly under the camera Brian stopped the video. Using the arrows on the keyboard and a function key, he zeroed in on the object on the tray.

"What the hell . . ."

"What is that? What's that old book?"

"She wasn't going to the vault. I figured she was going for one of the old bibles we have locked up. That priest actually was interested in something that was in my office. We recently got eight old manuscripts from a client for valuation. Seven of them are likely very rare – they're in the vault. The eighth is the one she's carrying. It's a ratty book that I think has no value. It's part of a set, the rest of which is missing, and it's in extremely poor condition. It was just thrown on a table in my office. Why did the priest want to see that particular book?"

"I want to come back to that. For now let's keep going."

Brian restarted the feed and they watched Collette put the tray on the counter in front of the priest. She donned cotton gloves as the priest glanced at his watch, then pressed a button on it.

"Stop the video!" Agent Underwood said abruptly. "What's he doing?"

Brian rewound then put the feed on slow mode. The frames crept along. Collette spoke to the priest, put on the gloves then looked in his face as the priest raised his left hand, checked his watch then moved his right hand to his left wrist. The Special Agent motioned for Brian to stop the video.

"Look at the time on the video feed. It's exactly 1 pm. Looks like an alarm went off on his watch. He glanced at it, said something then hit the button to silence it. Is that what it looks like to you?"

Brian and the agent agreed.

Underwood made a note on a legal pad. "Let's continue."

Collette opened one worn page of the book, then another. The priest absently looked at them. He appeared to be disinterested. Odd for a man who had made an appointment to see the book she was showing him.

Less than thirty seconds later all hell broke loose, the camera duly noting the action. In the background it was easy to see glass begin to fly into the showroom. Agent Underwood said, "Put it on slow motion."

"I have another camera that's aimed directly at the front door. Do you want to switch to that one?"

"No. Let's keep the camera on the priest while we watch the crash so we can see what he does."

Brian backed up to just before the glass breakage and restarted, keeping it on slow motion. They watched the frames slowly click by. The priest looked at the pages Collette had opened. Suddenly he reached under his cassock and drew up his arm.

"Stop and zoom in!"

Brian paused and increased the size of the image on the screen. The priest was aiming a pistol at Collette.

"Go forward a few frames."

Brian watched in shock. The picture couldn't be zoomed any larger but it was clear what was happening. In vivid detail the priest's hand moved back slightly as the gun recoiled. Blood spattered on Collette's chest as her mouth opened in surprise. Frame by horrible frame she began to fall to the floor behind the counter.

"I . . . I can't watch this," Brian said, his breath coming in short gasps. He was hyperventilating. "Oh my God. He killed her. He killed Collette." Brian began to sway and the agent moved closer to keep him from falling.

"Mr. Sadler," Underwood said soothingly, "we have to continue. I know this has to be devastatingly hard for you to see. Time is absolutely of the essence and if you can muster the strength to help us get through this it may help figure out what happened and why."

"I'll try," Brian said weakly. "I need some water."

The second agent brought Brian a bottle of water as Underwood moved him to a chair nearby. "We'll run it from here and get your help when we need to know something specific."

At the very instant Collette was shot, jagged shards of the huge plate glass windows overlooking Fifth Avenue began to shoot inward. Simultaneously the guard looked toward the priest and drew his weapon. A second later the front of a pickup could be seen as the entire front door caved in, pushed forward by the momentum of the vehicle. The truck turned toward the guard who fell under the front wheel on the driver side. In horror Brian watched each slow frame as the pickup very deliberately crushed the hapless guard.

Brian sobbed, chest heaving as he struggled to watch. It was difficult to do.

The pickup came to a stop in the middle of the showroom. Artifacts on display were strewn everywhere, broken and shredded. The priest calmly closed the manuscript Collette had shown him, picked it up and put it under his cassock. He glanced at the driver of the pickup but appeared to say nothing to him. Stepping over debris and glass, the priest walked to the front of the store and through what had been a large window. At that point the camera could no longer pick up his image.

"Stop for a second," the Special Agent said to the man at the computer. "Look in the bed of the pickup."

There were ten large canisters, the kind you store gasoline in. They were roped together and appeared to have wires running from each of their tops to all the others.

Restarting, the men watched the drama continue. Two seconds after the priest left, a single frame of the footage showed a small flame erupt from one of the gas cans in the pickup bed. The flame grew then suddenly the video stopped.

The computer screen went blank as Underwood spoke quietly. "As hard as this has to be, we now know the sequence of events that caused the explosion. It's no comfort but your assistance now can maybe help in some way stop the person or people who caused the deaths of your people. Are you up to continuing?"

"As long as I can, I'll try to help." His hands were shaking and sweat poured off his forehead.

Before they picked back up they enumerated the people who had been present. Brian himself had entered the building that morning but departed for the Fox broadcast. The priest had also entered and left. The video clearly showed that Collette, the guard, an apparently unrelated customer and the priest were the only people in the building when the truck hit. Collette and the guard were dead and the other customer lay on the floor, apparently unconscious. He must have died in the blast.

After the explosion their three bodies had been recovered, mostly intact. Then there was the driver. He had been in the cab of the truck and only small parts of his body were recovered due to his proximity to the gasoline cans that had created the blast.

"We have a clear head shot of the driver," Agent Underwood commented. "There wasn't much left of him but this may help us figure out who he was. As far as the priest, we did get one good image of him. Can we look at another camera to see him better?"

"The outside camera will show the priest as he enters the building and also when he leaves. The others inside won't be as specifically positioned as the one we just watched. I think you've seen the best inside shot but I'll guide you through all of them if you want."

"We'll watch them all but you won't have to stay," Underwood said. "We can take notes and ask questions later. I'd like to run through the outside camera footage with you, just from where the priest arrives until after the blast."

Brian explained there were two cameras outside, one mounted directly above the entry door and one on a pole at the curb. The former was aimed at the street, to capture people arriving, while the latter displayed the front of the building itself. Both would help determine what happened and when.

It took almost an hour to watch footage that captured less than twenty minutes of lapsed time. They went slowly over much of the video. They saw the priest arrive – his head was bowed slightly so his face was obscured. This angle wouldn't give them any help on identifying him.

Then they watched in slow motion as the driver jumped the curb, hit a pedestrian and sent him flying to the side. Underwood postulated the truck was going perhaps twenty miles an hour when it hit the building squarely at the front door, imploding the huge plate glass windows on either side of it and driving the door and frame into the building as momentum propelled the truck forward.

Brian watched silently as the footage showed the priest step onto the sidewalk, going through the hole where a plate glass window had been. This time there was a clear view of his face as he looked up. He walked a hundred feet to the north then reached his hand into his pocket. Removing it, he turned and extended his arm toward the building. Immediately the explosion occurred.

"He detonated the gasoline cans in the truck." Special Agent Underwood asked for the video to be rewound and they watched it again. "He used a remote device to set off the explosion. Keep this to yourself for now, Mr. Sadler. We won't release this to the press yet. In fact I'd appreciate your declining all interviews for the time being."

Brian agreed. He didn't think he had the stomach to talk about what had happened to a group of news-hungry reporters.

Watching the video up to when the first responders arrived, the FBI men saw no one who appeared to be involved with the bombing. Bodies of pedestrians lay on the sidewalk and cars were blown across Fifth Avenue, but frenzied activity consisted mostly of people using cellphones and peering inside to see if they could help. Others were running away, probably afraid of a second bomb.

Underwood said, "Mr. Sadler, thanks for your help. We'll be calling often, I'm sure. Our focus at this point is to find out who this priest was, how he arranged an appointment with your staff and why he did all this just to steal an old manuscript. Nothing makes sense now, but nothing usually does at the beginning. There's undoubtedly much more going on here than a single priest on a single mission. We want to figure out what it is. First thing tomorrow I want to know everything you can tell me about that book."

Agent Underwood also explained that an FBI agent from the Financial Services Unit would be calling Brian. "Please don't read anything into this. It's routine in cases like this that we ask for your financial records for the past few years, just to make sure you didn't have a financial motive yourself in this crime. Given what we just saw on video it appears unlikely but desperate people have done some pretty crazy things in the past."

"Are you kidding? This is bullshit. You think I could have done this? Blown up my gallery? Gotten a priest to steal something to throw you off? Kill my own employee? What the hell do you think I am? Some kind of psycho?"

"Please calm down. As I tried to explain, this is purely routine. We hope we're all on the same page here, but it's really early in this investigation and my job is to leave no stone unturned. That's how we do it."

He asked Brian where he would be over the next week or so.

"I haven't given it much thought. Maybe *you* ought to tell *me* where I'll be in the next week or so. Sounds like I'm a damned suspect myself here. I guess I'll be at my apartment while I'm in New York . . . speaking of which, am I free to travel overseas? I have a gallery in London that . . . " He swallowed hard. " . . . that I guess will be my headquarters now."

Agent Underwood spoke calmly. "You may travel anywhere you wish. As long as you're accessible to us by phone I'm fine with that for now. Right now nothing's certain, but I'm not considering you a person of interest at this point."

Brian's face registered the alarm evident when he said, "*At this point?* When the hell can I be considered on the same side as you?" Brian's voice trembled as he spoke.

"Please relax. You've been through an immense crisis. It's going to be hard for you for a long, long time. You have a lot to do as far as your company's future's concerned. You're free to travel to London since sadly there's not much left here. I do promise you we'll let you inside the gallery once we finish our preliminary investigation and the building inspectors determine it's safe. You're free to travel anywhere you wish, Mr. Sadler. Please consider us all on the same team. I don't see any reason why we shouldn't be. I'll keep you informed as much as possible about our findings. Please call me if you have any ideas, any thoughts at all, or if you hear anything I should know." He gave Brian a business card.

Brian dozed in the back seat as the FBI sedan took him uptown to his apartment. Every fiber of his body ached – he had never felt so drained, physically and emotionally.

He stumbled as the doorman held the door for him and plodded to the elevator like a zombie. Finally at his condo he fumbled, finding it difficult even to insert his key into the lock. He was exhausted and wondered if he should just collapse in bed without even undressing. At the moment that didn't seem like a bad idea at all.

He closed the door behind him and plodded into the living room. From his bedroom he heard, "About time you got here."

He felt a hundred percent better just hearing that totally unexpected voice. As exhausted as he was, everything was OK now.

CHAPTER EIGHT

"I can't tell you how glad I am to see you."

"Me too, sweetie. Sorry I wasn't here yesterday but I came as quickly as I could."

Yesterday in Dallas Nicole Farber had petitioned the Court for a postponement of the trial that was to begin today. She and the Judge were friends – not close, but well acquainted. He knew she would never request a postponement if something weren't seriously wrong. She was always just the opposite – pushing to go to trial while the prosecution tried to delay things.

Like most Americans, the Judge had heard the news reports from Manhattan about the explosion on Fifth Avenue. Nicole told him it was her boyfriend, Brian Sadler, who owned the gallery and was facing the trauma of the losses of his valued employees and his New York location. He quickly granted a ten-day continuance and Nicole had caught the first plane from DFW to LaGuardia this morning. She didn't tell Brian she was coming; he thought she was in trial and she hoped a surprise might perk him up.

And it did. She was wearing sweats when he walked in the bedroom and he commented that she was the most beautiful thing he'd ever seen. They kissed and held each other for what seemed like forever but was only a minute or so. He hated to let her go.

As he undressed she prepared a hot bath, got him settled into it and brought him one of his favorite things – an XO vodka martini in a glass he kept in the freezer along with the vodka bottle. It was ice-cold and wonderful. He lay back in the steaming bath and sipped on the drink. Meanwhile Nicole stuck a pizza in the oven.

When he stepped out she knelt and dried every inch of Brian's body. Ordinarily this would have been incredibly stimulating but they both knew better than to expect that tonight. Instead of the sexual overtone it normally would have, this was just another wonderful thing Nicole did to help Brian relax right now. She got him into bed, propped pillows behind him and brought in the pizza. They sat next to each other and ate.

"I want to know all about what's going on," she said softly, "but not tonight. Let's talk in the morning."

After a couple of pieces of pizza Brian felt himself drifting as though he were slipping into a coma. "How long . . . how long will you be here?" His words slurred.

She took the plate from his lap and helped him scrunch down into bed. "For as long as you need me." She pulled the covers up to his neck and he smiled.

As his eyes closed he murmured, "That could be a really, really long time." Then he was asleep.

She smiled, patted his arm and walked to the kitchen to clean things up before she came to bed.

Brian slept fitfully. His arms flailed and his thrashing woke Nicole more than once. In his sleep he yelled Collette's name. He was obviously dreaming, rehashing the horrible events of the day. Nicole put her hand on him to calm him down and it worked for a while. But the dreams returned.

She woke around 5:30 am and felt his side of the bed. He wasn't there. She got up quickly to find him and be sure he was OK. He was sitting on the couch in his living room, staring out the window. The sun was just rising and the view from his balcony was beautiful – Central Park and beyond that the tall buildings of Fifth Avenue on the east side of the park. She knew how much Brian loved the city and hoped this crisis wouldn't dim his appreciation for it.

"How's it going? Rough night, I think."

"Yeah. I feel like I've been run over."

She saw a coffee cup in front of him. "Need more?" she said, gesturing. He declined and she stuck a K-cup in the machine on the kitchen counter for herself. She took out a mug, added milk and a pack of sweetener and brought it to the couch. She sat close to him.

Nicole leaned over and kissed his cheek. "Sorry for the dragon breath."

"No problem. You're a dragon I'll deal with anytime. And hey, I don't think I ever said thanks for coming. I just can't tell you . . ." He broke down in heaving sobs. "I can't tell you how glad I am you're here."

She held him tight. "I've got some time, sweetie. I'll be here to help you with anything you need. And I've got some ideas on things I might be able to help with professionally. When you're ready we can talk. Not now, though. Let's just sit here and watch the sun rise."

"Let's get in bed and watch the sun rise, dragon breath." · Brian smiled as he wiped tears from his eyes, stood up and took her hand.

"I'll brush my teeth first. That might help," she laughed.

The view from Brian's bedroom window was the same spectacular one as in the living room. As they slowly, quietly made love the sun's rays peeped over the massive skyscrapers on the other side of the park and enveloped their bed with soothing sunshine.

When they finished Brian fell asleep. Thankful for his peaceful snores and afraid she might wake him, Nicole lay quietly next to him and ultimately dozed herself. The sound of Brian's cellphone vibrating woke them both. As he answered she glanced at the clock on the nightstand. Twelve noon.

Seeing several other calls they'd slept through, Brian answered this one, talked for a few minutes then said, "I'll check and let you know." He disconnected and told Nicole that was Agent Underwood from the FBI, who was running the investigation. He asked Brian to try to access Collette's email and also to give him everything he could about the missing book. He hoped to find something on the customer and the priest who had been in the gallery.

It was simple and if Brian hadn't been so emotionally drained yesterday he would have remembered that. He kicked himself for not thinking clearly when he was at the FBI office.

Invigorated from Nicole and his sleep, Brian went to work on Collette's account. He knew the user ID and password Collette used to access mail. She knew his too – they worked so closely together on projects they often checked each other's mail so no one missed anything. He also knew she always communicated with the guard by email so he would have a record. The guard viewed the mail on his phone then noted the information on the clipboard he carried. The clipboard was long gone at this point but email wasn't.

Brian accessed her account and quickly located the two mails she had sent to the guard. The first, sent the day before the bombing at 2:13 pm, read, "Paul Tremble from the Met will be here at 11:30 am." That would have been the customer in the gallery who was looking at old vases in one of Bijan's small offices.

By now the world had connected the name Paul Tremble to the tragedy. The Metropolitan Museum of Art contacted the FBI within minutes after the bombing to advise he was most likely in the gallery at the time it happened. Once the bodies were removed fingerprints verified the man's identity and the information was made public.

The critical thing now for Brian was to find out about the priest. He saw the mail, sent at 4:17 pm the day before the bombing. Collette had told the guard, "A Jesuit priest will be here at 12:45 pm."

Not a name. Just "a Jesuit priest." That was most unusual and certainly unhelpful. Now Brian had to figure out how Collette had been informed he was coming.

"I'm going to call the FBI back and tell them what I've found," he said to Nicole.

"Before you do that, sweetie, I have a suggestion for you. Let me put the agency on notice that you're represented by counsel. It won't interfere with anything and I'll explain that I'm also your friend. But it'll change the rules – you'll be less likely to give them anything they might use against you because they'll have boundaries."

"I don't have anything to hide."

"You know that and I know that but for now everybody's a suspect to them. It looks like you have no involvement but I promise they'll keep you on the watch list until they figure out what happened and why. They have to make sure you had no motive."

"OK, if you think that's a good idea. I sure don't want to make them start suspecting me because I ran out and got a criminal lawyer. And Underwood told me they want my financial records going back several years. Does that sound like I'm a suspect?"

"Don't worry about it. The FBI'll know why you got a lawyer – it's pretty common, after all. And the financial records request is the most routine one they make. Your records will help clear you of suspicion – they'll see that things were going great and you had no motive to kill the goose that laid the golden egg. Everything's going to be fine about that. No worries."

She called Special Agent-in-Charge Underwood and advised that she was both an attorney and a close personal friend of Brian's. She was in town and for the record she would be representing him. She asked that he keep her informed as to the agency's interest in Brian. If at any point his status changed from innocent gallery owner to possible suspect Nicole instructed that all questioning must stop.

The man acknowledged and said, "Does Mr. Sadler have anything for me at this point?"

She handed the phone to Brian. He told Agent Underwood about the two appointments and promised to work on every angle to see how Collette had been informed that a nameless priest would be coming to the gallery. Hopefully he could also find out why. He promised to get back with the agent as soon as he knew anything.

"Now can we talk about the book the priest took?

"It's one of eight we received on consignment from the heirs of a collector in Nova Scotia. I have a Times article that explains everything pretty well. I'll email it to you when we're done. Seven of the books were in pristine condition with beautiful pages. Three are bibles and four are works of literature, all hundreds of years old. The last one, the book that was stolen, is one volume of a set that chronicles the exploits of the Knights Templars. It's nothing special, one of a set the rest of which are missing, and it's in deplorable condition. It's three or four hundred years old but I'd value it at maybe a few hundred bucks whereas the other books are worth tens of thousands each."

"Strange. Did you look inside the book? Could there be something hidden in it that makes it valuable enough to kill for?"

"I thumbed through it. It's partially in Latin, partially in medieval French and maybe English – I didn't look too closely, frankly. There are random pages scattered throughout that are totally in symbols but I can't believe that's what made it so important. There was nothing hidden in it per se. It was just a moth-eaten ratty old book – in my opinion it had no value."

"But you'll agree it did to someone. That appears to be the sole purpose of this entire episode. Any idea how many other books are in the set, and where they might be?"

"There's absolutely no way to know. I think the one I saw covered maybe 1500 to 1700 – as I said, I didn't give it much of a look. The Templars started around 1100, if memory serves me. They were supposedly eradicated in the early 1300s but someone kept the Order alive. Today the Masons have a branch called the Knights Templars. I have no idea what connection, if any, it has with the original Templars.

"I also read there's a shadow group within the Catholic Church by the same name – Knights Templars. I saw an article once that said the Catholics have a secret sect of Templars led for hundreds of years by one Cardinal or another, answerable only to the Pope. I have no idea if that's true, what their mission would be, and why it would be a secret. The whole idea of a person dressed as a priest stealing the book and destroying the gallery just makes no sense."

"That's what we have to figure out. See if you can google the article you read on the Catholic connection to the Knights Templars. One thing I think's certain – some collector didn't stage all this just to get that last remaining book for his collection of Templar exploits. There's something in that book that someone was willing to commit murder for. We have to find out what it was."

CHAPTER NINE

Vatican City

Dominic Cardinal Conti had spent two weeks trying to get through to Benedict XVI, the former pontiff now retired. The Cardinal had been part of the inner circle when Benedict was Pope – reaching him by phone had been simple. It was not so now. Conti knew that the retired Pope remained out of touch on purpose. He would not take attention away from the new pontiff. He was out of the limelight – out of the picture – and he obviously intended to keep it that way.

Another call to the ex-Pope's secretary resulted in the same response he'd heard before. "Cardinal Conti, there is really no need to keep calling. I have given his Holiness your messages. He is aware that you have called. That is all I can do for you."

Frustrating.

Conti had to find out what Benedict had promised to reveal after he finished reading the last Templar manuscript.

The good news was that Giovanni Moretti had asked to meet. That could mean only one thing – he had what Conti wanted. They selected a different shady outdoor restaurant hidden in the twisted streets of Rome and spoke quietly over coffee.

Moretti smiled and said, "I have the manuscript you want."

The Cardinal's face was hard. "So I heard. Like everyone else on earth, I saw the news. A terrorist-type bombing of the gallery on Fifth Avenue? Really? Is that how you interpreted my instruction to be discreet?" Conti had been surprised at the ferocity of what Moretti had implemented. Obviously the man had a bone to pick with someone. Perhaps it involved that woman – the Conning woman who was shot in the gallery. Or maybe it was the owner. Who knew? Moretti had once been a dangerous man. Now, Cardinal Conti mused as he sat across the table from the old man, I think he's getting senile.

"I've done your dirty work for years, Cardinal. Surely you're not disappointed. I got what you wanted."

"I asked you to get a manuscript for me, not to kill eleven people and blow up a building. Are you crazy? Did you think I would condone this atrocity?"

"I followed your direction, Your Eminence. My enthusiasm in creating such a scene wasn't because of you. It was an old score that needed settling. Someone needed a lesson and through my efforts, that person got one. You needn't worry about how I handle my responsibilities. By now you should know that. We've worked together a long time, Dominic. Don't start second-guessing me now. You'll have your manuscript. Let it go, my friend."

The old man's voice quivered as he spoke angrily. He'd been on top of his game for years and it damned sure wasn't over yet. He didn't need this cleric telling him how to do his business. He had never bowed down to anyone, even a Cardinal – except in the literal sense, of course.

"Although I utilized what appeared to be a priest in the operation, it will ultimately be clear to the authorities that the Church was actually not involved at all. The man will easily be recognized as an impostor once they investigate."

That revelation was disturbing. Conti hadn't heard about the priest – that detail hadn't been released to the press yet. He would have done things differently. Regardless, nothing could be done now. For years Moretti had overseen operations of various sorts for Conti and he was very good at what he did. The Cardinal had to accept that the job had been accomplished since Moretti now had what the cleric wanted. The manuscript was now his.

"Give it to me."

"It isn't here, Eminence. I want to go over some things with you before I deliver it." Moretti smiled and leaned back in his chair.

The Cardinal's countenance hardened. His eyes grew cold and his words were clipped, harsh. He spoke in a whispered hiss through clenched teeth, his face contorting in rage.

"What are you doing? You owe me a great deal – your freedom, in fact. I'm sure you agree. You walk around Rome a free man with a Vatican passport, thanks to me. What can possibly be in your mind? Is this how you choose to repay me, by withholding the thing I asked of you in repayment of your debt? Don't test my patience." The Cardinal looked as though he were about to explode.

"Don't test mine either, Eminence."

"What things do you want to *go over* with me?"

"All in good time. All in good time." Moretti stood and left the café.

The Cardinal was speechless. No one had ever walked out on him before. *I hope you know what you're doing, Mr. Moretti. You're an old fool going down a hazardous path. Even for a once-dangerous man such as yourself. The Lord giveth. And He can take away what He hath given. I can make sure of that.*

Conti reached in his pocket and switched off a recording device. He finished his coffee and allowed himself to calm down before returning to the Vatican. As powerful and ruthless as Giovanni Moretti once had been, Conti had access to other useful resources. This man would regret his actions today. Dominic Cardinal Conti would see to it.

CHAPTER TEN

A week later one of Conti's good friends, a Cardinal in the Diocese of Rome, was honored on his retirement at a small gathering in the Vatican. Conti had debated going – he would rather have joined his fellow cleric in a quiet dinner and a good bottle of wine to celebrate his service to the Church, but Conti decided it was important he make an appearance at his close friend's gathering.

As he mingled with twenty-odd guests a hush came over the crowd. All eyes turned to the door as former Pope Benedict XVI entered the room. No one had expected the current pontiff to be present. He was in Brazil. But the attendees were pleased to see the reclusive ex-pontiff out and about. It was an important statement to the retiring Cardinal – the former Pope thought enough of him to attend his retirement celebration.

What an opportunity, Conti thought. *He can't avoid me here.*

Conti took his place in an impromptu receiving line as clerics walked one by one past the former Pope and spoke quietly with him. When it was his turn Conti greeted Benedict then said, "You've become a hard man to get hold of, Holiness."

"It is my wish not to interfere. The guard has changed. The seat is no longer mine. Your inquiries now must go to the new Pope."

"I need to know what you were going to show me when I finished the Templar manuscripts."

"At this point I will never again have access to the secret vault. I wanted to show you a parchment I came across. Although not a part of the four volumes of Templars adventures, I believe it is a key to the pages of puzzling symbols found throughout them. I think it may explain those pages."

The Cardinal's adrenalin flowed. "How can I see it, Holiness?"

"Ah, you've quickly identified the dilemma. *You* can't. Not without the new Pope's help. I told you earlier that in my office I kept a photocopy of the register of the items in the vault. But there's something else – another copy I made. I copied the parchment that might explain the pages of symbols in the manuscripts. It was only one page and I planned to show it to you after you finished all the books.

"Maybe that copy is still there, maybe not. If you can find the copy I made then you'll have what I wanted to give you. But fatefully," Benedict smiled, "I left it in the top right drawer of my desk. Now it's the *new* Pope's desk, in *his* office. I have no idea how you're going to get him to give it to you, or if it's even still there. If he came across it he would have had no idea what it was. He may have thrown it away. You have a daunting challenge, Cardinal Conti, but one that a resourceful man such as yourself might accomplish. Perhaps. It won't be easy." He patted Conti on the shoulder and turned to the next priest in line.

CHAPTER ELEVEN

New York City

The couple of days following the explosion became busier and busier for Brian. Working from home he handled a plethora of issues ranging from insurance claims to decisions about his lease and notifications to companies with whom the gallery had contracts for things like copiers and mail equipment.

He also pulled together audited financial statements for the past three years, plus unaudited monthly statements for the current year, and submitted everything to the Financial Services agent who had called him yesterday. He had discussed everything first with Nicole – she could have demanded a subpoena but since both of them knew Brian had nothing at all to do with the explosion, she saw no harm in producing what they wanted. His financials, prepared by one of America's top CPA firms, demonstrated the remarkable profitability of Bijan Rarities over the past few years. Since Brian took over he had paid himself half a million dollars a year and still left a million or more profit annually in the corporation. He needed cash all the time – opportunities to purchase significant rarities came up suddenly and he wanted to be able to pounce, to beat the competition. So the gallery was flush with profits and money, all legitimate, all legal and all accounted for.

When Brian submitted his financials all Nicole required from the FBI was that the financial statements be considered confidential so long as Brian was not a suspect. Shortly Agent Underwood reported to Nicole that the documents were fine and Brian was no longer under any scrutiny whatsoever.

Brian was told that insurance investigators had combed through the wreckage after the FBI released the scene and it appeared nothing was salvageable anywhere in the gallery except perhaps the vault and Brian's office. The massive vault door had been closed but unlocked when the explosion occurred. It was company policy that the door be closed during office hours. That may have protected the priceless antiquities inside, but no one would know until Brian opened it. Three hours after the bombing the door had automatically locked – it was programmed to lock after three hours without activity. Agent Underwood requested that Brian return soon to help them assess what, if anything, the vault held by way of clues. Brian's insurance company had posted round-the-clock off-duty policemen outside the boarded-up front entrance. If the vault had successfully withstood the blast, it was possible the items were still intact. That would be good news to both Brian and many customers whose consignments were there. About the only good news, Brian had mused.

So sometime soon, very soon, Brian Sadler had to face the situation at the gallery. Some critical things were on hold until he came back to Bijan Rarities. Today Brian had gotten a call from the insurance company. They couldn't wait any longer. Tomorrow was the day – arrangements were made to meet Brian at his ruined gallery.

He and Nicole had walked down Fifth Avenue yesterday, his first time since the blast to go to the site. They paused across the street to look at the boarded-up façade where Bijan had once been. Agony overwhelmed him and again he felt himself getting lightheaded. Suddenly he turned and vomited against a building, heaving and retching.

"I can't do this," he told Nicole as she wiped his brow. "I just can't face it. It's too hard." They turned the corner and hailed a cab back to his apartment.

This morning Nicole and Brian had taken a sedan to the Episcopal Church of the Epiphany on the Upper East Side, arriving fifteen minutes before the funeral of Collette Conning. Later this week they would attend two more funerals, those of the security guard and the client from the Met who had died in the explosion. Brian connected with the grief felt by those who attended funeral after funeral when the World Trade Center tragedy occurred on 9/11.

As they stood on the sidewalk before entering the church several regular clients of the gallery offered condolences and commented about the tragic loss. Afterwards Brian and Nicole visited with Collette's parents for a few minutes. The funeral was hard for Brian – he was in tears several times as friends gave heartfelt remembrances of a person Brian had respected and depended upon. She would be missed by many. Brian vowed to renew his strength and his efforts to help the FBI determine why this had happened.

When they left the church Brian switched his phone off mute and saw a call from Agent Underwood. On the way back to his apartment he returned the call with the phone on speaker.

"We have a number of things to go over with you. I was checking to see when we might get together."

"I've been watching the news reports. You haven't released much to the press."

"We didn't want to jump the gun. We had to be sure of our information and also not release anything that could harm the ongoing investigation. We plan to do a short press conference late this afternoon. Could we meet before that?"

"We can," Brian responded. "How about we meet up here this time instead of my coming downtown? I'll buy your lunch."

"Thanks but we're not allowed to accept gratuities, and I'm pretty sure I can't afford the places you go. May I meet you at your apartment at 1:45? And will Miss Farber be there as well?"

Brian glanced at her and she nodded.

"1:45 is fine. And yes, Nicole will be attending too."

"One thing to consider. In the next day or so you have to look inside the vault with your insurance adjuster and us. I'd appreciate your letting me know when that would fit into your schedule. Sorry to push you but some important steps are on hold until you can get inside."

"Actually I worked that out with the adjuster. I'm meeting him at ten am tomorrow at Bijan. I was going to tell you that when I saw you this afternoon."

Brian and Nicole had the car drop them at Harry Cipriani, one of his favorite restaurants, just a few blocks from where Bijan Rarities had been. He dismissed the driver – they would walk back after lunch – and glanced down Fifth Avenue. Now that four days had passed the concrete barriers had been removed. It was just too difficult to block this major street and the danger appeared to have been isolated to the one incident.

They ducked inside Cipriani's and were warmly greeted by the maître d', who offered his regret and condolences at the loss of life and property Brian had experienced. Brian was a regular and Nicole often joined him when she was in town. At a restaurant of this caliber, the senior staff knew its steady patrons well. "We're booked solid," he said, glancing at his reservations list, "but if you and Miss Farber will give me a few minutes I think we can accommodate you. Just have a seat at the bar and have a glass of wine on the house."

Within ten minutes they had a table in the busy restaurant. Through the windows Brian could see the Plaza Hotel across the street. Pedestrians jostled down the sidewalk as though nothing had happened. It was a little surreal, he thought, that life just goes on. But in Manhattan, like most huge cities, that was a fact.

"Hey," Nicole said softly. "Earth to Brian."

"Sorry. Was I daydreaming?"

"You were gone for a minute. You do that a lot lately. I worry about you. You've been through a lot. When I go back what are you planning to do next?" By asking about the future she hoped to get his mind off the present.

They hadn't talked much about what lay ahead since the event happened. Now they chatted about the new Bijan Gallery in Old Bond Street in London. It had only been open a year or so. The decision to open a second gallery had been easy for Brian. He loved London as much as New York and he thoroughly enjoyed having a business reason to make frequent trips to England. Nicole loved it too and joined him regularly when she could grab a few days here and there.

"Don't hold me to anything right now, but I'm thinking I'm not reopening in New York," Brian said. "I don't know if I can handle it, frankly. There's just too much that's been wrenched out of my soul and at the moment, without giving it a lot of thought, I think I might relocate to London."

He put into words what had only been vague thoughts until now. He immediately regretted it – his thoughts and ideas didn't even address his relationship with Nicole. He felt selfish. *I'm thinking only of myself, my sadness and loss, and not the person I care the most about.*

"I . . . I want you to know you mean the world to me. More than anything. I'm just thinking out loud – none of this is meant to hurt you or our relationship. I love you. I wish we were together a hundred percent of the time. You know that, right?"

"Sweetie, I do know that. And I feel the same way. I think it's too early to make long-term plans. I'd love for you to have a gallery in Dallas. I never said it before, because I couldn't have seen you splitting your time between New York, London *and* Texas, but now it might make sense if you wanted it. It's too soon to talk about anything. You need to concentrate on what you have – the gallery in London. Work from there for awhile until you come up with a battle plan. You know I'll support you in whatever you decide . . . just make a little place for me in there somewhere because I love you too!" She smiled at him and squeezed his hand.

As they ate, Brian talked about tomorrow. "I'm really nervous about going into the gallery. I have no idea what to expect. I'm not sure I can keep it together."

"You can do it. I know you and I know you're strong. You have to help the FBI figure out what happened, for the sake of your people who died if nothing else. I'm happy to go with you if you'd like."

"I need to do it by myself. This is going to be hard but I need to make this first step toward returning to the reality of what things will be going forward. I hope you understand. You're my rock right now. But I have to be able to stand alone too."

CHAPTER TWELVE

The doorman rang Brian's apartment and announced the arrival of the senior FBI agent. Once Underwood was settled into Brian's living room with a cup of coffee he gave Brian and Nicole an update.

Yesterday the FBI had learned the identity of the dead driver of the stolen truck, an American citizen named Hassan Palavi born here but raised in Iran.

"He's never broken the law in the USA and we can't find anything about him. He had an American passport and came to the States a lot in the past few years. We searched his apartment in Queens. It's a bare-bones place, a few pieces of furniture, the Koran and a couple of other foreign language books, and no food in the fridge. At this point I can say we're not considering this a terrorist act. No one's claimed responsibility and frankly, what's the point of such destruction just so a priest can steal a book? That's the mystery we have to figure out while we look for the perpetrator."

The conversation shifted to the man in clerical garb - the primary focus of the investigation so far. The agent explained they were carefully avoiding calling him a priest since no one knew who he was.

"We have two good shots of his face. We first called the Archdiocese since it's only a few blocks from you and he might have come from there. Every single person who works at St. Patrick's or the Archdiocese offices, including the Archbishop, looked at the shots. No one recognized him and we determined his appointment wasn't made by anyone there. That's not to say some other church in town didn't send a priest to blow up Bijan. But we now believe this guy was dressed as a priest to throw us off. We need to know if he was paid by someone or acting on his own behalf. What was his interest in the old Templar book, the one you originally thought was worthless. Obviously it was worth killing for."

Agent Underwood continued. "This was a very big job. Putting all the parts of this together, including a suicide bomber, a carefully timed operation, the shooting of Collette Conning and blowing up part of a Fifth Avenue building – all those things point to a large-scale operation with a lot of money behind it. I can't tell you everything we're working on right now, but I need you to think if there is someone who holds a grudge against you or the gallery. Could this have been a retaliatory strike – revenge for something? If it is, it must have been something major. If you can think of anything, it could be a tremendous help."

The agent explained that a press conference would be held at 5:45 pm in front of Bijan's boarded-up building. The FBI and police department would have representatives and Underwood himself would be the primary speaker.

"We're going to release details about the pickup driver, the method by which they blew up the gallery and pictures of the man dressed as a priest. We'll also reveal that Collette was shot prior to the bombing and the guard was run over by the pickup. Once we're finished, you're free to speak to the media yourself. One thing I ask – if there's ever anything you intend to tell the press that I don't know, tell me first. We consider you a victim and your cooperation is essential."

Brian looked at Nicole. She took his hand and replied, "You can count on Brian to work with you. He *is* a victim. He's lost a great deal. And we both want you to find out what happened here."

"I want to offer a reward," Brian said, looking at Nicole. "Is that OK for me to do?"

"I see nothing wrong with it. Agent Underwood?"

"It's usually a good idea. It could bring out someone who has information. What amount are you thinking?"

"A hundred thousand dollars."

"OK, with your permission I'll use the standard language about requiring arrest and conviction to claim the reward. That eliminates a lot of problems.

Underwood stood and extended his hand. "Unless I see you at the press conference I'll meet you at ten am tomorrow at the gallery. Thanks for your time. I can show myself out."

While they were meeting Brian's muted cellphone had vibrated several times as calls and voicemails were received. He checked it – none of the five numbers was one he recognized.

"I want to talk to you about our conversation," he told Nicole. "Just let me listen to one voicemail and see who these people are."

He put the phone on speaker and pressed the first voicemail number. "Mr. Sadler, this is Arlen Shadrick with the Post. I'll be at the FBI's press conference this afternoon. Wondered if you would be too and if I could grab you for a quick interview afterwards. Please call me back." He left a number.

"The rest are probably his contemporaries at the other news services," Nicole commented. "If you want to listen to them all now it's ok with me."

He did and she was right. They were from Fox, CNN, the Times and WNBC New York. He listened to each message long enough to ascertain who was calling, then deleted them. "I guess whichever one gets to me first will be the one I talk to," he said absently.

"My suggestion is we develop a few talking points that you're comfortable with. You stick to those and give a 'no comment' to anything else. That'll make it easier for you."

"I'm sure glad I have you. You think of everything. I'd have just gone out there and winged it."

"Yes, and that wouldn't have been good. These people are digging for dirt. They want something juicy and good. They'd love to catch you in an error or bring out a deep emotion no one has seen. We need to role-play before you do anything. Then I think you should hold a press conference yourself. Let them all attend at once instead of your having to endure this half a dozen times. Maybe you allow questions after your statement, maybe not. That's up to you. And just so I know, do you really think you should go to the FBI's press conference later on?"

"No way. Let's just watch it on TV from here."

"Agreed. You shouldn't be there. It'll just put the media into a feeding frenzy and you won't be ready for them."

They popped a bottle of good Chardonnay and talked about the meeting. Brian pondered the agent's question about revenge or retaliation.

"The reason for the entire bombing was obviously to steal the Templars manuscript. That's clear from the video. The priest or whatever shot Collette just before the truck crashed in. He took the book with him. I don't think this has anything to do with me."

Nicole sat quietly for a few minutes, slowly sipping her wine and thinking. Finally she said, "There's one person who once was powerful enough to pull this off. He had the connections, he had the money and he has the motive. He hates both of us." She looked Brian in the eyes. "You know who I'm talking about, don't you?"

"Sure. But that's impossible. He's in a Guatemalan prison serving a life sentence for murder. Right?"

"Far as we know. Do you think we should check and make sure he's still there?"

"I'm not sure who to call."

"Well, there's one person who owes you a debt of gratitude for past services rendered. I'll bet you can call the President of the United States and get your answer."

CHAPTER THIRTEEN

For thirty years John "Johnny Speed" Spedino was *the* godfather, the capo del capi, boss of bosses. Head of the powerful New York mob, he was the most dangerous criminal in America, seemingly beyond the clutches of law enforcement for decades. He was as elusive as John Gotti, who earned the nickname "Teflon Don" for his ability to slip out of the grip of federal agents. But Gotti had finally been taken down. Spedino too, as far as Brian Sadler knew.

Brian had first heard about Johnny Speed when he became involved with Bijan Rarities. Brian was a stockbroker at the investment firm Warren Taylor and Currant in Dallas. That high-flying operation attracted the attention of the Securities and Exchange Commission, then the FBI, as it led initial public offerings for companies that had no track record, no plans, no nothing. When WT&C was finished, those shell companies suddenly had millions of dollars, all of which was pushed back into the stockbroker's next deal. The firm's investors made money as long as new offerings could be pumped into the market. The next public offering fueled the last one. It was heady, exciting and crazy and the firm's brokers made serious money. The risk was high – they were right on the edge of ethics and the law – but the rewards were too.

A proposal from Darius Nazir, the owner of Bijan Rarities, oddly had landed on Brian Sadler's desk one day. Evaluating potential offerings for the firm wasn't part of Brian's job, but he was intrigued - he read every word of Bijan's business plan. This was a company he became interested in personally. He loved archaeology and ancient things. Bijan was fast becoming known as a major player in the world of rarities, from Egypt to South America to Turkey and elsewhere. Brian thought this could be his ticket out of the brokerage business into something that was his passion.

Brian flew to New York on his own time, became good friends with Nazir and helped the gallery go public in one of WT&C's last offerings before the Feds took it down over another company's deal that turned out to be a total fraud.

In a strange, bizarre turn of events Nazir ended up dead and Brian was handed ownership of the gallery. It was the most fortuitous moment in his life – a turning point that took him from small time stockbroker to Fifth Avenue businessman.

Mob boss John Spedino had somehow been involved with Darius Nazir. Brian was certain of that although he never found the connection. Spedino had enlisted Brian's help in obtaining one of the world's major rarities, the Bethlehem Scroll. Brian recalled how furious Nazir had been when he learned Brian was working with Spedino. He had chastised Brian, telling him the mobster was dangerous beyond belief. Nazir knew him well, Brian thought. That was disturbing. Brian wondered how the gallery owner knew Spedino but never found out – Nazir died before Brian could ask.

Spedino had inserted himself again into Brian Sadler's life when Brian was in Belize and Guatemala searching for an ancient lost city of the Mayas. People who were controlled by Spedino kidnapped both Brian and Nicole.

The man had even compromised Nicole's principles, using a date-rape drug to force her into total submission, corporately and personally.

A clever Brit with a hidden agenda brought the godfather to justice at long last. Facing charges in the USA and Guatemala, the boss of bosses had ended up in the latter country's Pavon Prison, serving a life sentence for murder.

Long story short, the problems the godfather of New York had right now were in large part due to the efforts of Brian Sadler and Nicole Farber. It was a fair statement to say Johnny Speed would hold a grudge against the people who had finally put him in prison . . . for life.

Brian looked at the contact list on his phone, scrolled down to the name *Harry* and called. Less than ten people on earth knew this particular number. Brian Sadler was one who did. Brian Sadler had the private cell number of the President of the United States.

As usual, the call went to voicemail. *He's the busiest man in the world*, Brian thought as a computer-generated voice said, "Please leave a message." Short and sweet. If anyone got this wrong number they'd never know whom they'd reached.

"Hey, Harry. It's Brian. Call me back when you can please. No rush. Just had a question. Say hi to Jennifer and the girls."

Once his college roommate had been inaugurated President, Brian had defaulted to addressing him as "Mr. President" out of respect. William Henry Harrison IV had quickly told him to knock it off, saying they knew each other too well for such formality in private. So Brian did it the President's way, even though it felt strange to him every time he called the leader of the free world "Harry."

Legal pad in hand, Nicole sat on the couch making a list of talking points. Brian went to the kitchen, retrieved the Chardonnay and poured them another glass. He sat next to her, saying nothing as she wrote.

The 5:45 press conference was scheduled strategically to coincide with the hour of local news coming up at six. Brian turned on his TV five minutes early and muted until he saw the newscaster in front of a screen. Displayed were a picture of his building and the words "Fifth Avenue Bombing." He turned up the sound.

There was a podium in front of the plywood barrier that covered what had been Bijan's two huge showroom windows. A newscaster recounted the events four days previously, explaining that a truck bomber had destroyed the famous antiquities gallery and part of the two floors above it, killing eleven people and injuring more than fifty, mostly pedestrians and drivers who had been unfortunate enough to be in close proximity to the blast.

Special Agent-in-Charge Underwood stepped to the podium, introduced himself and the New York City Police Chief, who stood by his side. Underwood presented the facts, explaining that most of the information they knew came from the gallery's video surveillance equipment. He identified the driver and gave a brief background on the Iranian-American. Then he shifted to the perpetrator.

"Pictures and parts of the surveillance video were distributed to the media a few minutes ago," Underwood said. "We enlist the public's help to identify the person, probably a male, dressed as a Jesuit priest, who shot Collette Conning, the assistant to the owner of the gallery and who detonated the gasoline cans that caused the massive explosion."

Next the Chief of Police spoke briefly, promising full cooperation from his agency to bring the perpetrators to justice. "This was a well-planned operation," he said. "There is someone who knows something about this. If you have information that might help please call police or the FBI immediately."

Underwood wrapped the conference with an announcement that Bijan Rarities owner Brian Sadler had offered a reward of $100,000 for the arrest and conviction of those involved in the bombing. As he spoke the networks broadcast the tip hotline phone number.

The conference lasted only eight minutes and the men took no questions from the media. Immediately following it, the news stations posted a picture of Hassan Palavi, the driver of the pickup. The photo had been obtained from his passport application and was two years old. It didn't matter. Palavi was dead.

The critical photos came next. They were the two of the person posing as a priest. Before the video footage was played an announcer told viewers how graphic the material would be. The film ran, showing the "priest" glancing at his watch precisely at one pm, pulling a gun and shooting Collette point-blank a few seconds later, then the truck crashing through the front window and toppling the guard. Finally the person was shown on the sidewalk pressing the detonator and walking away as the building exploded. It was tough to watch but the FBI hoped it might stir someone to offer information.

The moment the conference ended Brian's cellphone rang. The number showed "Blocked." Answering, he heard a voice familiar to him and most other Americans – the voice of the President. He put it on speaker.

"Hey buddy. Sorry I didn't call back earlier. I watched your press conference first. I'm so sorry about what happened. It must be devastating for you and I hope the FBI can quickly figure something out. I'm sure pushing them from this side. Is Nicole with you?"

"Thanks, Harry. Yes, she sure is and she's listening, so be careful what you say!

FYI she gave notice to the FBI that she was acting as my attorney, just in case. I hope you don't think . . ."

"Brian, come on. I think that's a very smart move. The FBI has to check everyone out. You and I know you're fine but they have a job to do. Nicole, you can rein them in if they get out of line."

"Hi, Harry. Thanks for the kind thoughts for Brian right now. He's been through a lot."

"He sure has. And Brian, the reward is a good idea too. Glad you're offering it. A hundred thousand bucks may bring out the information you need. So, what can I do to help?"

"The agent asked me this afternoon if I knew anyone who had a grudge against me. The only person Nicole and I could come up with was John Spedino. But the last I heard the godfather was tucked away in prison in Guatemala. I don't know who else to call, and I know how busy you are, but could you check on him and let me know?"

"Absolutely. That's simple and won't take long at all. We'll get on it and I'll let you know soon as I hear anything. Is there anything else we can do down here in Washington to help you?"

"I think that's it for the moment. If I get in a big jam I may call again."

"Always good to hear your voice, my friend. And listen. Once things settle down you and Nicole come see us and let's have dinner. We don't get a chance to have quiet times with old friends much anymore."

Promising to do so, Brian hung up. The President then turned to his computer and shot a message to his Chief of Staff. Within minutes Bob Parker stood in the Oval Office getting instructions from Harry Harrison.

Fifteen minutes later Brian's phone rang again. The same blocked message appeared.

"That was fast."

"Yeah, and not good, Brian. I'm furious at the Embassy in Guatemala City for not letting you know about this, but John Spedino went missing from his prison cell awhile back. The Ambassador said it's possible he had been gone for a couple of weeks when someone finally decided to check on him. Ask me can a guy like that go without being checked every day? Of course he can't. But he's the godfather. It's pretty simple to pay people off in a Guatemalan prison. Money talks. He was apparently living a life of luxury, such as it was, inside the prison and then just disappeared."

"Shit. Any clue where he might be?"

"My question exactly. And no. Nobody knows. And until my Chief of Staff called, it seems nobody gave it much attention. Just one less prisoner to deal with. You can damn well bet *that's* changing as we speak. I'm directing the FBI and CIA to get with Interpol and launch a worldwide top-priority search for him. Son of a bitch, it's hard sometimes to figure out what people are thinking. You think they might have considered letting somebody know this guy was gone? This really is irritating. Hey – do you want FBI give you and Nicole protection until we find something out? I'm happy to arrange it."

"We can't live like that. I can't imagine the godfather would come back to New York – that'd be pretty crazy in my opinion – and I don't want to have an agent with me every minute." Nicole was next to him, listening and shaking her head. "Neither does Nicole. We'll be fine."

"OK. For now I'm instructing the FBI's Manhattan office to look into the possibility that Spedino could be behind all of this. Again, I'm sorry the government dropped the ball on notifying you. I'm as upset as you are."

President Harrison promised to call the minute any information was available. Brian thanked him for all the effort and hung up. He looked at Nicole.

She spoke softly. "Well, this one doesn't take a rocket scientist to figure out. There's your guy with a grudge."

CHAPTER FOURTEEN

At ten am several people stood on the sidewalk in front of what had been Bijan Rarities. The police had taped off a large area outside of which several journalists with cameras watched the activity. Uniformed officers ensured those without permission remained outside the barrier.

An hour earlier a workman had removed two pieces of plywood that covered the ruined hole that had been the gallery's entrance and windows. He set up two very large Klieg lights, the kind used in filmmaking. They filled the ruined showroom with an intense light.

Brian, an adjuster from his insurance company, Agent Underwood, a second FBI agent and an NYPD detective waited for the arrival of a sixth person – a structural engineer who had been working with the building's owner to determine how extensive the damage to it actually was. He had observed the building over the past five days and saw no further collapse so he had declared it safe for Brian and the others to enter. As a precaution the engineer would be along with them.

Agent Underwood took Brian aside and said, "It's not often I get a call straight from the top. The Director called me yesterday and told me the President wants an investigation into John Spedino's possible involvement in the bombing. I'm not impressed by much any more, but I'd love to know how you got the President to intercede on your behalf. I also need everything you know about Spedino so we can move on the Director's . . . ah, request, I guess you'd say. More like a directive, actually."

"The President was my college roommate. He told me yesterday that Spedino escaped from the Guatemalan prison where he was serving a life sentence for murder."

The last member of their group walked up. "We'll talk later," Underwood said as they all approached the bombed gallery.

The structural engineer led the way, pointing out dangerous areas where shattered glass and steel lay strewn about the floor. Brian thought the scene was surreal. He was surprised to see one of his display cases still intact, glass and all, while others had simply been blown away. The twisted remains of the pickup sat almost exactly in the middle of the expansive showroom. A couple of large vases lay broken in a corner next to the pedestal displays where they had once stood. Brian pointed at them and casually remarked, "There lies a half million bucks worth of busted pots."

The day was already warm and there was no air circulating inside the bombed structure. The sickly sweet smell of decay pervaded the room. It was nauseating – Brian suddenly began to feel lightheaded.

Agent Underwood opened his briefcase and pulled out paper masks, the kind painters use, and a jar of Mentholatum. "The coroner wasn't able to remove everything from the site because of the extent of the damage to the driver's body. It's been a few hot days in here and you might want to use a mask. Just stick Mentholatum inside the mask and put it on. It'll hide the smell." Brian did and it helped a lot.

He turned to the others. "Anyone else need a mask?" The engineer and insurance adjuster gratefully accepted. The lawmen didn't. None of them wanted to be the first to admit they couldn't handle a death scene. For his part, Brian was glad the agent had thought to bring the masks. It made things tolerable.

Stepping over and around the debris from the gallery and its collapsed ceiling, they walked through the showroom to a hallway behind. The two FBI agents turned on powerful flashlights. On the left side was the closed door to Brian's office. He tried the knob; it was locked. He pulled out a key and opened the door.

Fortunately the wall at the back of the showroom was made of concrete. It had withstood the blast and his office was virtually intact albeit with a fine coating of dust on every surface. His chair sat behind the desk, the dock for his laptop was exactly where he had left it, and on the side table was an empty space where the missing manuscript had been. Collette Conning had taken it to the priest just before he killed her.

"Everything looks fine here," Brian said. "Let's see how the vault made out." He walked across the hall from his office to the massive door that was identical to those used in banks. He gave the large handle a tug – it was securely locked.

Explaining that the vault had a time delay, Brian entered a code on a keypad and an intermittent beep indicated the countdown process had begun. "So far so good," he muttered to no one in particular. Brian had been concerned the vault door might have been damaged in the blast. That could have required a demolition team to break through the thick, heavy door. Thanks to its location away from the showroom itself he was now hopeful the door and its hinges were okay. In a few minutes they'd find out.

Finally a series of louder beeps announced the end of the time-delay phase and Brian entered another code sequence onto the keypad. A noticeable thunk caused Brian to smile grimly. "Sounds like it's unlocked." He pulled down on the large handle and it moved noiselessly. Then he tugged on the door; it easily swung open.

Brian fished out another key to open the barred door that was next. He couldn't see inside the vault – the entrance was small and his body blocked the flashlight beams behind him.

He turned to Underwood. "Is it OK if I go in first? I'll need a light."

The agent nodded and handed the flashlight to him. Brian stepped inside the vault. Everything was exactly as it should have been. The vault itself was heavily reinforced like a bunker. It appeared the blast had had no effect on anything inside. Artifacts and ancient objects were lined up on shelves and pedestals and nothing had been damaged. Brian breathed a sigh of relief. The most valuable of the objects were in here, undamaged. And many of these belonged to others – they were held by Bijan on consignment, awaiting a sale or auction in the future.

The insurance adjuster said, "Will it be difficult to get me a list of the things that weren't in here, so we can know what was destroyed as compared to these things which weren't damaged?"

"Piece of cake," Brian replied, explaining that every morning Collette Conning prepared a list of items to bring from the vault for display in the gallery. The list from the morning of the bombing still lay on a counter just inside the vault. Only a fraction of the items were ever brought out, and none of the most expensive ones was. Those were brought to the showroom only if a client made an appointment to see one of them. Otherwise they were always securely locked up. That had been fortuitous on the day the bombing occurred. It made life considerably easier for Brian Sadler and his clients. And for the insurance company too. The adjuster took Brian's list with a promise to copy and return it. He also asked Brian to provide valuations and ownership details on the things that had been destroyed. That would also prove easy for Brian as everything was on the gallery's servers.

Agent Underwood asked Brian to show him the seven books from the Nova Scotia collector. The eighth had been the reason behind the bombing. Brian pointed to a shelf with the beam of the flashlight. "They're right here," he said. "I never got a chance to even look inside the covers."

Underwood asked if he and Brian could examine them more closely to make sure there was nothing in them that would help the investigation. Brian agreed and they decided to take them back to Brian's apartment when everyone was finished here. He and the FBI agent carried the books to Underwood's car while press photographers eagerly shot pictures of their activities.

While Brian walked around the showroom, recalling this piece or that which now lay on the floor in pieces, the FBI agents and policeman examined the area in the gallery where Collette Conning had been killed. A forensic team had previously scoured the room so new information was unlikely to be forthcoming but more sets of eyes might pick up something. The insurance adjuster jotted notes and took pictures with his phone. The engineer walked the perimeter of the gallery, checking the integrity of the steel beams.

In half an hour everyone was finished. Brian rode with Agent Underwood and the second agent to his apartment house. Over the next two hours they looked at the seven volumes from the Crane collection in Nova Scotia and talked extensively about John Spedino's involvement in the lives of Brian and Nicole.

The books revealed nothing of benefit to the FBI. They were exactly what they appeared to be – Bibles and works of literature. No notes hidden inside their pages, no secret inscriptions, nothing out of the ordinary. They were beautiful, valuable old books, Brian commented, but at this point the missing Templars volume was obviously the one someone cared about.

Underwood and his associate left with a promise to call if anything developed.

CHAPTER FIFTEEN

Vatican City

Dominic Cardinal Conti had made a decision. He had to get the photocopy from the papal office one way or another. He had to see what information it contained. He thought it might unravel the ancient mystery he was certain rested in the missing manuscript – the one Giovanni Moretti now possessed.

Speaking of whom, Moretti hadn't called so the Cardinal had decided to play his own game. He wouldn't make the first move. But it had been four days since the old man had walked out of their meeting here in Rome. *I'll give it twenty-four more hours. If he hasn't called I'll start things moving in a direction that will make life unpleasant for the ungrateful Mr. Moretti.*

Right now Conti had two choices – the overt one was to approach the Pope, tell him

Benedict had left a photocopy in the drawer and ask for it. That might work but it might backfire. First, he wasn't close to the new pontiff so he likely wouldn't cooperate. Instead of getting the document he might lose it forever. Second, that choice meant publicizing the document. The Pope might ask questions – what was it, and why did the Cardinal think it so important? No, an overt move wasn't the right one.

Which is why at 1:25 am the Cardinal was standing behind a tapestry in a long hallway that led to the papal offices fifty feet away. The pontiff was on a well-publicized trip back to his homeland in Buenos Aires, which meant the usual high security around here was almost non-existent tonight. The treasures of the Vatican were everywhere in the huge complex of buildings – but there was nothing that special in and of itself here in the somewhat austere papal office. If a thief sought riches he would go elsewhere.

Since the pontiff was away only one Swiss Guard sat in a chair outside the Pope's office. Dominic knew his routine. When the Pope was gone the same sentry sat from ten pm until four in the morning, taking a five-minute bathroom break every two hours and eating a meal out of his backpack around 1:30. Tonight should be no exception and the Cardinal waited for what always happened right now.

The guard stood, stretched and walked down the hall away from where Conti hid. He was going to a tiny pantry fifty feet away. He would fix a double espresso in a coffee maker, add milk and walk back to have his dinner. Based on the Cardinal's observation the past three nights, the guard would be away from the Pope's door between four and six minutes. Never less, never more. Hopefully tonight was typical.

As soon as the guard entered the pantry, Cardinal Conti clicked a stopwatch and moved. He expected the massive office door to be unlocked and it was. He entered, shut the door and walked to the Pope's desk. He pulled on the upper right drawer. The desk was locked. *Damn the luck,* the Cardinal involuntarily thought. He had brought a pick – as he looked at the drawer he saw there was no keyhole. *This drawer doesn't lock. It's the middle drawer that controls them all.*

Hoping this desk was like so many others, he pulled on the long middle drawer, the one above the kneehole space. *Come on, just be shut. Don't be locked.*

As the middle drawer slid out a noticeable click indicated the other drawers could now be opened as well. Conti glanced at his watch. Two and a half minutes down. He had ninety seconds to finish, leave and hide before the guard returned.

In the upper right drawer were a number of things including a stamp pad and rubber stamps, a number of old seals, the kind that work with wax, and a plethora of papers. Conti pulled them out and rummaged through them, starting at the bottom. Hopefully what Benedict had left was low in the pile and hadn't been discarded when the new Pope moved in.

He was getting nowhere. A quiet ding notified him there were thirty seconds left. Suddenly his hand pulled out a legal size piece of paper. It was a copy of something very old and it contained the same symbols he had seen in the four Templar manuscripts. Voila!

Conti stuck the paper in his pocket, closed the drawer and ran to the office door. He opened it carefully, glancing down the hallway toward the pantry. This was the tricky part. If the guard had been sitting back at his post when the door opened, the Cardinal would have had serious explaining to do. He would certainly have been detained, questioned and possibly sanctioned for his clandestine activities tonight.

But God was with him. At least that's what Conti attributed his good fortune to – maybe it was the devil at work instead but this cleric chose the former. The guard was still puttering around in the closet – the Cardinal could hear him – so Conti closed the door and ran back down the hall to his hiding place fifty feet away.

In less than fifteen seconds the guard strode back to his post, coffee in hand, and sat down. As he turned and reached for his backpack Cardinal Conti crept quietly away around a corner and left the papal office wing. Guards patrolled the corridors – when Conti met one he bowed his head as if on a late night meditative stroll. No one stopped the Cardinal – obviously this holy man, unable to sleep, had chosen to walk these sacred halls deep in prayer.

Reaching his own office, Conti entered and locked the door. He put the photocopy in his desk, walked to a nearby couch and lay down. He would spend the rest of the night here. It would raise less questions than if his late-night departure time were noted on a sentry's checkout sheet.

He fell asleep easily and dreamed about an ancient box so special it took a legion of Knights to protect it.

CHAPTER SIXTEEN

London

Brian preferred the daytime British Airways flight to London. Most planes from the States to Britain flew all night and arrived at the crack of dawn. That seemed counterproductive to Brian. He could leave Kennedy airport at 7:15 am, enjoy breakfast and a light lunch on the plane and arrive at seven pm local time. He rarely carried much luggage – the company flat in London was stocked with his clothes to allow him that convenience.

The express train from Heathrow to Paddington Station put him in central London by eight and he was at his flat in Cadogan Square twenty minutes later. After sitting on the plane all day he was ready for some exercise before bed – he put on his running gear and set off on a neighborhood run. Knightsbridge was busy this evening – pedestrians crowded Sloane Street, window-shopping at high-end boutiques that beckoned them and their money inside. He struggled with the crowds for a few blocks, then gave up. He turned onto Pont Street then up into trendy Beauchamp Place. Its one long block held stores, bars and Brian's favorite Thai restaurant in London. Patara Thai's open front door was inviting and the delicious smells wafting out made him hungry. Tomorrow night, he promised himself.

Heading east along Knightsbridge past Harrods, he turned behind the Sheraton into Lowndes Square then zigged and zagged back towards the building where his flat was located. Night had fallen and as he ran the last half-mile he took in the scenery. Street lamps created dim pockets of light along tree-lined sidewalks. This part of London had four-storied buildings in the Victorian style, each with a chimney pot backlit by the streetlights of Sloane Street a few blocks over. They reminded him of the antics of Bert, Dick Van Dyke's chimney sweep character in *Mary Poppins*. London was a city and an experience he never grew tired of. Like New York but in a different way, London was another place he loved.

Back at the flat he checked his phone. One call, about an hour ago. He listened to voicemail and heard a familiar Oxford accent.

"Brian, old boy, I hope this call finds you safely back in God's country. I know your plane was due to land a couple of hours ago so give me a call tonight if it's not too late, or tomorrow if you'd rather. I'm anxious to see you when you have time to catch up."

Lord Arthur Borland. The Earl of Weymouth. Brian smiled as he thought of his good friend and their adventures in Central America. He had become very fond of Arthur. He enjoyed the times with him more than with almost anyone else Brian knew. He glanced at his watch – almost ten pm. Not too late for a phone call to this night owl.

The two men talked for half an hour, first about the tragedy in New York involving Bijan Rarities, then recalling the adventures they'd shared in Guatemala and Belize. Arthur was the British aristocrat who worked with Brian to bring down the Mafia boss John Spedino. At first things had appeared grim for Lord Borland in that escapade a year or so ago but it turned out well and Spedino had been put behind bars for life. At least that had been the idea when he was convicted.

"Did you know John Spedino escaped from prison in Guatemala?"

"I hadn't heard. That's disturbing news. How did you find out?"

Brian explained that President Harrison had inquired and discovered Spedino had been missing for some time.

"That's serious, especially for us. Do you think he might have been involved in the bombing?"

"I can't imagine how or why Spedino would have done this. It looks more like this was a very elaborate move to steal what I originally considered to be a worthless eighteenth century manuscript. You could be right but I think it's something else. There's no doubt it took someone with a lot of power and a lot of money to orchestrate the bombing of a building on Fifth Avenue and the murders of eleven people including a suicide bomber. All that for one volume of a set of old Knights Templars books? It just doesn't make sense. Am I missing something?"

"Actually you are, if my hunches are right. I have an idea about that manuscript. Didn't you tell me earlier it was one of several old books found in Nova Scotia?"

"Yeah, it was. The collector bought it years ago, maybe around the same time as he acquired the other seven books. Some of those are virtually priceless – one of a kind and in unbelievable condition. All of those survived the explosion because they were locked in the vault."

"Interesting, but I don't think those seven have anything to do with this," Borland replied. "I think the Templar book does, and I'm certain Nova Scotia does as well. I've been doing a little research over at the

Monument Club and I have an interesting theory to present to you. Let me ask you, did you possibly make a copy of the manuscript that was stolen? Or any parts of it?"

"I didn't. I just didn't see the value in it and tossed it aside. I'm intrigued by your mysterious questions and I can't wait to hear your theory. Are you available for lunch one day this week?"

"I know you just got to town, old boy, but I could meet tomorrow. Is that too soon?"

"For you, my Lord? That suits me just fine. How about 1 pm at the Club?"

The Monument Club sits on the Victoria Embankment overlooking the Thames River. The massive building that has always been its home was erected in 1894, a few years after a group of men, linked by the common thread of archaeology, founded the club itself. There are a few women members today but its reading rooms, extensive library, bar and restaurant are dominated by men. The place is primarily a gentlemen's club, an aroma of fine cigars lingering in the dark bar, the clink of an obligatory gin and tonic or martini preceding a leisurely lunch or dinner.

Some of the members are professional archaeologists and anthropologists. Others are amateurs or those otherwise interested peripherally in ancient things and interesting stories of the past. One of the latter, Brian had hoped for years to become a member someday. Once he owned Bijan Rarities and began to make a name for himself in the world of rarities, he petitioned his old friend Oscar Carrington for help.

Carrington, the owner of an exclusive antiquities shop in London's posh Knightsbridge area, was pleased to put up his American friend for membership. It was convenient that the Monument Club had a location on Manhattan's Upper East Side as well as the one in London and before long Brian Sadler found himself frequently at one location or the other for drinks, lunch or dinner. He also occasionally used its world-class reference libraries; each location contained tens of thousands of books, manuscripts and articles that were invaluable for research. If a needed tome weren't available on one side of the pond, it was quickly dispatched from the other for a member's use.

Lord Borland was also a member of the Monument Club. He had been invested automatically as the descendant of a member. His deceased father, Sir John Borland, the eighth Earl of Weymouth, had been perhaps the club's most flamboyant and outspoken representative in its history. "Captain Jack," as Arthur's father was affectionately known to all, inherited a vast sum of money and spent much of it on adventure and treasure hunting.

Arthur Borland and Brian had met when the former requested help finding his father who had disappeared on an expedition to Guatemala. That search revealed far more than just the fate of Arthur's missing father. A vast horde of newly discovered Mayan codices and gold was now on display in a new museum at the ancient site of Tikal, Guatemala. Because of their significant involvements with the find, that museum bore the names of both Brian Sadler and Captain Jack Borland.

Lord Borland and Brian Sadler sat in the beautifully paneled bar enjoying glasses of Sancerre. Their table, Brian's favorite, was next to twenty-foot windows overlooking the Thames. Waterloo Bridge was only a few hundred yards east of the club. The ultramodern London Eye Ferris wheel had been erected around the river bend to the west, out of sight of the Club's lounge and restaurant. Brian was grateful not to have to gaze on that modern monstrosity every time he wanted to relax over a drink.

"Brian, it's really good to see you. Given the circumstances you look well. I know this tragedy has been a burden on you. And the loss of Collette. How horrible for her family and for you both personally and professionally. She was an asset to Bijan, I know. And you lost a friend as well."

They talked for half an hour about the bombing, possible reasons behind it and the ongoing investigation. Brian did most of the talking, Arthur interjecting a question or comment here and there. They finished the wine and moved to the dining room. More wine on the way, they placed their orders.

Brian began. "All right. You've kept me in suspense long enough. What's your theory on the stolen manuscript?"

"You're aware how extensive the Club's collection of very old works is."

Brian nodded.

"I'm sure you've heard of Oak Island in Nova Scotia."

He nodded again, a slight smile on his face.

Arthur sighed dramatically and reached into his briefcase, retrieving a sheaf of papers that appeared to be his notes.

"I see your smile. You're thinking I'm just another crazy treasure hunter with yet another hunch about the contents of the Money Pit. But I've come across something very interesting. So hear me out. You may just learn something new today!"

CHAPTER SEVENTEEN

Brian settled back in his chair, ready for a story about Oak Island. The British Earl was a great tale-teller. He managed to captivate Brian every time he had something new and mysterious to report. This time was no exception – the enigma of Oak Island was something that had interested Brian since he was a kid. A classic mystery set in North America – an ancient story involving pirates, treasure perhaps beyond imagination and someone who went to amazing lengths to create a booby-trapped pit. Who did it and why? Brian was surprised most of the world didn't even seem to wonder. Most people had never heard of Oak Island.

Lord Borland referred to his notes occasionally as he told the story. "As you know, the theories about what lies at the bottom of the Money Pit range from pirates to the Vikings to native Americans to Inca lords and much more. Some have speculated that the crown jewels of France were hidden there in the Middle Ages. Or the gold the Spanish were seeking from the Mayans in Mexico. Or the manuscripts that will tell who William Shakespeare really was. Or that aliens who came on spaceships secreted the knowledge of the ages. No one knows. But there is one theory, one possibility I haven't yet mentioned, that keeps turning up in my research. I think I know who built the Money Pit but I don't yet know why. Any ideas who?"

Brian smiled. "You're enjoying this guessing game, aren't you? I give up – at the moment I can't recall my Money Pit history well enough to think who you haven't mentioned."

"Then I'll tell you, dear boy. I've spent hours here in the Monument Club's library. They have copies, originals too sometimes, of the actual records of the earliest syndicates who tackled the Money Pit. I found the original journal of a man named Simeon Lynds. He lived near Oak Island and organized the first expedition. It was called the Onslow Syndicate."

"I've read about Lynds and the Syndicate. I think it's fascinating that our Club has his account of it."

"So do I. His old journal was written in 1804 and 1805 at the time these fellows took the Money Pit down nearly a hundred feet. According to Lynds' diary, they hit what he described as a wooden chest. When they arrived the next day the pit had flooded almost to the top. That was the first encounter with booby-traps in the shaft. A year later the syndicate dug a new pit alongside the existing one. They went down over a hundred feet, tunneled sideways to reach the Money Pit and that new shaft flooded too."

Brian said, "I remember this vaguely. That's when the Onslow Syndicate gave up, correct?"

"Right. They ran out of patience and money and apparently the syndicate members, like the three teenagers who had first dug out the pit, went their own ways. Interestingly, those teens grew up. One bought property on Oak Island; he and some former members of the Onslow Syndicate invested in the search again years later."

"So did you learn anything new from old Simeon's journal?"

"Ah, I haven't gotten to the interesting part yet. Patience, dear boy. Patience."

Over the next half hour Arthur Borland told Brian what else Simeon Lynds had written in his journal. Lynds was a well-educated and wealthy man and he was a member of the Masonic Lodge.

Borland pulled an index card from his pocket. "Pardon my relying on notes but this next part is tricky. In addition to being a Mason the diary says Simeon was the leader of a shadowy group called The United Religious, Military and Masonic Orders of the Temple and of Saint John of Jerusalem, Palestine, Rhodes and Malta. That name's a mouthful, and after using the complete moniker once Lynds only refers to it as 'The Order' afterwards.

"Lynds led the Order. He and other members invested in the Onslow Syndicate. Members of that mysterious secret group he called the Order wanted what lay hidden in the Money Pit."

Brian's interest was piqued now. He leaned forward, wanting more information. Taking another sip of the Sancerre he asked, "What else do you know about the Order? What are you holding back? Because I know you are. You weave too good a tale to give me everything up front."

Borland smiled. "The Order had several subsets, several of which became part of Freemasonry. These sub-orders include The Knights of Malta, the Knights of Saint Paul and the Knights of the Red Cross. Have you heard of any of them?"

"Not that I recall. Are they relevant to your story?"

"Not really."

"OK, I give up. Is there a point to this tale? I love Oak Island mysteries but what secrets are you holding back?" Brian smiled as he chided the British Earl.

Arthur gave him a wink. "Perhaps I forgot to mention one other sub-group that sprang out of this association which Simeon Lynds nicknamed the Order. The other part was called The Knights of the Temple." He stopped, leaned back in his chair and crossed his arms. He smiled as he watched Brian.

"The Knights of the Temple. That's awfully close to . . . wait a second. Are you saying . . .?"

"Am I saying what? Do you see where this is going?"

"Are you saying Simeon Lynds and the members of the Onslow Syndicate were *Knights Templars*?"

"That's exactly what I'm saying. Not the same Knights Templars as the ones who were exterminated in 1310, but directly related to them in terms of thought, deed and purpose. These later Templars restarted the order in secret in the 1400s. They were dedicated to preservation of what the early Templars began, they were committed to Templar ideals and they knew the secrets of the earlier group. These secrets were passed down in coded books over the centuries. Including, I'm certain, the answer to whatever was hidden at the bottom of the pit the Templars built on Oak Island."

"So these Templars were the Masonic Knights Templars? I think my grandfather might have been a member, actually."

"Absolutely not. The Templars I'm talking about have nothing to do with the Freemason Templars. Same name, different groups entirely. Simeon Lynds' Templars are directly tied to the tenth century Order through the Catholic Church."

"Really? Incredible. Does the secret Order of Templars in the Catholic Church still exist?"

"I'm still researching that but I believe so. If I can find out more about them it may explain why someone went to such lengths to get the manuscript that was at Bijan Rarities' gallery in New York."

The story stopped as the men ordered coffee. Thoughts swirled through Brian's head. Arthur said nothing, watching as Brian processed the information he had heard.

Finally Brian said, "So the manuscript that I got was part of a set. And I presume it's one of the books you're talking about – the ones with coded secrets of the Templars. Am I right so far?"

"Absolutely."

"Obviously the one given to me was very important to someone. Do you have any idea where the others are? Have they been stolen as well?"

"No, they haven't. They're safe and sound."

Brian saw Arthur's impish smile. The Earl was still playing games, revealing almost nothing.

"OK," Brian said, serious now. "Knock it off. Tell me the rest."

"All right. There are five volumes in all, each bearing the title *Opus Militum Xpisti* or *The Work of the Soldiers of Christ*. The first was recorded by the original Knights Templars, the ones who were rounded up in 1307 by King Philip of France and exterminated in 1310. It would have been a stand-alone account of the two hundred years of Templar existence had it not been for the men who came along in the 1400s and secretly resurrected the Order."

Arthur paused to allow Brian to soak in the information.

"So volumes two through five are records of the Knights Templars who followed the earlier ones? The volume that was the reason for the bombing of my gallery is part of that set?"

"It is."

"And you're certain of this how?"

"Because I've seen all the volumes except yours. Not originals, of course, but I have seen copies of them. Right here in this very building."

"The Club has copies of these volumes? Where are the originals?"

"The originals are in secret papal archives in Vatican City."

Brian was astonished. "Now I see why you hoped I had made a copy of my volume too. I know the Monument Club's library is something special, but tell me how in hell they could get copies of ancient manuscripts that are in the Vatican's archives?"

"A very wealthy Italian named Marco Caboto donated the originals to Pope Pius IX in 1875. But not before he paid to have them copied by hand. He secretly kept those copies in his own collection. After Caboto's death in 1930 one of his heirs, a member of our Club himself, donated this man's entire book collection to the Monument Club. Among thousands of old works were the copies - the four ancient manuscripts describing centuries of Knights Templars activities."

"But the volume I had wasn't copied."

"Up to this point everything indicates it wasn't. But I may have found something. In fact I just discovered it yesterday in the library. I haven't looked at it yet so I don't want to discuss it until I do. The book you saw covers the time from roughly 1475 to 1700. Until yesterday I believed the wealthy Italian never had that volume. He may not have known his four volumes were a chronological set. Or that a fifth book was missing. I think the manuscript you saw has been separated from the others for a very long time. But I'm trying to find out whether Marco Caboto ever owned the volume that's now been stolen. One thing's for sure – he copied four volumes of the Templars. If he ever had the fifth I'll wager he copied it too."

"Why is this particular one, the missing one, so important?"

"Think about it. Think about the time period it covers."

Once again Arthur sat back in his chair, impassive, watching Brian's face as the American's mind raced. He said nothing, letting Brian reach a conclusion.

"It's important because it records what happened at Oak Island. It's when they built the Money Pit. That's your theory, isn't it?"

"Exactly. And I'm close to proving it."

CHAPTER EIGHTEEN

It was nearly four pm when Brian and Arthur left the Monument Club. They set a dinner date for the day after tomorrow.

The men walked to Charing Cross train station.

"I'll be waiting for a report on the mysterious thing you found yesterday in the library. Don't keep me in suspense!"

Borland promised to get on the project in the morning. They parted company, Brian heading one direction and Arthur another, his briefcase in his hand as he waved goodbye.

Brian's mind was racing as he took the subway back to Green Park station, then a short walk down Piccadilly to the Bijan gallery on Old Bond Street. He took out an access card, opened the front door and stepped into the showroom. Although smaller than the New York gallery, it was tastefully appointed with displays of priceless artifacts for sale.

"Hi, Mr. Sadler! Nice lunch?"

Jason Hardesty had been with Bijan for a couple of years, working with Brian and Collette in New York before being moved to London a few months ago to assist the new UK gallery manager. Jason loved history. As a twenty-something single he had jumped at the chance to work in London. He had been grief-stricken to learn of the loss of his good friend Collette and the destruction of the company's New York headquarters. Brian and Jason had spent an hour talking about the Fifth Avenue bombing earlier this morning.

"A very interesting lunch. As every meeting with Arthur Borland is. I always end up with more food for thought than nourishment!"

"Sounds interesting! FYI Cory's at the Connaught Hotel meeting a client who wants to discuss consigning some pottery."

Brian went to his office. He glanced in the one next door. It belonged to Cory Spencer, the manager of Bijan's London location. Overcoming a very difficult youth, Cory had worked for Brian several years ago while he was in undergraduate school in New York City. Later as a Sussex University graduate student in archaeology Cory had led a dig at Palenque, Mexico. He discovered an incredibly strange, ancient artifact that had almost gotten him killed. Brian had become involved in that project to help the government after John Chapman, the President of the United States, disappeared deep inside a tomb at Palenque.

Not long after the Palenque adventure Cory graduated and called Brian about employment. It was a perfect fit – Brian trusted the man implicitly and had put him in charge of the growing London gallery. Brian was grateful to have Cory as his second-in-command, especially now that New York was history. The Old Bond Street location was critical – it was the only one left.

There was a large FedEx box sitting in the middle of Brian's desk. It contained most of the things Brian had been working on at the time of the bombing. Rather than checking the bulky, heavy box on the plane Brian had shipped it overnight to the London gallery. For a half hour he went through everything, sorting and arranging the contents for handling over the next couple of weeks he planned to be in London. This was his office now. His headquarters. It seemed odd but it was the new reality.

Around 5:30 Brian heard the soft buzz that indicated the front door had opened. Ten seconds later a voice boomed loudly from the showroom. "I hear the boss is back in town. Best behavior, everyone!"

Brian stood as Cory Spencer came into his office. They hugged each other – although they had spoken several times a day since the tragedy in New York Brian hadn't seen Cory in person. Tears welled up in both their eyes as they patted each other on the backs and Cory offered his condolences over the loss.

Pulling back, Brian composed himself and said, "I'm glad we're a team. I need your help and I'm deeply grateful to have you."

"Ditto, boss." Cory had the utmost admiration for Brian Sadler and appreciated the opportunity to learn from him and work at one of the nation's most respected antiquities dealers. Bijan had made quite a name in the past few years thanks to its involvement with the world's rarest objects such as the Bethlehem Scroll, Mayan codices long thought extinct and Egyptian mummies. The science networks, Discovery and History especially, had done several documentaries featuring Brian. And national news networks in the US and abroad called on him frequently for commentary about new discoveries around the world. Brian Sadler and Bijan Rarities were well known to those who loved the thrill of archaeology and ancient things.

"Are you free for dinner? We need to catch up and it might be easier outside the gallery than during the work day."

"Thought you'd never ask." Cory had hoped this would happen. He relished the time with his mentor and took every chance he could to be at Brian's side.

Jason locked up at six as Brian and Cory wrapped up the afternoon's work. They stopped by the Ritz Hotel on Piccadilly, three blocks from the gallery. In the quiet, refined Rivoli Bar they ordered martinis, clicked glasses and talked about how things were progressing on the case in New York. Brian brought Cory up to speed on the stolen manuscript and gave him a brief synopsis of the story Arthur Borland had told this afternoon. Cory was fascinated.

The men walked to Chinatown, just the other side of Piccadilly Circus less than fifteen minutes away from the Ritz. Soon they were seated at Dumplings' Legend, Brian's favorite place in London. It was nothing fancy but Brian considered it the best Chinese place in the world. He tended to eat here several times a week when he was left to his own devices in London.

Two glasses of wine and a couple of dim sum plates got them started.

"What's next on the manuscripts?" Cory asked. "Is it possible that rich Italian copied the stolen volume too?"

"I've given that a lot of thought since I left the lunch with Arthur. Arthur's not sure if this one was copied. Maybe the Italian never even had it. But I wonder. It's worth doing some digging. I'll get with you in the morning – I need your help to start the search. Think about it tonight and I'll do the same. I'm supposed to meet Arthur for dinner the day after tomorrow. I'd like you to join us. We can lay out our ideas to him then."

Cory was thrilled – the chance to meet Lord Borland was important to him both personally and professionally. He was of course fully aware of Brian's earlier adventures in Guatemala with the Earl of Weymouth and knew Brian had a great friendship with this man, the son of the late, great Captain Jack Borland, one of the world's most flamboyant explorers.

Brian's phone rang. "Speak of the devil," he said, glancing at the screen. "It's Arthur's home phone."

He answered with a smile. "Hello old boy. To what do I owe the honor of this call?"

Brian was suddenly quiet. Cory waited as his boss listened intently, his smile now gone.

"Brian, this is Carissa Borland. I'm so sorry to be a bother but wonder if you and Arthur have wrapped up yet. I know sometimes you both go on for hours and I hated to disturb you but his dinner's been on the stove for an hour and he's not picking up his mobile." He noticed her attempt to be lighthearted but could sense the concern in her shaky voice. She was worried.

"We left the club shortly before four pm. We walked to Charing Cross Station and I took the tube to the office. I'm pretty sure he was heading home then."

"He should have been here before five. That's three hours ago. I've tried his mobile a dozen times. It goes to voicemail." Her voice broke. "I'm worried, Brian. This isn't like him not to call and check in. And he's really late. Really late." She was crying now.

"What can I do to help?"

"I don't know. I'm sure you're at dinner and I'm probably imposing on you for nothing. Let me give it another half hour or so. If I don't hear anything by then I'll start checking hospitals, I guess. But I'll call you back first."

Brian filled Cory in on the situation as they snagged tiny dim sum pieces with chopsticks. They decided they would take on the task of calling the police and hospitals if Arthur hadn't shown up in a half hour.

Twenty minutes later Carissa Borland's home phone rang. She took the call, hung up and dialed Brian's number.

Brian's phone vibrated and he answered immediately. "Any news?"

He heard nothing but heaving sobs on the other end.

"Give me a moment," she finally whispered.

A few seconds later she composed herself and began to speak. "My phone rang – it was Arthur's number and I was prepared to give him a piece of my mind. But it wasn't him, Brian. It wasn't him." She sobbed. "It was an officer from the Metropolitan Police in London. He was calling me . . ." She stopped again. "Oh, Brian. He was calling me because he saw my number on Arthur's phone. He's dead." She stopped, unable to continue for a moment.

"Oh God. What . . . how did it happen?"

She was so overcome she couldn't speak. Brian knew she was probably by herself. They had no children and lived in a nearby suburb, in one of the row houses so common in outlying parts of London. She would need someone to be with her.

Finally Carissa Borland took a deep breath and said, "All right. I have to get through this. He was riding the train. All this time. Sometime after he got on at Charing Cross Station he died, somehow. The officer said his head was slumped on his chest and everyone thought he was asleep. He had just been sitting there riding the train for hours. Dead. His phone kept ringing –

those were my calls, of course - and finally one of the passengers heard it and alerted a policeman on the train.   That policeman called my number."

Brian pulled a notepad from his jacket pocket and jotted things down as she continued.   The body was being taken to a London hospital where the coroner's office would investigate the cause of death.   The policeman had assured her there was no reason to think foul play was involved but Carissa wondered.   She said he had no real health issues other than being slightly overweight, in his fifties and maybe drinking a little too much now and then.   Brian agreed with her.   The officer had given her his contact information and promised to call her in the morning.

"One thing that might be important, or maybe not.   Did the policeman tell you he had Arthur's briefcase?   When I last saw him at the station he was carrying it."

"He didn't mention it.   I'll check with him tomorrow about that.   I can't imagine anything in it's very important.   Arthur spent a lot of time researching a lot of strange things.   I doubt anyone would want what was in his case but people do steal.   Someone could have taken it."

Carissa thanked Brian when he offered to come be with her.   "Thanks but I'll be OK tonight.   I'm still in a daze and my dear friend next door is coming over to stay with me.   I told her I didn't need her to do that but . . ." oh, Brian, I'm going to miss Arthur so much." She cried.

Brian told her how much Arthur's friendship had meant to him. "A lot of other people are going to miss him too."

Brian said he would have a car pick her up first thing tomorrow to bring her to London. They would go to the police station together and talk to the investigating officer. He told her once again how sorry he was and renewed his offer to help, any way, any time. His words came from the heart – Arthur Borland had been one of Brian's best friends.

"He's dead. He died peacefully on the train heading home this afternoon."

"Very good. Everything's nice and quiet there?"

"Oh yes. He just went to sleep. Like we'd all want to go. All's well and no one will ever be the wiser."

"It seems so." The man hung up, satisfied.

One score settled, this one about halfway wrapped up, and one to go.

CHAPTER NINETEEN
Vatican City/New York

Cardinal Conti gazed for the hundredth time at the photocopied page he had taken from the Pope's office. He was anxious to compare it to the ancient manuscripts to see if it really represented a way to break the coded pages, but he was forced to be patient. He was playing a game of cat and mouse with Giovanni Moretti.

And when I am through playing the old man will be dead like the rat he has turned out to be. The Cardinal smiled.

As leader of the Church's Knights Templars, Dominic Conti knew that the four volumes in the papal archives weren't the ones he needed. He had read each one - they were for the wrong time period. The single volume that mattered was the one that had been missing for over a hundred years, the one that Moretti had. That volume held the coded secrets Conti needed to unlock. Something had happened between 1475 and 1700 – the years covered by the missing manuscript – and Dominic Conti believed he knew what it was. Nova Scotia. Legends of priceless treasures guarded by the Templars. A relic so important it required an engineering accomplishment almost beyond comprehension in the 1600s.

Oak Island. The Templars somehow went to Oak Island. That's what's in the missing manuscript, along with the answer to the riddle of what the relic actually is.

While the waiting game with Moretti was going on, it would have been good to see one of the existing volumes of Knights Templar exploits from the archives. Without one of the coded pages in front of him Conti couldn't try out the decryption page he had stolen from the papal office. He had to wait for Moretti's manuscript and the others were locked up in the secret archives. Pope Benedict would have retrieved a volume for him but that pontiff was gone. He couldn't ask the new Pope. Such a request would require too much explanation. And at this point Cardinal Conti was very close to unlocking a mystery. He needed to keep things quiet. So he had to be patient.

Two days later the Cardinal received a call on his cellphone.

"Hello, Giovanni," Conti answered. "Have you come to your senses?"

"Meet me day after tomorrow at Paolucci Restaurant in Little Italy on Mulberry Street. Twelve noon. You'll get what you want."

And you'll get what you deserve, *my friend.* "New York, Giovanni? I'm not sure I can clear time so quickly for a trip . . ."

"Your choice, Eminence. If you want the manuscript you'll be there."

"Isn't it a little dangerous for you to be traveling to the States, Giovanni?"

But there was no response. Moretti had hung up.

Fuming at the continued insolence of this man whose very existence Conti had saved, he forced himself to calm down. He summoned his secretary and booked a seat on tomorrow morning's Alitalia flight from Rome to New York. She also noted the Cardinal's request for a room at the Palace Hotel on Madison Avenue. It was unusual but not unheard of for Conti to stay somewhere other than the Archbishop's residence so she didn't question his instructions.

His next statement did surprise her, though.

"*I'll* notify the Archbishop in New York that I'm coming. Leave that with me."

It was policy that the Archbishop be notified when high-level members of the clergy would be spending the night in New York. She couldn't recall a time when Cardinal Conti had reserved that right to himself. Something was different this time but she didn't know what it was. And she certainly wasn't going to ask.

Wearing the black shirt and slacks of a priest instead of the distinctive red garb of a Cardinal, Dominic Conti flew to New York. He carried a Vatican City diplomatic passport, a privilege accorded to the highest members of the Church's entourage in Italy, and it enabled him to clear Customs in seconds. Ordinarily the Archdiocese would have had a limousine whisk the cleric to midtown but since no one had been told he was coming, he took a cab.

The desk clerks at the Palace gave the priest no more than a brief glance as they checked him in and swiped his personal credit card. The Palace dealt daily with dignitaries from around the world. When he presented his diplomatic passport from the home base of the Catholic Church no one so much as raised an eyebrow. The clerk might have recognized Conti's name but discretion was the byword at this posh New York hotel. No one said a thing and Cardinal Dominic Conti, the head of the Vatican Bank and one of the Church's most powerful people, was soon unpacking his light valise in his room, staying under the radar of his fellow clerics in Manhattan.

An hour later Conti stepped out onto the street. He was wearing a cotton shirt, sweater and blue jeans. This was a serious breach of church rules and Cardinal Conti felt strange wearing street clothing but he couldn't afford to be seen as a priest. He needed to blend in with thousands of other people hurrying up and down the crowded midtown sidewalks.

Careful to avoid the Archdiocese and St. Patrick's Cathedral less than two blocks away, Conti walked to Fifth Avenue and strolled past the boarded-up hole that had been Bijan Rarities. He wanted to look at the site but there turned out to be nothing to see. A lone NYPD officer stood guard on the sidewalk, nonchalantly watching pedestrian traffic go by. There seemed to be no activity – the wooden door that had been cut into the plywood was securely padlocked.

It was almost six pm and Conti was getting hungry. Thirsty too. He'd had a couple of glasses of wine on the plane but didn't overindulge. Wearing the clerical garb pointed him out as a man of God. But now he was out of God's clothes and he wanted a drink. It was dangerous to stay in this part of town so close to the hub of activity for the Archdiocese. Around here he could run into any one of a hundred people he knew so he hailed a cab and gave the driver a downtown address several miles away.

Traffic wasn't bad going south and within a half hour Dominic Conti was at the bar of Vincent's, a quiet place frequented by tourists that was across the street from the South Street Seaport. The Cardinal would have far preferred Harry's at Hanover Square, a great old bar three blocks from Wall Street and the New York Stock Exchange. He loved the place but in his position as head of the bank he was a well-known patron. Anonymity this time. Perhaps indulgence the next.

Vincent's was noisy and he sandwiched himself at the bar between two groups of people who had just visited Ground Zero only a few blocks west. Ignoring them as best he could, he ordered a Johnny Walker Blue, water back, and enjoyed the feeling as the premium Scotch went down smoothly. Fine Scotch was one of Dominic Conti's weaknesses. He had a few others but those wouldn't be satisfied on this trip. This time he had a mission. He would return with the manuscript. No matter what.

The next morning at 10:30 am Dominic Conti, again dressed in black as a priest, hailed a cab in front of the Palace Hotel and was dropped on Broadway in Chinatown, a teeming, bustling touristy place just north of downtown Manhattan. A hundred tiny stores in a two-block stretch sold knockoffs of everything from Coach bags to Hermes watches to Dior perfume. Barkers called to passersby browsing the crude displays.

"Priest!   Hey priest!"   A Chinese vendor motioned for Conti to come closer.   "Want Rolex? Genuine! Only twenty dollar!"

Dominic Conti kept moving, walking slowly and taking his time.   Making his way east along Broadway he would eventually come to Little Italy and Mulberry Street.   He meandered, looked at the knockoffs for sale and enjoyed the sunny morning.   He wanted to arrive at the restaurant ten minutes early so his apparently aimless stroll actually wasn't that at all.   He would be at Paolucci's a little before twelve.

The Cardinal thought about Giovanni Moretti.   Strange that he wanted to meet in Little Italy, a place Conti thought might frighten him at this point in his life.   Moretti had a lot of history, a lot of water under a very large bridge, and much of it had involved this scenic, historic part of New York.   Little Italy was an area of restaurants, shops and gelato stores today.   Once it had teemed with immigrants crowded into dirty tenement buildings.   La Cosa Nostra, the Mafia, had taken hold when Sicilians brought the ways of the old country to their new home in the United States.   A hundred years ago many of Little Italy's wretched residents looked up to the made men, the enforcers, numbers runners and drug dealers.   They were the few who made it out of the environment of the ghetto.   They became wealthy, albeit at the expense and lives of others.   They were revered, honored, considered great men.   But they were actually ruthless criminals –

murderers, thieves, bookmakers, creators of prostitution and drug rings. They didn't make life better. They made it worse.

He turned off Broadway onto Mulberry Street and walked north. The five- and six-story buildings that had been built in the late 1800s to house immigrants looked today much as they had then. It was an interesting, quaint part of New York with narrow streets and another group of street vendors selling clothing, purses and the like. Paolucci Restaurant was two blocks ahead on the left, just past Grand Street.

Conti arrived and saw a couple of waiters putting umbrellas on tables set up on the sidewalk. Another put place settings around – they were almost ready to open. As he walked in a couple of tourists entered behind him, hoping to catch an early lunch.

"Good morning, Father," the maître d' said as the Cardinal entered the restaurant. "We're opening in ten minutes but you're welcome to take a seat. Will there be just one?"

Conti requested a table for two in the back. He ordered a glass of Chablis, sipped and watched as arriving guests took a couple more tables. About 12:10 a man walked into the restaurant. Expecting Moretti, Conti looked closely. It wasn't him. Or was it? He watched the man walk straight toward his table. Then he pulled out a chair and sat.

"Who are you?" Conti asked.

The man was dressed in jeans and a polo shirt covered by a light jacket. A baseball cap and dark glasses obscured his face. The man had a moustache and neatly trimmed beard. He was easily four or five inches taller than Giovanni Moretti and had more girth.

"Why, Dominic. I'm disappointed in your abilities to recognize your old friend."

The Cardinal was astonished at the transformation. He noticed the platform shoes Moretti was wearing and saw that his jacket was well padded, giving the man a hefty look in his chest. "I didn't think you'd pick Little Italy without doing something to alter your appearance. So why go to all this trouble? Why didn't we just meet in Rome?"

Moretti ignored the cleric and raised a finger to the waiter, placing an order for a bottle of Italian Chardonnay. He said nothing until the bottle arrived, was uncorked and a glass filled. He sat back, savoring the taste.

"I can get this wine all over Italy but somehow it tastes better right here at Paolucci. It must be the atmosphere - the scenery of Mulberry Street just outside. Or maybe it's just memories."

The Cardinal sat impassively, seething inside but saying nothing. He let the old man waste time talking, doing it his way.

"I love this place. It was my favorite restaurant when I lived in New York. Our waiter – his name is Salvatore. He's from Sicily, where I'm originally from. He knew me well five years ago. But he doesn't recognize me now. I've transformed, Dominic. I'm a new man!" He looked smugly at the cleric.

"Everyone in Little Italy knew you well five years ago. Can we get to the subject?"

"You'll get indigestion if you don't stop worrying so much. We're going to have a nice lunch like old friends do when they get together. You're going to be civil and so am I. And in the end maybe everything will turn out the way you hope it will." He smiled broadly and opened his menu, ignoring the Cardinal's glare.

Dominic controlled his emotions. *Keep calm. Let him think he's winning. All I want is what I came for. We'll see who ultimately wins this battle.*

The men each ordered a light lunch. As they ate Moretti said, "It should be obvious why we're meeting in New York. The manuscript you want is here. You have a diplomatic passport. You can carry it back to Rome without so much as a raised eyebrow. I, on the other hand, would have a problem transporting the manuscript that precipitated the Fifth Avenue bombing. Thanks to the press the world knows there's a old book somewhere and a huge reward tied to it. So now do you see my logic?" He smiled.

The Cardinal was tired of all this. "All right. Enough games. Where's the manuscript?"

The old man ignored the question. "This job was expensive. I have plenty, yes, but the Knights Templars order is gaining something you obviously want very much. A priceless object, I think. Am I correct?"

It took all the patience Conti had to maintain his composure. What on earth was this idiot doing? Was this an extortion attempt?

"Are you holding the manuscript for ransom?" the Cardinal said calmly.

"The Church has unlimited assets. And I, I'm just a poor peasant from Sicily who's made a few fortuitous investments in the past. I've been blessed, certainly, but one can always use a bit more to ensure a comfortable retirement. I think five million dollars would be fair for this document you want so badly. What do you think?" Moretti smiled and leaned back in his chair.

"*Bastardo!* You made your millions running a drug syndicate. You helped untold thousands of American children become drug addicts. You smug *bastardo*. You and I had a deal. A quid pro quo. You owe me for your very existence and I asked you to repay the favor. Now you're trying to extort five million dollars? How quickly you've forgotten how confining your prison cell was. Perhaps I can help you learn again. What do you think about that?"

"Now, Now. Don't lose your temper. It's not good for your heart. Do you want the manuscript or not? It's up to you. I'm sure I can sell it elsewhere – surely someone else thinks it's as important as you obviously do."

The Cardinal's mind raced and a solution quickly emerged. It made him smile.

"Yes. I want the manuscript. And of course I'll pay your ransom. The Church needs the book. You don't need to know why. Hand over the manuscript and I'll pay you five million dollars."

"Of course you will," Moretti said. "I trust you implicitly. Why shouldn't I? I owe you everything, as you constantly remind me. But let's be practical." He pulled a slip of paper from his pocket along with a key. "Wire the money to this account in Turkey. When the money's in my account I'll tell you what lock this key fits. Then you can have your manuscript. I have your number. You'll hear from me when I confirm the funds have arrived. And thank you for lunch."

Giovanni Moretti stood, turned and walked out of the restaurant. He thanked his waiter, who registered not a trace of recognition of the man he had served often just a few years ago.

CHAPTER TWENTY

New York/Rome

Giovanni Moretti took a taxi directly from the restaurant in Little Italy to JFK Airport. Waiting in the Alitalia first class lounge for his flight to Rome, he checked the bank account in Ankara. Nothing so far, but that was of no concern to Moretti. He knew it would take time for Cardinal Conti to move funds. As head of the Vatican Bank Conti could singlehandedly accomplish the transfer of much more than five million dollars but there were other factors, the greatest of which was the time difference between the USA and Turkey. It would be the next morning before funds arrived and Moretti would be safely back in Italy.

Riding the train from Fiumicino Airport into central Rome, Moretti checked the bank again. It was now 9:50 am in Turkey and the funds had been deposited in his account just as he had demanded. He smiled. *I pulled*

*one over on Dominic Conti. Bastardo, eh?
Well, I'm a richer bastardo now, thanks to you.*

He called Conti's cellphone and said,
"Many thanks, my friend. There's a gym at
the corner of Ninth Avenue and 23rd Street.
Locker number fourteen in the men's locker
room." He hung up without waiting for a
response.

Dressed again in civilian clothes to
avoid attention, Conti bought a membership
in the gym in order to gain access. He paid
thirty dollars cash for a month's trial, walked
straight to the locker room, opened the door
and saw a bulky manila folder inside. He
glanced around – no one was paying him any
attention. He opened the folder and saw the
stolen manuscript. It was unmistakably
genuine and obviously was a match to the
ones Dominic had previously read. He slid
the book back into the folder and walked out.

In order to carry the manuscript to
Rome in a diplomatic pouch Conti would
have had to visit the Vatican Consulate on
West 34th Street. People would have asked
questions about why he was in New York.
Since he was traveling under the radar and
wished to attract no attention, he took a
chance that the authorities wouldn't
challenge him as he left the United States.
Once he arrived in Rome his diplomatic
status would give him instant passage
through the immigration process. Everything
went as he had predicted and within twenty-
four hours he was at his office in the Vatican.

The manuscript was laid out on his desk, its first page bearing the now-familiar words *Opus Militum Xpisti,* the same words that appeared in the Vatican's other four Templar manuscripts. Conti flipped through to one of the pages covered in symbols – a page of code.

Dominic Cardinal Conti had one more task to complete before turning his full attention to the manuscript. He pulled up some information on his computer, called a trusted friend in the Vatican's passport control office, and had Giovanni Moretti's passport number flagged as fraudulent. Without a valid passport Moretti no longer had legal status anywhere on earth.

CHAPTER TWENTY-ONE

London

After the events Brian had experienced the last two weeks, the death of Arthur Borland affected him greatly. Two days after the apparent death by natural causes of his fellow explorer and close personal friend, Brian sat alone in the flat in Cadogan Square. It was eight pm and a martini sat on the coffee table in front of him, his third of the evening.

Arthur's sudden death became the catalyst for a grim reality for Brian Sadler. Until now Brian hadn't allowed himself to really let go, to fully embrace the fact of how much his life had changed in two weeks. One of his dearest friends, a man whom Brian looked forward to spending time with, a man whose calls and emails always brightened Brian's day – that man was suddenly gone forever. Just days before, his friend and colleague Collette Conning died a tragic death along with many others and Brian lost the gallery that had been his baby, his project, his life.

In the past Nicole jokingly referred to Bijan as Brian's "favorite thing." Each time it came up he laughingly assured her she was also up there somewhere among his favorite things. It became an ongoing joke but it was true that Brian had never enjoyed anything as much as he had loved life and his place in it since he took over the gallery. And in an instant, in a flash, the New York flagship store was gone. So were a dozen people.

Collette was special. She had been with the gallery when Darius Nazir owned it. Collette had agreed to stay on after Nazir's death when Brian assumed ownership. Brian had been grateful; her knowledge of both clients and artifacts made his life much easier as he learned the ropes. She was a confidant – in the know on all of Brian's plans for the business – and he had depended on her for advice and input. Now all that was over. He felt alone, truly alone for the first time in a long, long time.

As he sat in the dark in his London flat he thought of Nicole. They had had a wonderful life when they both lived in Dallas a few years back. When Brian left for Manhattan the relationship suffered but they still worked at keeping it as good as possible.

But it's not good, Brian thought. *It's not good. She's not here. She never is.*

The judge had postponed Nicole's trial for ten days while she was with Brian in New York after the tragedy. Now she was in the courtroom eight hours a day representing a wealthy client whose freedom depended on her legal skills. He was the chief financial officer of a Dallas wealth management firm. The company invested hundreds of millions of dollars for its multimillionaire clients. All went well until a low-level accountant got fired for being chronically late. Mad as hell, she went to the Feds with a story about phony accounts, a Madoff-like Ponzi scheme and – just to make it even spicier – money laundering for a Mexican drug cartel. The angry ex-employee also took her story to a local TV station. It had made the evening news.

Even though her allegations weren't true, the repercussion from the story in ritzy Dallas neighborhoods like the Park Cities was devastating for the firm. Lots of money was demanded by lots of clients. The firm was unable to sell assets quickly enough to avoid massive losses; it subsequently defaulted on some of its obligations. The company filed bankruptcy but the government continued its misguided, relentless pursuit of justice. The firm had no money left – insurance companies stepped in to provide defense for the key officers indicted, but those funds proved inadequate to cover all the costs. The government's lawyers kept after this case like wolves on their prey. And the innocent defendants were paying enormous legal fees out of their own pockets.

Nicole's client had done nothing wrong. Nothing at all. She was certain he would be exonerated but sadly she couldn't convince the U.S. Attorney to drop the case against him. The former CFO was now spending hundreds of thousands of dollars of his own money with Carter and Wells, hoping Nicole could keep him out of prison.

So while Brian sat in the darkened apartment in London nursing another martini, she was in her fourth day of trial in Dallas, unable to be with him. They spoke every day around 5:30 am Brian's time, 11:30 pm in Dallas. Nicole was home by then, preparing for the next day of trial and getting ready for bed. Brian was starting another day in London.

He began to cry as he pondered his life two weeks ago compared to today. Arthur was gone. Collette was gone. So were many innocent people. Brian's pride and joy, Bijan Rarities on Fifth Avenue in New York, was gone. And for all intents and purposes, Brian decided, Nicole was gone too. As the tears flowed he said out loud, "All she and I do is pretend. We pretend to be as close as we used to be. We pretend it's all going to be OK. Well, dammit, it's NOT going to be OK. I might as well realize that now. My whole world has gone to shit. For what? What the hell's going on?"

By now he was shouting. He threw his glass at the fireplace as hard as he could. The Waterford crystal martini glass shattered into a thousand pieces as Brian fell back into the chair, sobbing and holding his head in his hands. *Did John Spedino do all this? That's impossible. How could he have enough power to pull something this big off? And why? What's really behind all this?*

Through the haze of vodka a thought crept into Brian's mind. He sat up abruptly. Nicole. Was Nicole going to be harmed too?

Brian picked up his phone, dialed a number and reached the FBI's Manhattan office. When Agent Underwood answered Brian told him about Arthur Borland's death and Brian's suspicion that it wasn't from natural causes. His words slurred and he paused occasionally, attempting to arrange his thoughts. The agent finally stopped him.

"Mr. Sadler, are you all right? You don't sound like yourself."

"Oh, absolutely. I'm just terrific. I'm sitting here on top of the world having a martini. Everything's just wonderful and I have yet another funeral to go to this week." Brian stopped. He could talk no longer. He began to cry, heaving chest-racking sobs.

The agent had known it would all hit Brian Sadler eventually. No one could be a rock forever. He waited, saying nothing, until Brian composed himself.

"I'm afraid for Nicole. I think John Spedino may be behind this after all. Whoever's doing this has hurt me and killed Arthur. Nicole's the only one left of the three of us who put Johnny Speed in prison for life." He paused again. "That's a laugh, isn't it, Agent Underwood? You put a guy in prison for life, then suddenly he's gone! And no one gives a rat's ass until he's out killing people. Then it suddenly becomes important. At least to me. You know what I mean, *Agent Underwood?*" Brian shouted into the phone. "You get it? I think he's going to kill Nicole next. What the hell are you all going to do about *that?*"

Brian hung up.

CHAPTER TWENTY-TWO

The ringing of Brian's phone jolted him awake. In a fog, he struggled to remember why he was asleep in his living room chair, fully dressed, with shattered glass all over the hearth. He glanced at the phone; it was 5:35 am and Nicole was doing her daily check-in. He slid the arrow to answer the call.

"Well, it took you a while to answer. I almost gave up on you," she said, concern in her voice. "Are you OK, Brian?"

"Oh shit," he mumbled. "Oh shit. I feel terrible."

"What's the matter? Are you OK? I got a call from the FBI . . ."

"Hell, that's my fault. I got a little drunk . . . a lot drunk, actually . . . and I called Underwood. I was feeling sorry for myself last night. I'm still in my clothes, asleep in the chair in the living room. And my head feels like someone's jack-hammering inside it. Give me a minute. I'll be right back."

He stood unsteadily and walked to the bathroom to find a couple of Ibuprofens. He took them with a large glass of water and immediately felt as though he were going to throw up. He forced himself to stop thinking about it and choked down the warm acid rising in the back of his throat. He returned to the living room and picked up the phone. "You still there?"

"I'm here. I talked to Agent Underwood after today's trial wrapped up. He had left an urgent message to call him and I had no idea if you were in trouble or what was up. I'm fine. I appreciate your worrying about me but I don't think John Spedino is behind all that's been done. I think there's something else going on here, something that obviously involves you and Arthur but I don't see any connection with me."

She told Brian to get in bed and rest for a few hours before tackling work. "I'll call you sometime after noon your time when your head clears and we can talk this through. I know right now probably isn't a good time for you to carry on a conversation." She was right. His temples throbbed.

"I need to go, Nicole. Now."

After exchanging I-love-you's they hung up, allowing Brian roughly ten seconds to make it to the commode. Thankfully he arrived in time. Afterwards he felt a little better. Naked under the bedcovers with a wet washcloth on his forehead, Brian slept fitfully for three hours trying to recover and awoke vowing he would never drink again. Ever.

Around noon Brian took a taxi to the office. He'd showered and shaved and felt much better but didn't want to tackle the subway and bounce along the tracks to Green Park Station. He had forced himself to eat some toast and drink a little club soda. He was maybe seventy percent, he told himself optimistically.

He played back the last couple of days. He and Carissa had gone to the police station the morning after Arthur's death. She was allowed to identify the body via a video hookup with the morgue. Brian was grateful - that was far better than her having to see him in person. The coroner had requested an autopsy and she consented, hoping to learn what had actually happened to her husband.

Every train car in London is monitored by at least one video camera. Depending on where that camera is positioned they can be more or less helpful for viewing activities of riders. The Metropolitan Police had requested footage from the car Arthur Borland had taken. The officer promised to view it as quickly as possible and report back.

Carissa Borland signed a consent document allowing Brian to be notified about all aspects of the investigation of Arthur's death. She told Brian and the officer it would be easier on her to get information through her good friend than from the police.

Carissa told Brian she would call the funeral director and have Arthur picked up once the police released his body. There was little family and she planned a graveside service in a few days. "I hope you'll come," she told him. "Arthur thought the world of you." Brian assured her he would be there.

Borland's briefcase had not been recovered. The policeman said it was not with him when his body was removed from the train, but that Carissa Borland shouldn't read too much into that. People take things on trains, especially when a person appears to be sound asleep. Brian didn't know if the person who took Arthur's case with nothing but a thick sheaf of notes about the Knights Templars did it on purpose. More likely the thief thought he might score big – a laptop or iPad, something to fence for drug money. Surely that was it. It made more sense, at least.

That afternoon in one phone call Brian received both the autopsy results and the information gleaned from the camera in the train car. The autopsy was startling. In Arthur's system at the time of death were two drugs – sodium pentothal and potassium chloride. They had apparently been injected through his clothing into his upper left arm – the coroner found tiny needle holes puncturing his jacket and shirt and an entry in the arm itself.

These two drugs were familiar to the coroner and were frequently used together. Not in the UK, where capital punishment has been illegal for years. But in half of the states in the USA these two drugs are used to execute criminals. The policeman gave Brian the coroner's opinion. After an injection of these drugs he would have been unconscious in five seconds and dead in perhaps twenty minutes. There would have been no spasms, no outward sign of distress. He would have appeared to be asleep.

The officer turned to the next report, the video footage from the train car. At first it didn't appear helpful. The camera was mounted in the front of the train and Arthur had sat on the first row. Therefore Arthur himself was not in the recording – the camera's angle didn't include his seat but it did show the one next to him. That seat was empty at first but then an older man in a trenchcoat had taken the seat next to Arthur's for perhaps two minutes. From the camera's angle the police could see almost straight down onto the man's balding pate. But they had one important four-second piece of footage that showed the man turn toward Arthur and, using his hand, possibly graze Arthur's arm. It was impossible to tell for sure – Arthur's arm itself wasn't in the picture – but the policeman surmised from the seat placement and the camera angle that the man could have bumped Arthur's arm in the place where the injection had occurred.

Five seconds later the man left his seat and ten seconds after that he exited the train. The police had very little – they knew the station at which the man left the train and they had a very vague description of a balding older probably Caucasian man with gray hair wearing a trenchcoat. There was no frontal shot from the camera so they had no idea what he looked like.

Brian asked, "Are you treating this as a homicide?"

"We areI wish I could be optimistic about the chances of successfully finding this man who sat next to your friend, but we have very little to go on. I promise to give it my best shot and keep you informed." He gave Brian his phone number and email address for future contact.

Brian then gave the officer a brief background of the bombing in New York and Arthur's connection to the vanished mobster John Spedino. He also provided the number of Special Agent Underwood in the Manhattan office of the FBI. If there were a connection between the events in New York and Arthur's death these two men needed to communicate.

At four pm Nicole called. Brian gave her the news that Arthur Borland's death was a homicide. Carissa wasn't strong, he said, and he was going to try to convince her to move into central London for a week or so in order that he could be of more help to her.

"I feel so sorry for her. She has nobody but some neighbors. Her mother lives in South Africa and is very old and Arthur's mother is in a dementia facility north of London. She hasn't been lucid in months. I want to help Carissa but I have to work too. It would be so much easier if I could have her staying nearby. I'm going to offer the second bedroom in the flat. If she refuses I'm going to try to put her up in a hotel near here. That's the least I can do for old friends."

Nicole changed the subject. "Agent Underwood called me again and reiterated your concerns for my safety. I wish you'd talked to me first. I'm a big girl; I don't need you arranging a baby-sitting service for me."

"I know it's no excuse but I told him all that when I was drunk. I agree I should have called you but I knew you wouldn't do the security if I asked you. Are you going to do it?"

"No. I don't want to live like that, watching over my shoulder every second. I agree with you John Spedino might have had something to do with the bombing and Arthur's death. But remember something. In fact, I'm sure you remember it every single day. I do. John Spedino got his revenge on me already. He raped me, Brian. He violated me like the animal he is. His score with me is even already." She began to cry.

"I don't think about it, Nicole. I know how traumatic that was and I love you more than I ever have. You were a victim. And you're right - he was an animal. That doesn't mean he thinks the score's settled. But it's your decision. I can't do it for you."

After his conversation with Nicole, Brian called Carissa Borland. To his surprise, she immediately accepted his offer to use the second bedroom at the flat in Cadogan Square.

"I won't be a bother," she told him, "and I think I need to be in the city to deal with everything right now. A hotel would be expensive for me but your flat would be a welcome change to this old house where Arthur and I have lived for decades." Her voice quivered. "It's really hard without him, you know."

"I know the loss *I* feel," Brian replied. "I can't comprehend the depth of yours."

Brian sent a car to pick up Carissa late that afternoon. He arrived at the flat before she did, cleaned things up from his episode last evening and presented her a key when she arrived. By seven pm she had settled in so they popped around the corner to a quiet pub for a pint and a sandwich. So much for Brian's vow to stop drinking.

Earlier Brian had told Carissa about the lunch with Arthur and the manuscripts he was working on. Now he brought up a subject he'd been waiting for the right time to broach with Carissa. "Would you mind after things settle down if I come out to your house and look through Arthur's papers? I'm wondering if he might have photocopies or other notes. This Knights Templars thing somehow is involved with the crimes that have been committed."

She was more than happy to have Brian come out. "Arthur was a bit of a packrat, as you may know. When he's on a mission, like he has been lately with this Knights Templars thing, he has his laptop, books, papers, you-name-it, all over the place. I can't even dust in his study, it's so cluttered! I guess . . ." her voice broke, "I guess I can clean it up now, can't I?"

"Leave everything until I come, please. Let me go through things. I need to know what he'd been researching – it might help figure out the reason for his death."

They agreed Brian would come to the house soon, after the funeral was over and things calmed down a bit.

"There was nothing in the briefcase other than his notes, sir. Maybe fifty pages of scribbling about this and that."

"Any reference to manuscripts?"

"Everywhere. Apparently he was working on something involving copies of old manuscripts. You want to see the notes? I can scan and email them to you."

Copies of old manuscripts? There are copies? "Yes. Do that but do this too. Get in his house and find those copies. I didn't know copies existed so I need you to get them. This is critical. Don't let anyone know you were there."

"His wife lives in the house – right? What about her?"

"What *about* her? Find the copies of those books. Do I need to tell you how to do this job or can you handle it by yourself?"

"Yes, I can handle it, sir. Just wanted to be sure how big a priority finding the copies is. Dirty work costs more – but you already know that. It'll be done. Tonight."

At three am the ringing of the cellphone on his nightstand awoke Brian. He listened, speechless, responded briefly and hung up. He walked down the hallway and knocked softly on the second bedroom door.

"Carissa, it's Brian."

She was a light sleeper, especially in a strange place. "Come in," she immediately responded.

She saw the grim look on his face and cringed. No news in the middle of the night was ever good.

"I just got a call. I'm so sorry. I'm so sorry to have to tell you this but your house is on fire. Totally engulfed in flames. It's a total loss, the policeman said."

"Oh Brian. What's going on?" She cried quietly.

"I wish I knew. Dear God, I wish I knew."

CHAPTER TWENTY-THREE

As police and arson investigators combed through the ruins that had been Arthur and Carissa Borland's house outside London, Giovanni Moretti sat at his office desk in his apartment in Rome. It was a beautiful morning and he had his French doors open wide. The bustling noises of the street below were somehow soothing. He had come so far – on top of the world, down again and now back up. At this point nothing could go wrong and he was going to make sure it stayed that way.

On his desk lay a cheap cellphone he had bought yesterday on the street. It was a throwaway – the kind people use who can't afford a cell plan. The phone rang and Moretti picked it up – only one person had the number so he skipped straight to business. "What did you find?"

"Nothing. We tossed the entire house, top to bottom. We spent a lot of time in his study and looked for anything that might involve manuscripts. Especially we looked for copies of books, like you requested. I didn't see a laptop, although there was a computer desk and some wires. It looks like he used his study for research – there were open books all over the place – pretty messy. But no copies of manuscripts. Oh by the way, his wife wasn't there so that wasn't an issue. So we torched the house. They'll never know we were there."

Moretti digested that information. "Before you set the fire you made sure there was no evidence that could tie this to you or me. Is that correct?"

"Are you kidding?" the man said haughtily. "This ain't my first job, mister." He didn't know who his employer was and frankly could care less. After the job he was to call this number and report. Then he would receive fifty thousand Euros in his Swiss account. Same as the last time. Regardless, nobody questioned his abilities. He was good at this and that made him angry. "You do your job, buddy, whatever it is, and I'll do mine. Capisce?"

Moretti hung up, made a few keystrokes on his computer and transferred the money to the arsonist's account. He hadn't expected the man to find anything and frankly could care less about the manuscript. That was Cardinal Conti's baby, not his. He just wanted Borland's house searched with no loose ends. He had hoped Borland's wife would be out of the picture too, just for the sake of wrapping everything up neatly. That last part hadn't happened but he felt satisfaction anyway. An eye for an eye. Vindication. Job complete.

After the call Giovanni Moretti concentrated on the next project. He furiously jotted notes on a legal pad, finalizing a plan for vendetta number three. The first two, he mused, had gone exceedingly well. He had wanted Brian Sadler dead but the antiquities dealer was too high profile for that. One of Sadler's best friends was President of the United States. Even an accident would have been given the highest possible scrutiny.

No, Moretti mused, I handled that correctly. Conti wanted the book, the book was in Brian Sadler's beloved gallery, and now both it and his associate Collette Conning were gone. The investigation appeared to be geared completely toward the theft of the manuscript, and why not? Blowing up a Fifth Avenue store was a big deal, but that just added an element of mystery to everything. No one had a clue that it was in retribution for what Brian Sadler had done to him. Yes, that one had gone well.

So did Arthur Borland's unfortunate demise. Moretti had checked the Internet for any information that might indicate Borland had been murdered – there was nothing. Being an Earl and a member of the House of Lords, his obituary understandably had been prominently featured. His flamboyant father Captain Jack Borland was also mentioned, but from what Moretti read in the newspapers the Earl's death was presumed from natural causes.

All's well with those two, Moretti thought. Two people who have caused me more inconvenience than any others on earth have now been dealt with satisfactorily. And there's only one left to teach a lesson. And what a lesson she's going to get!

He picked up his throwaway cellphone and made a call to the 214 area code in the United States.

Dallas, Texas.

After a twenty minute conversation the plan was in place to exact retribution from the third of his enemies.

CHAPTER TWENTY-FOUR

The morning after Cardinal Conti returned to Rome Giovanni Moretti's cellphone rang.

The Cardinal sounded ecstatic. "I just wanted to offer my apology. The manuscript is everything I hoped it would be and more. It's undoubtedly the most interesting thing I have ever read – without your resourcefulness I wouldn't have it. Although your late-stage negotiating irritated me, everything was worth it. Five million US was a small price to pay for what I've seen so far. And I've hardly begun, Giovanni."

Moretti was surprised but cautious. He and Cardinal Conti had been good friends once but everything had gotten strained over the manuscript. Giovanni Moretti owed the cleric a debt – there was no doubt about that – and he had decided to demand money for the ancient volume mostly as a matter of principle. Moretti had plenty of money already but everyone could use a little more, he reasoned, and the Church had plenty to spare. Besides, he could keep his friend the Cardinal on edge. That was always pleasant. A little game he played.

Wary but choosing the high road, he said, "Thank you, my friend. I regret your anger earlier but I'm glad to see you feel you got value for your hard-earned money." Moretti laughed and, surprisingly, so did Cardinal Conti. Moretti's initial concerns eased slightly.

"You drove a hard bargain, but you had me in a tight place and you bargained well. I want to show you what the manuscript revealed. I think you will be astounded. The information in this book will change history, and you were an integral part of bringing it to light. Meet me for lunch on Thursday and I'll give you the revelation of your life."

Moretti couldn't help but be intrigued. He agreed and they picked a time and place.

At the appointed hour Cardinal Conti sat in a booth at the back of Ristorantino Moccia facing the entrance so he could watch for Giovanni Moretti. The tiny place near the Coliseum had only eight tables. Except for Conti the place was empty when Moretti entered, a tinkle from a bell over the door announcing his arrival. He slid in the booth across from Conti and smiled.

"Good to see you under better circumstances, Eminence."

"And you. It's good indeed to see you as well." And it was. The Cardinal was practically ecstatic.

Moretti was pleased to see the cleric so happy. He had been concerned when they met in New York that this powerful man might try to retaliate. But it seemed they were back on familiar ground – two old friends who had just consummated a deal that benefitted both sides.

Moretti recognized the folder sitting on the table, the one he had placed in the locker at the New York gym, the one that had held the manuscript. The old man motioned to it. "What do you have to show me?"

"Patience, my good man. A friend once told me to have patience." Conti laughed heartily and Moretti smiled.

"I suppose I had that coming, my friend."

A waiter took Cardinal Conti's order for a bottle of Chianti as the doorbell tinkled lightly again. Conti glanced up then looked at Giovanni Moretti.

"I don't know how I can repay you for all you've done. I can only hope I've been fair with you."

"Fair? I got exactly what I asked for, Cardinal . . ."

The cleric's face beamed with a broad smile as he quietly said, "And now, my friend, you'll get exactly what you deserve."

"What did you say?" Moretti stopped as two men came to their booth. They were dressed identically in black suits and ties with white shirts.

One of the men acknowledged the Cardinal, looked at Moretti and pulled out a badge and ID card. "I am Inspector Gamboli and this is my associate. We are from the DIA."

Moretti blanched. The Direzione Investigativa Antimafia is a branch of the national Italian police force aimed at fighting organized crime. He was well familiar with the DIA.

"I'm afraid there's been a mistake."

The Inspector looked at Cardinal Conti who jovially answered Moretti. "John, you know there's no mistake." He gestured expansively toward Moretti. "This is your man, inspector."

"John Spedino, you're under arrest for murder, drug trafficking and unlawful flight to avoid prosecution." The men pulled Moretti out of the booth, handcuffs ready.

And suddenly John Spedino, the missing godfather who had become Giovanni Moretti, was a fugitive no longer. He glared at Dominic Cardinal Conti who was positively beaming with delight. If looks could kill, as the saying goes, there would have been one dead Cardinal in the restaurant.

As the officers began to roughly usher Spedino out, he turned to Conti and hissed, "Don't I even get a kiss, Judas?"

CHAPTER TWENTY-FIVE

Vatican City

Now that Giovanni Moretti had been properly repaid for his insolence Dominic Cardinal Conti could get to work. Conti was amused at how easily he had flushed Moretti into the hands the DIA. The man had grown old and complacent. There was a time, the Cardinal reflected, when Spedino would have been too wary and crafty to be caught like a fish in a barrel. But not this time. John Spedino wouldn't get away again – after the godfather's escape from Pavon Prison in Guatemala the President ordered the FBI to find and recapture him. The drug trafficking charges lodged against Spedino in the States hadn't gone away when he was convicted of murder in the Central American country. The American government wouldn't let him go now. He was going to prison in the United States this time.

Getting the attention of the authorities had been simple. Once Cardinal Conti arrived back in Rome with the manuscript he placed a call to the FBI's Manhattan office. Once he mentioned the reason for the call and who he was, it took only a moment for the prestigious official of the Catholic Church to be connected with Special Agent-in-Charge Jack Underwood.

Apologetically Conti explained that he might have inadvertently helped precipitate the bombing in New York because of his request to a man named Giovanni Moretti.

"I wanted a manuscript for the Vatican Archives – one volume that had been missing from a set for hundreds of years," the Cardinal said. "The Church has the others. Once I read in the New York Times that the last volume was extant I asked Mr. Moretti to obtain it for us. In past years he has been a major benefactor of the church and I was aware he collects rare works of literature. It seemed natural to use him as an intermediary. We do this often. When sellers learn the Church wants something the price usually skyrockets. It happens all the time when we evidence interest in an antiquity. So we use middle-men to help us discreetly acquire items of interest."

Conti continued his lie. "I became concerned as I spoke more with Mr. Moretti about this project. He seemed eager, like a schoolboy almost. When I saw the news and realized he had obviously been behind the bombing on Fifth Avenue, not to mention having someone steal the manuscript itself, I recorded my next meeting with him."

He had heavily edited the recording. At this point it had become simply an excerpt from the middle of their conversation during the aborted lunch meeting in Rome. Regardless, Moretti's language was clear. What was omitted completely was the rest of the conversation – the part that showed Conti's complicity in the crime.

Underwood asked the Cardinal to play the recording.

As it began the agent listened closely. First he heard Cardinal Conti's voice.

"I asked you to get a manuscript for me, Giovanni. Not to kill eleven people and blow up a building. Are you crazy? Did you think I would condone this atrocity?"

"I followed your direction, Your Eminence. My enthusiasm in creating such a scene wasn't because of you. It was an old score that needed settling. Someone needed a lesson and through my efforts, that person got one. You needn't worry about how I handle my responsibilities. By now you should know that. We've worked together a long time, Dominic. Don't start second-guessing me now. You'll have your manuscript. Let it go, my friend.

"Although I utilized what appeared to be a priest in the operation, it will ultimately be

clear to the authorities that the Church was actually not involved at all. The man will easily be recognized as an impostor once they investigate."

Agent Underwood was speechless. Here was the major break he'd needed – convincing evidence that Giovanni Moretti, whoever he was, had masterminded the Fifth Avenue bombing. He spent another few minutes talking with Conti, who advised nothing of substance followed that dialogue and he had erased the balance. If it had been anyone else, Agent Underwood might have been suspicious. But this man was one of the highest-ranking people in the Vatican, head of the Church's bank. He was above reproach.

The FBI agent arranged to have a man from the US Embassy in Rome pick up a copy of the recording.

Cardinal Conti had done one more thing to help the FBI. In order to get a Vatican passport John Spedino had been fingerprinted. It was a requirement no one could avoid, but behind the scenes the cleric had ensured the fingerprint card of this "friend of the Church" wasn't processed through Interpol. Before contacting the authorities Conti had made a call. Suddenly the prints were distributed to the international police agency for comparison to known criminals worldwide.

Four days later Special Agent Underwood called the Cardinal. Moretti, the agent said, was actually John Spedino, the missing godfather of the New York mob who had fled Guatemala while serving a life sentence for murder. He was a dangerous man and had once been the most powerful mobster in America, the agent told a seemingly incredulous Cardinal.

"How did he get to Italy?"

"Eminence, he somehow obtained a Vatican City passport and used it to travel from Central America to Italy. Interpol confirms the number of the passport he carries is not in the Vatican's system. It's probably forged."

Conti knew all this of course, having been instrumental in Spedino's relocation to Italy after his escape. On the phone with the FBI agent Conti managed to sound suitably appalled. Despite expressing concern for his own safety, the Cardinal generously offered to try to help the FBI and Italian DIA flush Spedino out of hiding, since even Cardinal Conti actually didn't know where Spedino lived in Rome. Spedino had taken the bait and the rest was history. The FBI got their man without spending too much time checking the doctored tape. The Cardinal was free from involvement. He had become a key asset in the apprehension of an international criminal instead of an accessory to a major crime. And the FBI agent had assured him that Conti's own involvement in the entire matter would remain completely confidential. There was no need for a high-ranking official of the Church to be linked to an international crime and a Mafia godfather, they both agreed.

That first afternoon after arriving from New York with the manuscript Conti had had one goal - to ensure the photocopy Conti had taken from the Pope's office really was the key to decoding the manuscripts. And it had worked perfectly. It appeared that this single sheet was the key to unlocking the secret pages in the Templars volumes.

The manuscript that had been stolen from Bijan Rarities contained over two hundred pages handwritten in Latin, medieval French and English by unknown Templar scribes.

Today Conti examined the first page of the volume to make sure it was what he expected. And it was – this was definitely the missing book from the set. Its cover bore the same bold words in Latin – *Opus Militum Xpisti. The Work of the Soldiers of Christ.* And this volume started with an entry in the year 1475. Perfect. The cleric then flipped to the end – the last few pages were the same strange symbols, the coded pages that he hoped he could now decipher. However, the last entry not in code was dated 1699. Again perfect. Chronologically this book dovetailed precisely in between two others that Dominic

Conti had already seen, two of the four that resided in the Pope's secret vault. This was indeed the missing book – the one that told what the Knights Templars were doing at the time the Money Pit on Oak Island was being constructed.

Although he desperately wanted to tackle the coded pages first the cleric forced himself to be patient. He read the first four pages. They were in Latin. On page five Conti came to the first page of symbols. He stopped and reflected - he had learned nothing new so far; the book was basically a diary and these four pages were as routine as most of the material in the other volumes had been. They told of adventures and riches but Dominic was looking for secrets.

Now that he had reached the page of symbols Conti picked up the sheet that would decode the information. The symbols in the manuscript were small and intricately drawn; there were several hundred of them on the page like letters in words. He looked at each symbol then painstakingly referred to the decoder, being extremely careful to get the solution right the first time. He decoded a few words, stopped and glanced at what he had written. This time the language was medieval French; the Cardinal was thankful for the monotonous classes he'd endured in parochial school learning arcane languages. He never thought he'd have the slightest use for it but his efforts paid off today. Choosing not to read the translation until he finished the whole page, he continued his decryption.

At one pm the cleric had to stop. His eyes were burning from squinting and his mind was numb from the tedious work. He was three-fourths of the way through the first encoded page but he had to take a break. He closed the ancient manuscript and put it and his code sheet into his desk drawer. He needed air so he walked down Via Tunisi to Via Candia and came to Piacere Molise. It was the cleric's favorite restaurant and so close to the Vatican he could be there in ten minutes. The owners were a husband and wife team who knew Cardinal Conti well. He was ushered to his favorite table and a glass of good white wine was soon in front of him.

He ordered lunch but hardly touched his food, deep in thought about the work he was doing. He figured he had maybe a couple of hours left before this page was done. Then he could read the whole thing. In less than an hour he was back at his desk hunched over the manuscript, painstakingly decoding one symbol after another. By four pm he was finished. One encoded page down, twelve to go.

Just to be safe Cardinal Conti scanned the decoded page into his computer. He folded the original, put it in his pocket and left his office. At his apartment Conti poured himself a double Scotch and water with a couple cubes of ice then settled into a comfortable chair in his living room. Eager to see what was so important that it had warranted encryption, he began to read.

CHAPTER TWENTY-SIX

According to the New Testament book of John, Jesus was crucified on a hill called Golgotha. He hung on the Cross for several hours. At one point Mary the mother of Jesus stood at the foot of the Cross with "the disciple whom Jesus loved," presumably John, most scholars believe.

Looking down at her, Jesus said to his mother, "Woman, behold thy son." He said to John, "Behold thy mother." The Bible says from that point on the disciple took her "to his own home."

After Jesus died, a wealthy man named Joseph of Arimathea claimed the body. Joseph took the body of Jesus to his own new tomb and buried him. A very heavy stone was rolled into place to block the entrance and keep enemies from snatching the body of the man many had worshipped as the Messiah.

Three days later Mary Magdalene came to the tomb and saw that the stone was rolled away and it was open. Thinking the body of Jesus had indeed been stolen, she ran to tell his disciples. Arriving at the tomb, these men confirmed Mary's story. The body of Jesus Christ was not there.

Cardinal Conti began to read the words he had written down, the first fully decoded page of symbols. He skipped to the middle, then the end, translating the ancient French as he went, just to confirm he was seeing what he thought he was seeing. How odd, he thought.

The words were familiar to him. It seemed strange to come across them in code in a Templars diary that otherwise related events in the late fifteenth century.

Conti reached for a Bible sitting two feet away on his coffee table. He wanted to ensure the translation was not altered. It hadn't been - it was the same. Verbatim. In medieval French, Dominic Conti had decoded John 19:25-27 and John 20:1-8. It was the account of Christ on the Cross, entrusting his mother's care to John, then the body of Jesus disappearing from the tomb where he had been buried, presumably resurrected to fulfill prophecy.

Conti was dumbfounded. Why would anyone go to such painstaking effort, writing by hand one symbol at a time, to encode a simple passage from the Bible? Were the other coded pages the same – encoded verses from the best selling book in the world? Could the verses themselves be yet another code, meant to guide the reader to a different solution?

He was absolutely exhausted after the day's painstaking work. He had hunched over his desk squinting through a magnifying glass at a thousand symbols, decoding each one. Although the verses obviously must mean more than what they seemed, it was frustrating that he'd spent so much time on something he could have easily read in the Bible. Tomorrow he'd see what the next page of code said. Hopefully it would be more revealing. He downed the rest of his Scotch and poured another.

CHAPTER TWENTY-SEVEN

London

The call from Special Agent-in-Charge Underwood came at 4 pm London time. He reported to Brian that John Spedino had been captured in Rome earlier today. The mobster had been living in Italy for a few months with a new identity, apparently having somehow obtained a Vatican passport.

Despite the Vatican connection, the agent said at this point the FBI believed the man dressed as a priest who stole the manuscript was just that – a person using a costume as a diversion.

Underwood told Brian they had information which, if genuine, proved Spedino orchestrated the bombing of Bijan Rarities. To his old drug trafficking charges they intended to add murder and unlawful flight. He said other charges might come later.

"From our source we understand John Spedino had the stolen manuscript. It's now in the hands of the Catholic Church in Vatican City." That was important information – the book rightfully belonged to the Crane family who had given it to Brian for valuation. Agent Underwood said he was contacting the Church to see if they would return the manuscript to Brian.

Brian said, "Do you think John Spedino caused the murder of Arthur Borland here in London?" He thought it couldn't be a coincidence.

"Sorry I can't answer that. I don't have details on the Borland case. That's being handled in London. I'm certain my counterparts there are going to investigate the possibility and once they know something we'll see if anything ties together."

"Which brings me to one last question. Is there anything in all of this that would cause you to think my friend Nicole Farber is in danger?"

"We don't have anything concrete. I know you think Spedino was systematically retaliating against the three of you. Maybe that's true, but I think we got him before he could put anything in place against Miss Farber. And I'm sure you know she turned down my offer to give her some added protection. We'll continue to keep an eye on that angle though. You have my word on that."

Later Brian called Nicole and gave her the news. She was relieved that Spedino was in custody and theoretically no longer a potential threat to either of them.

Then she brightly said, "I'm rearranging some things at the office, sweetie, and I'm taking off a few days. In a couple of weeks will you still be in London or will you come back to New York by then? I'm hoping London – I haven't been there in forever and you know how much I love it!"

He said his plans were to remain in London for now – there was nothing other than checking on his New York apartment that couldn't be handled by phone or email. And his neighbor was periodically ensuring things were good at home. She offered to fly over for a week and Brian jumped on it. He'd be damned glad to see her again. It seemed like ages since they were last together.

There was a comfortable feeling in both libraries of the Monument Club. Brian was an occasional user of the one in New York, which was almost as extensive as the library here in London. The Club was famous for having the world's largest collection of reference works on archaeology, anthropology and a plethora of related subjects. As in New York, the top two floors of the London building contained shelf after shelf of books, manuscripts and other written documents, just like a traditional library. Carrels were placed here and there, allowing members a quiet place to study and do research. Each carrel contained a computer that accessed the Club's microfiche archives. Although many members preferred for one reason or another to see the original book or copy thereof, others preferred microfiche. There were several advantages – all documents held by the Monument Club in either location were on one computer and every single thing had been microfilmed. Members therefore could find one of nearly a hundred and fifty thousand works, examine it at their leisure, photocopy anything they needed from fiche, and order up the original item if necessary. It was very helpful and one of the things that made the Monument Club so popular among archaeologists, explorers and the like. Research was critical in the world of antiquities and for that, this place was the best on earth.

Armed with a letter of authorization from Carissa Borland, Brian sat in the office of Jeffrey Montfort, the librarian who managed the sixty thousand volumes at the London Monument Club. The man was gaunt, pale, bookish – exactly as you'd expect for a librarian, Brian thought - and had held his position for twenty years. He was reputed to be extremely knowledgeable about the resources he oversaw.

The man gave Carissa's letter a brief glance, smiled and said, "Jeffrey Montfort, at your service. Please, call me Jeffrey. What can we do for you, Mr. Sadler?" He appeared glad to have a visitor. The place was otherwise as solemn as a church.

"Call me Brian, please. You're aware, I'm sure, of the death of Lord Borland. I'm interested in seeing anything you can give me about the research he was doing."

"Ah, yes. I was saddened to hear of the Earl's demise. Of late he had become my best customer, as it were. He was here almost every day for the past few months. I'll be glad to show you everything I can." The men talked for fifteen minutes about Lord Borland, recounting how much both of them enjoyed his company.

Finally Jeffrey wheeled his chair to a computer on a side table, typed some entries and peered at the screen.

"He looked at several things early on. Most recently he had been spending time with a set of Knights Templars manuscripts. Our volumes are copies. They were donated by the Caboto family of Italy. Marco Caboto died and his heirs donated a few thousand books, manuscripts, drawings and other documents to the Monument Club. Caboto gave the original Knights Templars books to the Vatican in the late 1800s, I believe.

"Lord Borland told me there was a missing volume, one covering roughly the fifteenth and sixteenth centuries. He and I spent a lot of effort trying to ascertain if the Club had a copy. The day before he died, in fact, I finally acknowledged drawing a blank on the search. He didn't seem disappointed. In fact I gathered he had an idea. I'm not certain, but he just wasn't as upset as I thought he'd be."

The librarian was savoring the conversation. Brian figured he spent a good deal of time alone.

"Please go on."

"Since Lord Borland was so determined to find that manuscript I presume it holds information he desperately needed for whatever project he was working on. You know, I rarely know what's behind the searches our members do. Sometimes I find out – now and then a book gets written, I read it and think to myself, 'I found the information he's using in that description.' That's gratifying, to think I can help people find things they need. You know? Sort of makes you feel good inside!"

Brian smiled and nodded.

"We've been talking about his search for a copy of a missing manuscript. The book itself actually exists - a week or so ago Arthur told me the missing volume had turned up. He said it was found in a collector's library in

Nova Scotia and that man's heirs turned it over to a gallery in New York City – a friend of his owned the gallery, I think he said. Then I heard on the news something about a terrible accident at the gallery. The book was either destroyed or somehow went missing. I can't recall which. Surely you heard of the bombing, being a Yank yourself . . ."

"The explosion at the gallery was no accident," Brian said quietly.

"Oh, so you heard about it too . . . oh my." His face suddenly showed recognition. "Please forgive me, sir. I just recalled what else Arthur told me about his friend. The gallery belonged to one of our members, a Yank who owned a London gallery as well. Oh my. Oh my. That would be you, wouldn't it? My apologies, sir, if I spoke out of turn. I do that sometimes." He smiled ruefully.

"No problem. Yes, it was my gallery. It was bombed and the manuscript was stolen. Several people died. I'm here to find out why."

"Oh my God. So there really is something very important in that missing volume, it appears. If it's here, I'll help you find it, in memory of my good friend Arthur Borland. I also want to help you figure out why someone stole the manuscript after bombing your shop. What a reprehensible crime."

CHAPTER TWENTY-EIGHT

Vatican City

As Cardinal Conti read six more pages of the Templars manuscript he saw the same routine diary entries as were in the Vatican's own volumes. There was nothing surprising. Many months separated the individual entries – the six pages he had just finished covered a twelve-year timespan. Like the others, this book contained the highlights of events in the lives of crusading soldiers, this time from the late 1400s to around 1700. Battles were fought, church relics saved from marauding bands of heathens, tribute demanded and collected from those under the protection of these roaming knights. The entries in the book were consistent with the activities generally attributed to the Knights Templars as the Middle Ages transitioned into the European rebirth, the Renaissance.

Skimming the routine entries, Dominic saw nothing that captured his interest. He was in the year 1496. He turned the page and his adrenalin spiked – here were more tiny symbols. Conti had a quarterly bank meeting in thirty minutes so he quelled the urge to start decoding. Although it was frustrating, his project would have to wait until the afternoon.

It was a beautiful morning as Cardinal Conti walked to the medieval tower that housed the Institute for the Works of Religion, the Vatican Bank. Every quarter the five men who served on the Supervisory Commission of Cardinals gathered from around the world to review the bank's activities and results.

Conti had been elected President of the Commission two years previously with the overt blessing of Pope Benedict. The bank's meetings were held behind closed doors and no minutes were recorded. Cellphones were not allowed in the room. The five members therefore were free to discuss anything they wished; what happened in the bank's conference room was revealed to the outside world only if all of those men determined it would be so.

Cardinal Conti presided over today's meeting, hastily pushing agenda items through the process and frequently gazing out the ancient tower windows as mundane fact-filled reports were presented. His lack of attention wasn't lost on the others. The Archbishop of Santiago sat next to Conti – he leaned over at one point and whispered,

"Dominic, are you all right? You seem preoccupied."

"Yes, yes. I'm fine. I just have a lot going on right now. You can't imagine how busy things are."

The Archbishop truly couldn't imagine. He had no desire to work in Vatican City. There were many, many men here whose political ambitions were as strong as their godly ones. He loved being in Chile, a vast ocean and a continent away from the politics and intrigue that festered in any seat of government, including the holiest one on earth. *Put the Church and the State together in one place,* the Archbishop thought with a smile, *and you get nothing but problems.*

Cardinal Conti forced his mind back on the issues at hand as the presentations droned on. Everything on today's agenda was totally routine – if he hadn't been President of the group he might have begged off and stayed with his exciting project. But he had to carry on for another hour or so.

His mind drifted again to the Templars manuscript. He felt both excitement and dread at the prospect of tackling the symbols. He hoped to find information so secret, so important that it was painstakingly encoded for protection. At the same time he feared he would find nothing but another page of Bible verses. If the latter happened he'd have to figure out why someone went to that effort. There had to be more than there appeared.

"Ahem. Eminence, may we proceed?"

Dominic was jolted back to the reality of the bank meeting from his reverie. The Vatican Secretary of State and the other men around the table looked expectantly at him.

"Ah, my apologies, gentlemen." He glanced at the agenda in front of him and had no idea whose report had just concluded. "Let's see. Who's next?" He smiled as one of his colleagues gave him a quizzical glance and began the next discussion.

Mercifully the meeting ended around noon, Conti having kept his mind on the subjects at hand for the remainder of the session. He avoided the usual small talk and conversation that followed each meeting – these men only saw each other quarterly and all had become good friends. There was always a period of catching up, usually including lunch, but today Dominic Conti excused himself and hurried back to his office.

Ensuring he had nothing on his agenda for the afternoon and all calls were held, Dominic poured himself a glass of wine from a small refrigerator in an adjoining pantry, took it, a piece of cheese and a slice of crusty bread to the table. He sat and began to decipher.

As before, the process was painstakingly slow. The symbols were so tiny his eyes ached. After about an hour he had several lines printed out in the ancient French language. He stopped, poured another glass of wine and walked around his office a few times to loosen his aching shoulders and legs. Then he sat down to read what he had decoded.

O Lord, hear our prayer. By the grace of God our Father and his Son Jesus the Christ our Lord we have been appointed defenders and guardians of the faith. Let our words and deeds be pleasing to Him and through His holy guidance may we steadfastly continue our mission, guarding the secret with which we have been entrusted for these three hundred sixty-seven years.

Conti stopped and reread the words in front of him. *A prayer. But what does it mean? What secret have the Templars guarded for 367 years?* The date of the last diary entry was 1496. Three hundred and sixty-seven years previously would be the year 1129.

As head of the Knights Templars today, Conti was familiar with the historical significance of that time period. Led by Hugues de Payens, the original Knights Templars were officially endorsed by the Catholic Church at the Council of Troyes in 1128. Thus began two centuries of religious and martial fervor, the meteoric rise of the soldiers of the order and its deadly eradication in the early 1300s.

In 1129 the original Templars would have been immensely popular among the population, revered as soldiers of the cross, defenders of the faith and guardians of the church. And if the prayer he just translated were true, these crusading Christian soldiers were entrusted with a secret in that year. Those early Templars had been completely wiped out in 1310, their members burned to death. But as Dominic Conti knew well, that wasn't the end of the Knights Templars. Successors arose, in secret at first. These were dangerous times but men bravely continued the work. The Templars secrets were passed to them. According to legend they knew where vast treasure was hidden, spoils of the Templars' activities. That knowledge had gone missing over the centuries but the rumors of unimaginable riches persisted.

Of course this wasn't the group also called Knights Templars who ultimately became a subset of the Masonic organization. These Templars were part of the Church just as the original ones had been. And that continued today.

What had they been entrusted with? What had they guarded for three and a half centuries? Hopefully the rest of the coded symbols would provide the answer.

The phone on the desk across the room rang, startling Cardinal Conti. He had explicitly instructed his secretary that no calls were to be put through. Angrily he strode across the expansive office, punched a button on his phone and curtly said to his assistant, "This better be important."

"The secretary to His Holiness is on the line, sir. I'm so sorry to disturb you. I told him you were in conference and he insisted on being put through immediately."

Wonder what this is all about? Dominic punched a flashing button on his phone and said, "Good afternoon. This is Dominic Conti."

"Good afternoon, Eminence. My apologies for disturbing you but His Holiness asks that you meet with him today at four pm. Is that time acceptable?"

Is that time acceptable? How ridiculous, Conti thought. There's not a person in Vatican City who wouldn't drop anything when the Pope asked for a meeting.

"Of course. I'll be there. May I ask what is the subject of our meeting?"

"I'm afraid I wasn't told, Eminence. We'll see you at four."

There was a time when things had been different. When Benedict was Pope the call would have come directly from him, not through an assistant. He and the retired pontiff had had a close working relationship, one of mutual respect. Not so with the new one. Although he was widely respected and admired, he was also just that – new. No one knew exactly what to expect, and he didn't yet have an infrastructure of colleagues. That would come in time but at this early stage he was an enigma. Dominic Conti could speculate forever on the purpose of his summons to the papal office but he had no idea what the meeting would be about. And he was disappointed that his decoding project would have to wait for another day. He had just over an hour to wrap things up, walk to the Pope's office and be on time for the meeting.

CHAPTER TWENTY-NINE

Cardinal Conti felt uneasy standing at the same office doors he had surreptitiously entered just a few nights ago. Since the Pope was in his office today, two Swiss Guards stood at attention outside the office, a marked difference from the solitary guard who had lounged in a chair the other night.

The papal secretary opened the door and gestured Conti inside, closing it behind him. The pontiff sat behind the desk where Dominic had gone through drawers and stolen the photocopy that decrypted the Templars manuscript. Suddenly he became aware of another person in the room. He glanced to his left and saw a man sitting in a chair.

The Pope came around his desk and presented his ring to the Cardinal, who knelt and kissed it. The Pope said, "Cardinal Conti, do you know Frederico Messina?" He gestured to the man sitting in the chair, who rose and extended his hand.

A wave of fear swept over Dominic Conti, causing him to shudder. He struggled to control his emotions, averting his eyes downward as he looked at the man. He had never seen Messina although the name was immediately familiar to him and to everyone else in Vatican City. Frederico Messina was head of the Directorate of Security and Civil Protection Services. More directly to the point, he was commandant of the Gendarmerie Corps. This was the police and security organization of the tiny country of Vatican City. Unlike the Swiss Guard, who provides personal security for the Pope and his offices, the Gendarmerie Corps was the national police force, roughly equivalent to the FBI.

Conti forced himself to be calm. His mind raced – at first he thought this was about his breaking into the Pope's office – somehow he had been caught on camera or otherwise compromised. But if that were the case the head of the Swiss Guard would have been here, not Frederico Messina. So this was about something else. But what?

The Pope introduced the two then said, "Please sit. May I arrange some coffee for you, Cardinal Conti?"

He declined. The pontiff then sat down behind his desk.

"A matter has come to my attention, Eminence, and I thought it best to get first-hand answers to a few questions Officer Messina has."

"Of course, Holiness.   Anything I can do to help . . ."

The Pope interrupted.   "Officer Messina, please take over from here.   I'll interject when I feel it necessary."

Dominic Conti could feel drops of sweat beading up on his neck and in his armpits. *Where was this headed?*

Within a matter of seconds he knew the answer.

"Eminence," the policeman began, "does the name Giovanni Moretti ring a bell with you?"

CHAPTER THIRTY

London

Brian spent the morning at the gallery, ate a quick lunch at his desk, wrapped up and took the tube to the Club. At three pm he walked into the library. A man dressed in khaki slacks and a sweater stood at the front desk, completing a short check-in form.

Jeffrey Montfort was helping the man. He looked up and said, "Good afternoon, Brian. Ready to tackle our project? I'll be with you in a moment. Let me get this gentleman situated."

Jeffrey seemed eager to get to work. He hummed as the man at the desk handed in his paperwork and requested a couple of books. He led the stranger to a carrel, held up a finger to Brian to indicate he'd be right back, and trotted off to the stacks. He returned in a couple of minutes with two books, handed them off to the new guest and returned to his desk and Brian.

"All yours!" He was effusive, Brian noticed. Working on a mystery was likely the most interesting thing that had happened in the Monument Club library in years. And Jeffrey Montfort was ready for some detective work.

"The easiest way to start will be to provide you with everything Lord Borland was working on that last few days before his death. I'll print out a list of the items he had checked out that last week. He was here every day. As excited as he became there at the end I'm sure he was on to something. He'd come in every morning around ten, have a cup of tea with me then get started. He checked out several things each day and returned them every evening. That's our policy, you know. Everything checked out gets returned the same day. That's my job! Library policeman!"

Brian listened patiently to Jeffrey Montfort ramble. The librarian craved conversation - that much was obvious. He was friendly and probably very intelligent, but his pasty skin and disheveled appearance revealed a man who got outdoors very little and cared nothing for how he looked.

Jeffrey Montfort went to work. "All right then," the librarian said shortly, "here's our printout. I'll find all these things for you. Meanwhile let me stick you in a carrel – here, let's just use the same one Arthur worked in for the last few months. Seems fitting, don't you think?" The carrel was twenty feet away from the only other person in the library. That man had his head buried in a book, hard at work in his own cubicle.

The librarian scurried away, perusing his list as he stuck a pencil behind his ear. In his carrel Brian unpacked the case he had brought, putting pen, pencil, highlighter and paper on his desk.

"I haven't sat in a carrel since college," he thought, remembering the old days at Oklahoma University with his roommate Harry Harrison. Harry had followed his father's career in politics, ultimately becoming Vice President of the United States, and then assuming the highest office when his predecessor went missing in Mexico. Brian had been instrumental in helping find the former President some time back.

The librarian returned with an armful of things – a couple of books, several three-ring binders filled with papers and a couple of magazines. But he looked puzzled.

"Find everything OK?" Brian asked.

"Not exactly. This is odd. Yes it is. This is odd."

As Brian's grandfather would have put it, the man was in a tizzy. He was upset about something; he kept looking at his printout, then the items he had in his arms, then back to the sheet. He shook his head. "I can't explain how this could have happened."

"What's the problem?"

"Well, it appears our friend Lord Borland broke the rules. Or more accurately, we both did. It looks like that last day he forgot to turn in one of the things he checked out. And I'm an accomplice! I neglected to double-check what he returned. Instead, I must have simply marked off everything as back in its place."

"So one of the items isn't on the shelf?"

"Exactly. Lord Borland must have forgotten to turn it in."

"Could he actually have handed it back, and you either misfiled it or someone else took it off the shelf where it belonged?"

Jeffrey Montfort became even more miffed. "I haven't misfiled an item in ten years. Some people call me OCD. I prefer to call myself meticulous, careful even. I care deeply for each one of these sixty thousand documents. They're my family, you might say. I treat each with respect and care. And I ensure our members do the same."

This is a little creepy, Brian thought. *This guy really needs a life.*

"And no one took this item off the shelf. Before Lord Borland asked for it no one had requested it in the entire time I've been here. Twenty-one years next month."   Obviously distressed, he pulled a handkerchief from his back pocket and wiped his brow.   He was sweating profusely.   Brian was afraid he was going to have a heart attack.

"Let's just think this through.   What is the thing that's missing?"

"It's a two-inch three-ring binder, one of several copies of books that Marco Caboto's heirs donated to the Club in 1930.   I told you earlier that Arthur was very interested in the Knights Templars manuscripts, the ones Caboto turned over to the Vatican around 1875.   The Club received copies of those manuscripts in 1930 along with the rest of Marco Caboto's library.   One day or another over the past few weeks Arthur Borland had checked out every Templars copy we had, but lately he began requesting unrelated things.   This missing binder is one of those.   I think he was looking at every copy of anything from the Caboto collection.   Not original volumes, mind you.   Just copies.   I figure he was probably making sure none of them might accidentally be the copy of that last volume – the Templar manuscript that was stolen from your gallery.   The name of the item that's missing is 'Journal des Pauperes Commilitones'.   It's a copy of an original which was dated 1699."

The title meant nothing to Brian. "So you think Arthur had to have put this binder into his briefcase in order for it to be missing? Correct? Do you inspect the carrels before closing at night to ensure no one left anything out?"

Jeffrey Montfort puffed up like a balloon. He was livid – Brian could see veins in his temples and his face was red. His voice rose slightly and was strangely high-pitched.

"*Mister Sadler!* I would think from what I've told you that you daren't question my diligence in maintaining this roomful of my children, my books. Of *course* I check everything at night. I make sure every chair is pushed back in each carrel. I turn off every single light. There was nothing left behind. *Nothing.*"

Brian had unintentionally gone too far. "I apologize, Jeffrey. I'm just vocalizing every thought I can come up with, trying to conceptualize what could have happened. I met Arthur downstairs for lunch the day after his last visit here. If the case he had then is the same as he carried here I don't see how he could have put a two-inch binder in it. It wasn't that big – certainly not large enough to hold a binder that size."

"He always carried the same brown case."

"That's the one. Do you have storage lockers here?"

"No. Well actually, yes. But no one's used them in years."

"Can we take a look at them?"

"Follow me." With a frustrated sigh, Montfort led Brian to a closet near the entrance to the library. He opened the door; inside was a dusty room lined with shelves of cubbyholes, each one covered by a hinged wooden door. Each was perhaps a foot square and two feet deep. The librarian was right – they looked as though nobody had been in the room for ages.

"Look," Brian said, pointing to the floor. There were shoe prints in the dust. They led into the room four feet to a wall of ancient wooden lockers, some doors open with hinges hanging askew. Others were closed and one had a small padlock on it. Brian pointed at the lock.

"I've never seen that before in my life," Montfort said.

"It looks pretty new, at least a whole lot newer than the shelves in this room," Brian replied. "Can I open it?"

"Absolutely you can. Whoever put that lock on did so without my permission. We need to see what's in there."

They decided it would be easier to pry off the very old hasp than deal with the modern lock. Montfort got a letter opener from his desk and Brian jimmied the hasp and it broke in seconds. He opened the door and looked inside.

"Take a look," he told the librarian.

There lay a white binder. Underneath it was a laptop.

The men wondered out loud why Arthur Borland would have purposely hidden the book he should have returned, and why he would have left his laptop.

They didn't notice the man who had come in earlier. He now stood just outside the closet door, listening to every word they said.

CHAPTER THIRTY-ONE

Vatican City

The head of the Gendarmerie Corps fired questions at Cardinal Conti for half an hour. He had been briefed on everything that Special Agent-in-Charge Jack Underwood knew. So much for the FBI's promise to keep Conti's involvement under wraps, the Cardinal reflected.

I suppose there's a code of honor among international law enforcement agencies, Conti thought. *It was foolish to think I could remain anonymous.* But as the questioning continued, the Cardinal found it easier and easier to settle in to the lie he had created.

Yes, he had used Moretti as an intermediary to get the manuscript. No, he wasn't aware of the man's past. No, he had no idea how he got a Vatican passport or that he was actually John Spedino, the escaped prisoner whose identity had been altered immediately prior to his arrival in Europe.

Dominic Conti felt more and more confident as he smoothly fielded every question with a glib answer. This is going quite well, he thought, becoming ever more bold and fearless with every lie he tossed out.

Suddenly the Pope spoke. He hadn't said a word in over twenty minutes and his quiet voice startled Dominic.

"How much money did you spend to get this Templars manuscript?"

Dominic quickly considered if there were any way to trace the five million US he had transferred to John Spedino's account in Turkey. His confidence was solid. He had made sure things were well covered.

"Only a few thousand dollars, Holiness. A pittance compared with the historic value of such a unique document."

The Pope thought about Conti's answer. "Only a few thousand dollars. That's surprising. Almost unbelievable, in fact, that you could get it for that. Why did you deem this old book so important?"

"Your predecessor generously allowed me to read the four Knights Templars volumes which reside in the secret vault, Holiness. I believe I was the first to determine that one volume was missing from what had been a set. As head of the Templars today I thought it important to find this priceless manuscript and obtain it for the Church's archives to complete the record of Templars exploits."

"Where is the book now?"

Dominic Conti lowered his eyes. He couldn't look the Pope in the face as he uttered a blatant lie. "It's in my office, Holiness. I'm reading it in my spare time. There's nothing special about it. It's simply part of a chronology of a thousand years or more of Templars history. This volume covers the Middle Ages and the Renaissance period."

The Pope's words were stern now. "I understand that you want to read it. However it doesn't belong to you. Finish reviewing it by this time tomorrow. Then contact the FBI in New York City and ask what they want you to do with it."

There was nothing Dominic could do but nod. He'd have to get the book photocopied. Once it was out of his hands he'd never see it again.

The policeman waited respectfully until the Pope gestured for him to proceed, then resumed his inquiry. "Many people died in New York the day that manuscript was stolen. At what point did you become aware that Signore Moretti, directly or through others, was committing multiple crimes to obtain the manuscript you ordered him to get?"

"I, uh . . . I saw the news of the Fifth Avenue bombing on television like everyone else. At some point after that Moretti told me he had the manuscript. It wasn't until later that I realized that book must have been the one that was stolen from the gallery when the explosion occurred."

"With all respect, Eminence, I have listened to the recording you made of Giovanni Moretti's meeting with you. In that recording you tell him you did not authorize him to use force to obtain the manuscript. So at that time you were aware he was probably behind the bombing. Is that correct?"

Nervous again, Conti backpedaled. "Of course. By then I had put two and two together, as they say, and concluded that Moretti was behind the bombing. That's why I recorded our meeting, which was fortunate. Thanks to my foresight a major Mafia figure has been brought to justice."

The policeman pushed harder. "Excuse me, Cardinal Conti, for my not completely understanding everything. You told Agent Underwood that Signore Moretti had in the past been a major benefactor to the Church. I believe you also stated you knew that he had an interest in rare books. Are both those statements accurate?"

Conti stopped and turned to the pontiff. "I'm not sure where all this is going, Holiness. Am I under investigation here? Should I retain an attorney? I thought I had done something beneficial for the Church in obtaining the missing manuscript. I was also instrumental in bringing a criminal to justice. Why do I suddenly feel as though this man" - he gestured at Officer Messina – "considers me a criminal too?"

The Pope said nothing.

"My deepest apologies, Eminence," Officer Messina responded quietly to the Cardinal once he knew the Pope intended to remain silent. "My only desire is to understand exactly how everything happened so that we may put this matter to rest. I had earlier asked His Holiness if he would allow you come to our offices for an interview but he declined."

"Dominic," the Pope said. "I told Officer Messina we would talk here in my office instead of making this a formal interrogation. There's no need for outsiders to question why a Cardinal, the head of the Vatican Bank nonetheless, is being questioned at a police station. I refused to allow that."

The pontiff spoke harshly, a surprising change from his typically quiet demeanor. "You must understand that it is this man's job to solve this case. You are here, Cardinal Conti, because of your own actions. Without seeking advice or approval from your superiors, you chose to involve the American FBI in an operation to catch a criminal on Italian soil. The FBI in turn called upon the Italian anti-Mafia police to capture Signore Moretti, or Signore Spedino as we now know. It is imperative the Vatican police ensure nothing further needs to be done. We are keeping our own house clean. A high-ranking Church official is involved in apprehending a criminal. Very strange, you'd agree. You're out of line, Cardinal, in your protest of what is nothing more than a fact-finding mission by the police."

The officer was trained to listen to words and hear more than what was being said. The pontiff didn't trust Conti. He was sure of it. His face remained impassive as he watched the Pope dress down this senior Church official.

"I'm sure you have nothing to hide, so I'll ask Officer Messina to keep going now. We must move along as expeditiously as possible."

Messina picked up the questioning again, emboldened by the pontiff's tacit approval of his interrogation. "Let's see, where were we? I think I asked about two of your statements. I believe you said Moretti was a major benefactor to the Church and that you were aware he had an interest in rare books. What is the basis of those statements and how did you know these things?"

Weaving a web of deceit is not an easy matter. Lies pile upon lies and one must be on his toes to keep from being caught in one's own web. Dominic Conti had come into this meeting unprepared for questioning by a member of law enforcement. He hadn't completely thought through his stories and at this point he was frankly getting tired. His answers became less structured, more vague.

"I really don't recall, Officer Messina. I heard some time ago that Giovanni Moretti was a generous man to his church and that he was a bibliophile. I think it may have been . . ."

The officer stopped him. "Pardon me, Cardinal Conti, but Signore Moretti was only in Italy less than a year before he was captured . . . with your significant help, as you pointed out. Before that he was John Spedino, a Mafia chieftain in prison for murder in Guatemala. Are you saying you knew John Spedino was generous to the Church, or Giovanni Moretti? If the latter, his generosity must have appeared only very recently. He wasn't using that name for very long."

"Possibly it was Spedino . . ." Conti was backing himself into a corner. "No, I'm obviously mistaken. I had no idea Moretti was actually John Spedino. So of course I couldn't have known."

The Cardinal turned to the Pope, sitting impassively behind his desk, his hands folded over his waist. "Holiness, I respectfully ask that we terminate this interrogation. I have nothing to hide but I feel as though I'm on the witness stand. I'm angered at this man's insinuations."

The pontiff said, "I've listened to every word, Dominic. I heard no insinuations. I heard a man of the law ask a man of the cloth questions about some things he doesn't fully understand. I'm willing to accede to your request to stop now because I have other matters at hand. Gentlemen, this meeting is concluded for today. Officer Messina, if you have further questions you may contact Cardinal Conti directly. For the time being you will not require him to come to your police headquarters. Any discussions will be held here in the Vatican and you, Eminence, will make yourself available on reasonable notice from Officer Messina. I will be involved in future conversations if I deem it necessary. Should your interest in Cardinal Conti become more than it is today, you will notify me and I will give further direction then. Please give Signore Messina your contact information, Cardinal Conti."

Everyone stood, the visitors bowed and left the room. In the hallway outside the papal offices Conti handed the policeman a card with his email address and office phone number. Messina said, "I appreciate your help, Eminence. I apologize if I seemed aggressive. I certainly meant no disrespect."

Conti looked at him stonily and said nothing. He turned and strode angrily down the hall.

Officer Messina walked to a staircase fifty feet away and took the broad stone steps down three flights to ground level.

"I wonder what Cardinal Conti has to hide," he thought to himself as he walked back to police headquarters. "He's definitely lying about something. Even the Pope knows it. I'll have to find out what it is."

CHAPTER THIRTY-TWO

London

Brian and the librarian returned to the front desk with the things they'd discovered in the locker. They noticed the other visitor walking to the restrooms.

Jeffrey Montfort glanced at the cover of the binder and confirmed it was the one that hadn't been returned. He then handed it to Brian. "I know you're going to want to peruse this. Hopefully something here will help figure out what Lord Borland was doing."

Brian carried the laptop and binder to the carrel he had been assigned. He tackled the computer first; although an older Lenovo it powered up promptly then asked for a password. He had no idea what Arthur might have used so the laptop would have to wait until he could talk to Carissa Borland.

He turned to the book. The binder's spine was blank. On the front cover someone had written "Journal des Pauperes Commilitones." He opened it and gasped. The title page said *Opus Militum Xpisti. The Work of the Soldiers of Christ.* Excitedly he turned to the next page – the entry was dated 1475. Brian was ecstatic. This was the missing book, a copy of the manuscript that had been stolen in the Fifth Avenue bombing. He flipped quickly through pages to the end. It looked as though it had a couple hundred pages. This could be a complete copy!

He looked at Google on the computer in front of him then said, "Jeffrey, take a look at this." The librarian walked from his desk to the carrel. "You said the library's description of this book is 'Journal des Pauperes Commilitones' and it's dated 1699. Right?"

"Absolutely correct, Brian."

"I looked it up. Do you know what Journal des Pauperes Commilitones roughly translates to in English? It's the diary of the poor soldiers."

"From my rusty schoolboy French I think that's accurate. And your point?"

"Arthur said that the original Knights Templars were called the Poor Fellow-Soldiers of Christ and of the Temple of Solomon. So it doesn't really matter what the listing in your records showed. This is what matters." He opened the book to the first page. *Opus Militum Xpisti.*

He spoke almost in a whisper. "It's the missing volume. It's a copy of the book that was stolen when my gallery was bombed."

"My God! Is this what Arthur was looking for?"

"I think it must have been. I need to do more work on this but I have to go to a meeting at the gallery shortly. Do you have a high-speed copier here?"

"Yes. Even better, I could scan it."

"Excellent! Can you get to work on that while I call Lord Borland's wife? I know I don't need to tell you to be careful. That's the only copy in existence, I guarantee!"

The librarian smiled at Brian, saying nothing. He would be careful. He always was.

Jeffrey Montfort took the binder back to his desk, snapped the rings open and removed the pages. He turned on a scanner and got everything ready. He hit the green button and the pages rapidly began to feed into the machine.

The man who was using the other carrel had heard everything. He entered a text message into his phone.

"There's a copy of the manuscript. Sadler has seen it."

"Take care of it. Get me that copy. Do you understand?"

"Affirmative, Eminence."

CHAPTER THIRTY-THREE

Vatican City

It was nearly five pm when Dominic got back to his office. His secretary was wrapping things up for the day. Conti gave him a curt nod, walked into his office and slammed the door. He turned the lock on it, walked to the pantry by his office and put two cubes of ice in a highball glass. Sitting at his desk he reached into the bottom left drawer and pulled out a fifth of Chivas Regal. He poured the glass half full, knocked it back in a few steady gulps and fixed another. His heart rate slowed as the alcohol did its work.

What the hell was this guy doing? How dare he treat a senior official of the Catholic Church like a common street thief? *I didn't appreciate his condescending attitude but I have to be careful now. He's asking questions that could get me in trouble. I need to think this entire thing through, come up with an airtight story and stick to it. I can outwit this man.*

Nursing his next drink, Dominic Conti took out a legal pad and began to make a list. In one column were the events that had actually transpired with Moretti aka Spedino. Opposite those entries were the things Conti would *say* had happened. By the time the liquor began to dull his brain he had filled two pages – one side of each page with actual events and the other with fictitious explanations. Satisfied that he was on the right track, he hid the pad of paper where it would be safe. He turned off the lights, locked his office door from the outside and walked to his apartment.

At 2:30 am Conti sat straight up in bed. A million hammers banged inside his head. He shouldn't have come home and had another scotch. Or was it two? He had awakened with a sudden dread in his clouded mind. He shouldn't have left that legal pad at the office. It had everything on it that would create his alibi. No one could challenge it except Spedino and he was in jail. But he should have brought it home. It wouldn't do for that to get in the wrong hands. What if it were missing? What if someone had taken it?

It was rare that a Cardinal would come to his office in the wee hours, but it wasn't unprecedented. The security guard dutifully checked Conti's ID even though he knew the man well. That was the rule and they both followed it. Conti signed in and noted the time – 3:13 am.

"I won't be long," he said. "I left something in my office that I need."

He took the stairs to his floor then went to the wing where his office was located. Everything was completely quiet, the hallways and rooms dark. There were no security guards in this area; only the papal offices had such protection. Conti pulled out his key, unlocked the office door and turned on the light.

He walked to his desk and pulled the middle drawer wide open to get the legal pad from the back where he had put it.

But it wasn't there.

CHAPTER THIRTY-FOUR

The Cardinal frantically searched his desk. He had forgotten exactly where he had hidden the notepad. He had been a little tipsy, in fact he still was, he admitted to himself. So he had put it somewhere else. He went through every drawer, examined folders and files in and on his desk and even looked in the wastebasket. It was empty; the cleaning crew had already been through. And he knew he hadn't accidentally thrown it away. As fuzzy as his mind was, that little pad was too important. He wouldn't have done that.

The cleaning crew! There's a spy here! They took my notepad!

He spent ten minutes mulling that possibility in his addled brain, then decided he was making too much of all this. When people lose keys or other things it usually pays to forget about it. Then what you've lost turns up and you remember that's where you put it in the first place.

He was nervous. But he wasn't going to panic. He hadn't been in the best of shape when he put the pad away. It was somewhere. He just needed to wait until the naked light of day. It would turn up.

Before he left he made sure the manuscript and decoder page were safely in a drawer of his credenza, well hidden underneath a stack of mundane reports no one cared about. Then he went home to bed, tossing and turning the rest of the night.

The next morning Dominic had pressing business with the bank. There was no time to think about the missing legal pad or the coded page in the ancient manuscript. Two Ibuprofens and massive quantities of coffee had helped a little but he still felt sluggish and drowsy. Thank God the things on his agenda were handled via emails and phone calls. He didn't need the hassle of face-to-face meetings this morning.

He found himself opening his middle desk drawer and peering into the back of it perhaps a dozen times during the morning. Every time he thought maybe he'd overlooked the pad or maybe it had slipped behind the drawer – a quick withdrawal of the entire drawer proved that theory wrong. So far he had no idea where it had gone but he still hoped against hope it would turn up. It had to.

At noon he went out for lunch. A plate of pasta with shrimps and two glasses of Chianti at a nearby sidewalk café made things much better. By two pm he decided he would live to fight another day.

Conti blocked off the remainder of the afternoon for the book project. He settled down at the worktable in his office and started decoding the remainder of the page he had worked on yesterday. His headache was gone and he felt practically human again; it would have been hard to work on this project earlier today, he knew. The intense concentration wouldn't have been easy.

Three hours later he was well down the page of symbols. His secretary gave a brief knock. Conti unlocked the door and bade the young cleric good evening. He decided to give it one more hour to see how far he could get. Today he hadn't stopped to read what he was decoding. He wanted to concentrate on the difficult part – decoding each single symbol into a letter. He wouldn't stop to read the decoded words until he was finished.

It was nearly seven pm when Dominic put down his pen, leaned back in his chair and stretched. He had taken short breaks several times but for the most part he had been at the decoding job for four hours straight. It was tiresome at best; today it was doubly so given Conti's lack of sleep the night before and his rather precarious condition before lunch.

He put the manuscript and code page back into the credenza. As he turned he dropped his pen on the floor beside his desk. He bent to pick it up and saw something under the desk pedestal that held its drawers.

On hands and knees he peered into the small space and saw a pad of paper. He pulled it out; it was his notes from the night before.

He thought for a few minutes and then shook his head, relieved beyond belief that the pad was safe and sound. *I must be losing my mind,* he thought to himself. Undoubtedly the pad was exactly where he had hidden it. He gathered it and the couple of pages of words he had written from the code in the book. Sticking them both in an underarm leather satchel he walked home.

Dominic fixed a light dinner and a glass of wine and then returned to the project. He picked up the folio into which he'd scribbled hours of translated material and began to read from the beginning of that page. He'd read the prayer yesterday but wanted to see it in context with the translation.

O Lord, hear our prayer. By the grace of God our Father and his Son Jesus the Christ our Lord we have been appointed defenders and guardians of the faith. Let our words and deeds be pleasing to Him and through His holy guidance may we steadfastly continue

our mission, guarding the secret with which
we have been entrusted for these three
hundred sixty-seven years.

Now Conti read the new words he had decrypted.

Carrying on the tradition of our forefathers,
Pauvres Chevaliers du Temple, we the
Templars risen from the ashes of our brethren
like the Phoenix, do pledge to uphold the
secrets given to us, to be faithful stewards of
the wealth and treasure amassed and hidden
by our forebears and to continue the good
works of the Order.

Conti paused. Pauvres Chevaliers du Temple was one of a number of titles by which the first Knights Templars were known. It meant "poor Knights of the Temple" – others called them simply the "Order of the Temple" or the more scholarly title Poor Soldiers of Christ and the Temple of Solomon.

In the twelfth century, the early days of the Order, the Templars truly had been poor. They did services for people as they traveled and received donations in return. One important aspect of their work was to serve as escorts or guardians for people making pilgrimages from Europe to Jerusalem, Conti recalled. Over a few years as the organization grew and received sanction from the Church their fortunes took a major turn for the better. It was well known that the Knights Templars were immensely wealthy when they finally were rounded up and murdered through the efforts of a weak Pope and a jealous French king.

Dominic was intrigued by the paragraph he had just read. The writer spoke of the Templars' pledge *"to be faithful stewards of the wealth and treasure amassed and hidden by our forebears."* Very interesting. Many legends spoke of significant Templars treasure and money amassed during their crusades and put in secret places before their demise in 1310. None of it had ever been found, but here was yet another indication that the stories might be true. He resumed reading the medieval French, considering every exciting word carefully.

We have willingly assumed the responsibility to maintain the precious objects, religious artifacts, silver and gold we have been given through the grace of God our Father. As the ancients have written in the Bible, "Through wisdom is an house builded; and by understanding it is established. And by knowledge shall the chambers be filled with all precious and pleasant riches." We the sixteen who lead the Templars are humbled by the mighty weight of the responsibility God has laid upon us.

A quiet ding on Conti's phone interrupted the fascinating words pouring off the page in front of him. He had received an email, a rare event for him this time of the evening. Conti picked up his phone and read the message. The words were few but frightening. His hands shook and the phone fell to the carpet beside him. He leaned back in his chair, his chest contracting as breathing became labored.

Calm down, Dominic.

He forced panic from his mind.

Everything will work out. You just have to think this through.

Dominic Conti had developed a good plan on paper to explain the events that transpired between him and Giovanni Moretti. But he hadn't thought about this.

The email was from Frederico Messina, the head of the Gendarmerie Corps who had grilled the Cardinal earlier this afternoon.

"Eminence, I'd like the original of the recording you made of your meeting with Giovanni Moretti, please. I'll arrange to have it picked up from your office. Let's say ten am tomorrow. If you're not available please leave it with your secretary. Thank you in advance for your cooperation in this matter."

In a panic, the Cardinal put aside the decryption project. Lying in bed he ran scenarios through his head. He slept an hour at most, only when he forced himself not to think about what a deep hole he had dug for himself.

At last daylight arrived. Despite a second restless night, Dominic was ready. His plan wasn't perfect but it would have to do. He would tell the officer he couldn't find the recording. He was sure he'd put it in his desk at the office but it wasn't there. Perhaps it had been stolen – more likely he had misplaced it. After all, he had given the relevant portion to the FBI – there actually hadn't been any need to keep it. So that was believable. Hopefully.

The more he went over the explanation the better it sounded. It was weak – there was no question about that – but he couldn't think of anything better.

He arrived at his office around nine and walked to a beautiful eighteenth-century inlaid wood table sitting by a grouping of chairs. He opened the top drawer, pulled it out and reached into the space behind it. His hands wrapped around the microcassette that contained the entire recording of his meeting with the godfather. He slipped the incriminating tape it into his pocket. Tonight at home he would crush it with a hammer and throw the pieces into the dumpster behind the apartment complex.

He composed an email in response to Officer Messina's request.

"I'm afraid I have misplaced the cassette. I've searched my office but it's nowhere to be found. Fortunately the FBI has the relevant portion I provided and by now I'm

sure you do too. That's what you need. If at some point the cassette turns up I will let you know."

A short response appeared within seconds.

"I will be at your office at ten am."

Precisely at ten the Cardinal's secretary advised Conti that the policeman was here to see him.

"I'm sorry but I'm not available this morning," was Conti's cocky response. *This man needs to learn who's in charge here. I'll call the shots, not him.*

In a moment his assistant replied. "He's choosing to stay in hopes you can work a few minutes into your schedule."

Fine. Let him stay. Let him sit here all day, for all I care.

For two hours Dominic read reports, made calls and found himself unable to concentrate on anything. Every few minutes his hand went into his pocket to ensure the microcassette was still there. He was afraid to start working on the decoded Templars information with the policeman sitting just outside his office door. What he needed desperately to do was to copy the manuscript. He couldn't do it here in the Vatican without arousing suspicion. The head of the Vatican Bank personally using a photocopier, instead of having a subordinate do it? And copying an obviously ancient book? No, that wouldn't work. He had to copy the book elsewhere.

At 12:30 Cardinal Conti emailed his secretary and learned that the policeman was still in the waiting area. Dominic was getting hungry but so was the officer, he presumed. Five minutes later his secretary called, advising that Officer Messina had gone to the bathroom. "Instead of letting him use the one here, Eminence, I directed him to the public restrooms on the second floor. I thought it might give you a chance to leave your office if you wish."

"Good thinking," Conti said to himself. He put the Templars manuscript in his satchel along with the legal pad containing the story he'd created about his involvement with Spedino. Laying the code solution sheet in his desk drawer he walked out of his office with the satchel under his arm.

In the hallway outside his office he turned to go to the elevator. Frederico Messina was standing just across the hall, obviously waiting for him. *Damn this man. He was clever.*

"I'm so glad to have run into you, Eminence," the officer said as though it were purely by chance. "I won't take long but I need to ask you more about this missing tape. This is very disturbing news at this point in my investigation."

"I'm actually on my way to a luncheon," Conti replied breezily, his hand involuntarily closing around the tape in his pocket. His other arm clutched the satchel tightly as if he thought Messina was going to grab it. "Perhaps another time."

"I'll just walk with you if you don't mind. We can talk a moment while we go downstairs."

The Cardinal had no options if he wanted to appear helpful. They took the elevator then walked across the expansive square toward the walls that separated Vatican City from the sprawling mass that was Rome. As they walked the policeman talked.

"Do you mind if I offer some assistance? I have a team of men who are experts at finding things. I'd like to have them do a complete search of your office. We can be in and out in an hour. Perhaps this afternoon? Would that be satisfactory?"

Conti looked at him coldly. "No, it wouldn't. I've told you I will let you know if the tape turns up. And I will do just that."

"This is all critical because it will give me a feel for exactly what was said by you both. I can hear the conversation before and after the segment where Moretti admits complicity in the New York bombing. I really must insist on your cooperation, sir. It's so much easier with your help than . . . well, than getting a search warrant, for instance. I'm sure the Pope . . ."

The Cardinal's face went ashen. He swallowed hard, hoping the officer couldn't see his discomfort.

"Don't you think you're carrying all this a bit too far?"

"In my business you follow every trail as far as you can and see where it takes you. This missing cassette is vitally important in my opinion. It may gain us nothing but I really do intend to hear it. And I'd appreciate your cooperation." He touched the Cardinal gently on the sleeve and Conti involuntarily jerked back. His satchel fell on the ground and the top came open. The legal pad was partially exposed.

"My apologies if I startled you." The policeman bent down to pick up the case for the cleric. He was close enough to read the words on the pad.

Conti stooped, retrieved the case from the ground and stuck the legal pad inside. He closed the flap, tucked it under his arm and said, "I have nothing to hide. I get the impression you think I do, but you're wrong. I'm a very busy man. I will cooperate with you. I have told you twice I will keep looking for the cassette. There will be no policemen searching my office. There will be no search warrant, my friend, unless you can convince the Pope himself to allow it. You have nothing on me. I have done nothing but assist you in bringing a violent criminal to justice. And your thanks for this is to harass me?"

Conti walked to the taxi line in front of him, Messina following behind. "Eminence, my apologies but I am not harassing. I'm doing my job . . ."

The Cardinal entered the cab and shut the door as the policeman was talking. The car drove away leaving Frederico Messina standing at the curb wondering why Dominic Conti was so afraid.

Conti had the cab take him to a restaurant a few miles away. He had intended to go home but once Messina saw him the cleric had no choice but to get away. He spent an hour having lunch then took another taxi to his apartment.

At home Conti destroyed the cassette, crushing it into tiny pieces, putting all of them in an envelope that he placed in his satchel. He changed from his robe to a sweater and jeans, tennis shoes and a ball cap. With dark glasses he looked like a tourist. Perfect. No one would recognize him.

He took the satchel, walked downstairs and hailed another taxi. Soon he was in a photocopy shop far from the Vatican and people who might know him. He paid some Euros and began to copy the two hundred-page book. Some of the pages were brittle so it took time. He was careful.

When he left the shop he emptied the envelope containing the crushed pieces of microcassette into a trash bin on the street. No one would find the tape now. That eased his mind.

Back at home Cardinal Conti did something that pained him deeply because he appreciated old things – he loved the history that surrounded the Church and his Order, the present-day Knights Templars.

He carefully took the Templar manuscript that had been stolen from Brian Sadler's gallery, turned through it carefully and tore out the thirteen pages of coded symbols. They came out easily – the book was old and the binding was in poor shape at best.

Cardinal Conti would now skim the diary entries one last time while he still had the original. Then he'd give the FBI the manuscript. "They'll never know it had extra pages," he told himself.

That evening Dominic flipped through the entire book and read the entries from the 1400s to the late 1600s. He saw nothing except historical exploits, pillaging of enemy villages and references to tribute paid and booty claimed. At this point the Cardinal believed the coded pages would tell specifics of where all that treasure was. And when the time was right he would get back to deciphering the code.

The next day Conti called Agent Jack Underwood in Manhattan. Underwood thanked him for his efforts to get the manuscript back to its rightful owner. He suggested Conti contact Brian Sadler, the man from whose gallery the book was stolen. The Cardinal and Brian could deal with it going forward. Underwood gave the cleric Brian's cellphone number.

Conti felt as though he already knew Brian Sadler from his conversations with Giovanni Moretti. He would call Mr. Sadler and work out the handover of the document.

CHAPTER THIRTY-FIVE

London

The stranger in the Monument Club's library surveyed the situation. Brian was reaching for his cellphone and the librarian's back was turned as he monitored the scanner's progress.

Suddenly Brian became aware of someone standing just behind him - that was the last thing he was aware of. Everything suddenly went black as he slumped onto the desk in front of him.

The man withdrew a tiny needle from Brian's neck. He'd be incapacitated for fifteen minutes and wake with a headache, but he'd be fine. He turned and saw the librarian looking at him from across the room.

"What are you doing?" Jeffrey Montfort shouted. "What do you want?"

The man walked quickly toward the librarian, another tiny needle tight in his fingers. He smiled and said, "You really need to cooperate and everything will be fine."

Montfort backed up, his fingers grazing the top of the scanner. As the man plunged the needle into the librarian's arm Montfort pressed a button then he collapsed in a heap. The man took the pages from the scanner tray and threw the machine to the floor. It crashed into a dozen pieces.

Next he rushed to Brian's carrel and attempted to lift Brian's upper body off the laptop where it lay, but the tiny booth was too small. He'd have to pull Brian backwards onto the floor. He didn't know if the laptop was important or not; his boss hadn't mentioned it but he thought he'd get it if he could. Since it was found in that locker with the copy, maybe it was important.

As he grabbed Brian's shoulders and prepared to give a heave the front door of the library suddenly swung open. Engaged in conversation, two men entered the room and walked toward the front desk. They hadn't noticed him. Now he had no time to get the laptop; he moved to a shadowed corner and waited for the chance to escape.

The newcomers stood for a moment at the desk. "Jeffrey?" one called out. "This is odd," he told his friend. "Jeffrey's always here."

"Look! He's there, on the floor!"

The men rushed behind the front desk area and knelt down to feel the librarian's pulse. As they did the stranger calmly walked out, took an elevator to the ground floor and left the building. He had accomplished exactly what he was told to do – he had the copy of the manuscript. He was certain he had destroyed the scanner. Hopefully the pages that had been scanned wouldn't be retrievable from the ruined machine. Too bad that he had been interrupted, but it couldn't be helped. He'd make his fee by delivering the copy. He wouldn't mention the laptop or the scanner. What the boss doesn't know won't hurt *me*, the man thought.

Later that afternoon he dropped a bulky envelope into a UPS box on Charing Cross Road in central London. It would end up at the Vatican tomorrow. Job complete. Twenty thousand dollars earned. Another satisfied customer.

CHAPTER THIRTY-SIX
London/Dallas

The library's entryway buzzed with activity. Paramedics attended to Jeffrey Montfort and Brian Sadler, who lay on the floor awake but woozy. The two members who had happened upon the crime in progress sat at a desk with a policeman giving their statements. The general manager of the Monument Club conversed quietly with a detective from Scotland Yard who was glad to learn there were security cameras everywhere.

Brian and the librarian declined to go to the hospital; although their heads throbbed mercilessly they were otherwise OK. The EMTs drew blood for testing; it was their opinion the men had been drugged with a powerful, fast-acting sedative.

Within a couple of hours the Scotland Yard man had gathered facts and viewed video footage. What he learned was that a man entered the Club through a door that opened to the alleyway behind the building. As they did every day at the same time, the kitchen help had taken a smoke break, propping the door open to allow re-entry. The man easily slipped into the building unnoticed. The first video camera showed him walking down the rear service hall and through an empty kitchen.

He rode an elevator to the third floor library where he presented a fake membership card to Jeffrey Montfort and requested to see two volumes. Montfort had dutifully registered the man's fictitious name and brought the books he requested. The stranger had sat in his own carrel as Brian and Jeffrey worked on the Borland project. After accosting the men and stealing the binder, the intruder had left the building through the front entrance, simply blending into the pedestrian traffic along the Thames.

"The intruder wanted the laptop," the detective said. "What's the significance of it?"

Brian explained that it had belonged to the late Lord Arthur Borland, who was working on a project to find a lost manuscript. He truthfully told the officer that he had no idea exactly what the significance of the book was and explained how it played a part in the Fifth Avenue bombing.

Brian was left with the laptop and a promise to call Scotland Yard immediately if he had anything more to report. After everyone cleared out he and Jeffrey went downstairs to the bar. As a member of the staff the librarian ordinarily wouldn't be allowed in the member areas, but after today's events the general manager made an exception. They sat by the window, Brian with his usual late afternoon martini and Jeffrey with a gin and tonic.

They discussed the events of the afternoon. Their heads were clearing, thanks both to the passage of time and the soothing effects of the alcohol. Brian mentioned how unfortunate it was, when they were so close to having the manuscript copy, they had lost it to the thief.

Suddenly Jeffrey Montfort perked up and said, "How hard do you think it would be to get into Lord Montfort's email account?"

Surprised that the librarian had suddenly changed the subject, Brian responded, "I don't get where you're going with this, but all I'd need to know is how big a password freak he was – if both his laptop and his mail account are password-protected it might be a challenge. Maybe his wife knows what passwords he used. I'll check it all out tonight at the flat. Why do you ask?"

"If you can get in, I feel confident we'll have the manuscript again!" Jeffrey explained that Lord Borland had requested scans often as he reviewed things in the library. To make it simpler Jeffrey had programmed Borland's email address into the scanner. He could press a single button and send the scan to Arthur's email account instead of having to enter the information every time.

"While the pages were scanning today I scrolled to Lord Borland's information so all I had to do was push a button when the scan was finished. The last page went through just as the intruder came towards me and I tried to push the 'send' button before I passed out. I hope it worked. The man destroyed the scanner but I would think the scan would have been sent instantly when I pushed the button. Don't you?"

"We can only hope," Brian said excitedly. "Good thinking. Keep your fingers crossed."

Later that evening Brian sat in the flat with Arthur's laptop on his dining table. He called Carissa Borland and gave her a rundown of the afternoon's events. She was shocked at what she heard and apologized for his involvement in Arthur's problem.

"I was already involved, Carissa. Remember this all started with the bombing in New York."

Brian told her how he had found Arthur's laptop. He requested permission to try to access it and she immediately agreed.

"You may not find much. I think he used it mostly to organize things. He had email but we really didn't use it. He used the Internet for research but that's about it."

They talked about passwords. She had no idea what his might have been. Brian asked her for a lot of things to try – names of current and past pets, dates of birth, mother's and maiden names and nicknames they called each other. He thanked her for the help and soon was entering word and number combinations. It proved less difficult than Brian had expected. On the eleventh try he entered "CarissaSwann0917," her maiden name and date of birth. The locked screen went away and desktop icons appeared.

He clicked on Mail and entered the same password. It worked. "Arthur, you should have been more careful," he murmured, "but thanks for being low-tech." He eagerly opened the inbox and saw just a few entries. One was new – from the library of the Monument Club. He opened the mail and its attachment and saw the now-familiar first page of the Templar Manuscript. He was thrilled. "I'll be damned. Thank God for Jeffrey's quick thinking." He emailed the librarian and told him the good news.

Just to be safe he forwarded the email to his own mailbox then he hid the laptop behind the gas logs in his fireplace. He called Nicole's office but got her voicemail. He gave her a summary of the afternoon's events and said he was off to bed. He asked her to call tomorrow when she got a minute.

After the things he had gone through, Brian Sadler slept like a rock. He heard nothing until his phone alarm woke him at six am.

This afternoon in Dallas had been spectacular. After a long week of trial and another stunning victory for Nicole Farber, she had taken the afternoon off. Dallas was hot as hell in the summer but in the months before and after it was a wonderful place for those who loved to be outdoors. She put the top down on her Mercedes convertible and drove from her office in Uptown to the West Village. She took a table on the shaded patio at Cru Wine Bar and ordered a glass of her favorite, which happened to be the best Chardonnay offered. Nicole certainly could afford it – she was the highest paid female lawyer in Dallas and her success rate at defending those accused of white-collar crimes was unparalleled. After her lunch she relaxed a bit longer over a second glass, then drove to the Ritz-Carlton Residences where she lived. She parked her car in the building's garage, raised the top and took an elevator to her condo.

Nicole changed into shorts and a t-shirt and walked to a park a few blocks away. She jogged for awhile, stopping when the wine from lunch made her more tired than usual.

She sat on a park bench under a tree for an hour and enjoyed the day. Walking home in a small breeze felt nice. As she strolled down McKinney Avenue she glanced at her phone and saw she'd missed a call from Brian. She listened to his voicemail, concerned when she heard that he'd been accosted but relieved to hear everything was OK. Part of her wanted to call him back – this news was one more reason to be concerned about what was going on - but it was after ten in London. He'd be dead to the world by now. She had to wait until tomorrow, as he had asked her to do.

She walked to the grocery store around the corner from her condo building and grabbed a few things for dinner. *Dinner on the patio tonight after this gorgeous day.*

At home she opened two huge sliding patio doors of glass. The breeze made her place feel better – there was no need for air conditioning today, although it wouldn't be long before it was a necessity.

After a hot shower she stayed in her bathrobe, fixed a martini and sat on the patio watching the sun sink behind the downtown buildings a couple of miles away. She thought a lot about Brian and hoped everything was OK. *He loves adventure so much but I don't want him to get hurt.* She had never loved anyone before and she wasn't sure what it was supposed to feel like. But her pragmatic legal mind had analyzed her feelings and concluded that this was it. She had been in love with Brian Sadler for a while. Sadly they were literally a world apart on opposite sides of the Atlantic Ocean.

Be content, she told herself. As the old song went, true love never runs smooth. She went to bed and thought of Brian, hoping he was not in danger and wondering what she could do to help him.

Nicole awoke at six am, opened her floor-to-ceiling shades and the patio doors. It was a breezy Dallas morning and the sun was ready to pop over the horizon. She climbed back into bed and called Brian – it was noon in London and he was at work. He told her all about the events at the library.

"What's going on with all this? Do you think John Spedino's still orchestrating all this even now?"

"I'm not sure. Maybe he put things in place before he was arrested and they're just now playing out. Or it could be someone else. I haven't figured out why the manuscript's so important but now that I have a copy I can start working on it. I just wish I knew who's behind all this. Spedino's the logical choice but I can't figure out why he would want the manuscript."

Brian expressed his continuing concern for her safety. "The godfather's settling scores. The way I see it you're the only one left to settle and even from jail he's dangerous. I wish you'd let the FBI give you protection."

She thanked him for his concern and promised to watch her step, telling him to watch his too. "Frankly I was relieved to hear he was arrested. I think that puts an end to the problems he might have created for me."

Brian said he wasn't so sure.

They talked for a minute about her plans to come to London soon. He told her how excited he was to be with her again soon. They agreed to talk again after six his time tonight.

She had to be at the County Courts building downtown at nine am for a hearing. It wasn't far; she drove the Mercedes from the garage south onto Pearl Street and began to wind through the canyons of buildings. Traffic was moderate as she started down a hill on Akard Street. The light ahead was red; she hit her brakes but got no response. She pumped harder, frantically pushing over and over. Instead of stopping, her convertible was gaining downhill momentum. She had seconds to decide what to do before she'd run the light and enter an intersection full of opposing traffic. She jerked the emergency brake but nothing happened.

Cars were right beside her in the next lane; she couldn't move to the curb and hit a parked car so she decided to take a chance. She slammed her palm onto the horn as she continued to pump the useless brake pedal. Her other hand gripped the steering wheel as she sailed through the light and entered the busy downtown intersection at nearly thirty miles per hour.

Everything happened in a split second. She heard honking as she clipped a car, swerved to the right then saw a Dallas city bus ten feet away from her passenger door. She jerked the wheel to the left as the massive vehicle crashed into her. Airbags deployed - the entire right side of her little car caved in as the safety bumper of the bus pushed her Mercedes through the intersection and into other cars. By the time it was over four vehicles were totaled and her body lay twisted in the driver seat of her destroyed convertible.

CHAPTER THIRTY-SEVEN

A little after four pm Brian's cellphone rang. Agent Jack Underwood advised that Dominic Cardinal Conti, head of the Vatican Bank, was in possession of the manuscript that had been stolen. The cleric would be calling Brian to arrange its return. The agent had no knowledge of how the book got there, he said, maintaining his promise to Conti to keep his involvement with Spedino secret.

Brian filled in Underwood about the events at the Monument Club and said he now had a copy of the manuscript. He promised Underwood he would start to work immediately on the book in an attempt to discover why it was so important to someone.

Within an hour Brian got another call. Europe – Italy, if memory served him on the country code. He knew who this caller was. The person on the phone identified himself as secretary to Cardinal Conti.

"Do you have a few minutes to speak to him?" he asked Brian, and then put him on hold.

As Brian waited he received a third call. *A busy afternoon,* Brian casually thought. He looked at the number on his screen - he knew the area code and prefix but didn't recognize the number. The call was from Carter and Wells, the law firm Nicole worked for, but not from her. He hit decline as he waited for Cardinal Conti. He'd have to call the law firm back.

Before the cleric came on the line Brian received another call from the same Dallas number. Something must be wrong. He disconnected and accepted the call from Carter and Wells. He heard the familiar voice of Nicole's boss Randall Carter, the lead partner in the firm.

"Brian, I'm afraid I have some bad news. Nicole's been in an accident." The words hit Brian like a brick.

The rest of the call was a blur. He tried to concentrate but he was dizzy and lightheaded. He cried as he heard Carter's explanation of the wreck a couple of hours earlier in downtown Dallas. Nicole was in critical condition at Baylor Hospital, on life support and not expected to live. Witnesses said she had driven through a red light at a high rate of speed and been T-boned by a city bus. Her tiny Mercedes had given her little protection. He said the police would investigate the destroyed convertible to see if mechanical failure was the cause.

Brian rambled. "What . . . what do I do? Listen, keep me informed . . ." His mind couldn't wrap around the words he had heard. He didn't know what to say, what to do next.

Carter promised to call immediately when they knew more. As soon as Brian put the phone down it rang again – the Cardinal from Italy. He declined the call. Now was no time for business.

From his adjoining office Cory Spencer heard Brian on the call with Nicole's boss. He knew something was terribly wrong. When the call was done he stuck his head in and saw Brian weeping uncontrollably, his head in his hands. Brian told him what had happened.

"What can I do, Brian? Do you want to go? How can I help?"

"How can I get there fast? I'm afraid she's going to die before I get there, Cory. I want to see her." He sobbed. "I want to hold her one more time."

"OK, leave it with me for a few minutes." Cory knew money wasn't an issue but he checked commercial flights first just in case. It was too late – the day's last flight to Dallas had departed a couple of hours ago.

He went online and found a charter service. Within fifteen minutes he'd made a call and had information for Brian. It was a fortune but it would be worth it to his boss.

Ninety minutes later Brian sat in the cabin of a Gulfstream G350 taxiing to the departure runway at Stansted Airport in rural London. In eight hours he would be at Love Field in Dallas. It would be around eight pm local time when he arrived.

It was a little after six in England, noon in Dallas. He would never have made it without the calm guidance and direction of Cory Spencer. Thinking logically when Brian couldn't, Cory had thrown together Brian's overnighter suitcase with a change of clothes. Brian kept them in his office closet in case a quick trip came up.

Cory ensured the air charter company would have food, a phone and an amenities kit on board so Brian could shave and clean up before arrival. He put Brian's iPad, phone and some reading material into his briefcase. He made sure the copy of the Templars manuscript was included; it might keep his mind occupied if he needed a diversion.

Given Brian's state, Cory decided to accompany his boss in a cab to the nearby Liverpool Street train station and stayed with him on the Stansted Express to the airport. The trip would take a little less than an hour.

While they were on the train Cory called Randall Carter's office and left the number of the plane's satellite phone with Carter's secretary. There had been no update to Nicole's condition, she reported. Cory relayed that information to Brian then handed him a sheet of paper with familiar numbers on it. Nicole's assistant, Cory's cellphone, Randall Carter's office - most were numbers Brian knew by heart but with his mind reeling and his emotions running wild Cory figured it might help to have them available. No need to rely on memory when your mind was going crazy with worry. He even added Brian's parents' number and those of Nicole's mother and father.

"Thanks for everything, Cory," he said as the pilots did last-minute preflight checks. He glanced at the phone list and thought of something. "Oh hey, call my parents and tell them what's up. Tell them I plan to go right to the hospital as soon as we land. Tell them . . . Oh hell, Cory. I can't even think straight. Just take care of it. And one more thing – you have a key to the flat. Go by there and pick up Arthur Borland's laptop. It's hidden in the fireplace behind the gas logs. Keep it locked in the vault at the gallery until I get back."

"Got it, boss. There'll be a sedan to meet you at Love Field. I'll call the plane if anything comes up. Call me if you need anything, anything at all. I'll be praying for Nicole."

Spencer waited in the terminal building as the jet's mighty engines screamed and it rolled briskly toward the taxiway. He left only after it streaked into the evening sky.

Brian tried to sleep, tried to eat, tried to read, tried almost everything to take his mind off Nicole lying in a hospital bed on life support. "She's a fighter," he told himself as tears flowed. "If anybody can make it, she can." But he really didn't know. How bad was she? How many internal injuries? How many broken bones? Nobody had told him any of that yet.

Brian went to the plane's bedroom and lay down. He stared at the ceiling as the plane flew west through the night sky. Suddenly a strange chirping sound awoke Brian from the brief troubled sleep he had finally managed. A green light blinked on the phone console on the desk next to his bed. He answered.

"Brian, this is Randall Carter again. I know you're on your way – Cory Spencer told me you'd be in Dallas around eight our time. I'll meet you at the airport – I told Cory to cancel the limo he'd arranged."

"Any news?" Brian held his breath. News probably wasn't a good thing but he had to ask.

"She's stable. She can't breathe on her own but she's in no pain. She's hasn't been conscious since the accident. They don't know at this point about brain damage but she has a broken arm and both legs and massive internal injuries. If she's strong enough they may do surgery tonight to relieve pressure in her chest. They're trying to keep her comfortable so she's on a lot of morphine. It's serious. No two ways about it. But she's got courage, as we both well know."

Carter promised to keep him abreast of any changes in the situation. Brian prayed fervently for Nicole and in the middle of his prayer he fell asleep, exhausted but finally able to catch a couple of hours of slumber. When he awoke the skies outside were lighter. The jet was catching up to the setting sun as they headed west across America.

One of the pilots knocked lightly on his door and Brian answered. "May I fix you a cup of coffee, Mr. Sadler? We should be landing in Dallas in ninety minutes."

Brian gratefully accepted. He'd need the caffeine to keep his head clear. The jet was equipped with a full bathroom – Brian showered, shaved and donned the change of clothes Cory had packed. He felt better after another cup of coffee and a piece of fruit.

He suddenly remembered the two calls from the Vatican. Brian left Cory Spencer a voicemail with the number, asking him to arrange getting the manuscript from the Cardinal.

Before long the plane descended into the city Brian had lived in for years. He saw one familiar landmark after another as it dropped lower and lower, crossed Mockingbird Lane and touched down at Love Field. They taxied to a private air charter company's terminal where Randall Carter waited.

As Carter's driver took them to Baylor Hospital her boss gave Brian an update. "The police say the brake lines on her car were sabotaged. Someone put a small hole in the front brake line – she had had brakes for a short time but then they failed. Also the emergency brake line was cut completely through, so she didn't stand a chance."

"Any idea how that happened? It couldn't possibly be accidental, right?"

"Apparently not. I'm no mechanic so I can't answer that myself. The cops think it was deliberate. They're calling this attempted murder."

"Attempted . . ." Brian repeated slowly. "Let's hope it stays attempted."

"Your parents and hers are at the hospital. Her sister from Houston's there too."

"Calling in all the family . . ." Brian murmured. Suddenly he lost it. He began to cry, shaking hard. "I'm sorry . . . I can't help it."

Carter got him a box of Kleenex. "No apologies necessary. I can't imagine how hard this is for you. It's gut-wrenching for all of us."

Brian joined a group of people in the ICU waiting room. It was usually a happy time when he saw family but tonight it was awful. Ryan Coleman, Nicole's assistant, was there and so were a few other people from her office that Brian didn't know.

"Can I see her?"

Brian's mother explained the ICU rules. "As guarded as her condition is, only one person can go in every thirty minutes. You can only stay five minutes. We've all seen her so it's your turn."

Seeing Nicole lying in the bed hooked up to a million tubes and monitors was the hardest thing Brian Sadler had ever done. A nurse stood quietly in the corner, ready to move quickly in case her condition worsened.

He touched her arm lightly. It was discolored and in a temporary cast to hold it firm until the swelling subsided. They hadn't done surgery yet, he learned later, but they had casted it and her legs to keep them straight until surgery could be performed.

Nicole looked so frail. "I love you, baby," he murmured, squeezing one finger of her hand. He thought he might have felt a tiny squeeze back but wasn't sure. Given how she looked he figured that was wishful thinking.

He stood next to her and gingerly held her hand until the nurse quietly said that his time was up. He bent down and kissed Nicole's bruised forehead. "Come back to me, sweetie. If you will I promise I'll never let you go away again."

CHAPTER THIRTY-EIGHT

Cory Spencer had two voicemails from Brian when he arrived at work the next morning. The first asked him to return Cardinal Conti's call and handle whatever the man needed. The second was an update on Nicole's condition and the news that the car crash was deliberately caused. Brian expressed his appreciation to Cory for taking charge and getting him to Dallas quickly. No one knew how much time Nicole had left and Brian was grateful to be with her.

After the usual morning routine to open Bijan Rarities, Cory called the number at the Vatican. Conti's secretary answered and Cory explained what had happened yesterday. "Mr. Sadler received news of a family emergency while he was waiting for the Cardinal to come on the line. He had to terminate the call and he flew to the States late yesterday. Please apologize to Cardinal Conti for his inability to speak with him at this time and tell his Eminence I am happy to assist if I can."

The assistant promised to relay the message and call Cory back. That afternoon the men spoke. The Cardinal told Cory that a man named Giovanni Moretti had given the missing manuscript from the Fifth Avenue bombing to the Church. The way Conti told it, it sounded like a donation - Conti omitted any reference to his having hired Moretti to get the book. He knew this whole story would have to be refined by the time he talked to Brian Sadler but for now it would do. He didn't tell the assistant that Moretti was Spedino or that he'd paid for the stolen manuscript.

Cory promised to speak with his boss about arranging a meeting in Rome to get the manuscript. After the call he emailed Brian with an update.

Outside the Baylor Hospital ICU waiting room Brian placed a call to the FBI in New York. He told Agent Underwood the cause behind Nicole's near-fatal crash this morning. They agreed the possible involvement of John Spedino should be investigated. Underwood promised to get on it immediately.

Brian scanned his emails and saw one from Cory that said, "Cardinal Conti is president of the Vatican Bank. He has the stolen manuscript and wants to know when you can come to Rome to get it back."

Brian responded quickly, "Tell him I'll do it absolutely as quickly as I can. I won't know for a while when I'll be back there. I'll advise when I know more. Relay that to the Cardinal please." Cory Spencer did so.

Brian spent most of the next three days at the hospital, using his iPad as his primary means of work and recreation. He alternated nights with Nicole's mother and father – one of them stayed each night in the hospital's on-site hotel just in case anything changed suddenly. Both he and Nicole's parents had a key to her condo and they all used it as their base when not at the hospital. His parents had gone home, promising to come back in a flash if they were needed. Her sister stayed on to help.

The surgeons repaired Nicole's broken arm and legs once they determined she was strong enough to survive the surgery. A doctor also did non-invasive examinations of her chest and abdomen. There appeared to be less internal damage than earlier thought; the internist would investigate further once she was more stable. Nicole's brain scan was clear but a neurologist warned the trauma could have caused damage that wasn't immediately apparent. They would monitor her brain activity closely.

Her primary physician reported that Nicole's condition remained critical and cautioned everyone that she was very seriously injured. Nicole lay in a coma and he wouldn't speculate on her chances for recovery until she was awake. The good news, the doctor said, was that she was young, strong and in good health.

It was convenient that Brian kept clothes at Nicole's place for his visits to Dallas. Thanks to that and a rental car, he had everything he needed to stay for a period of time.

On that third morning Brian had made a decision to work on something that had been in both their minds for a long time. Without mentioning anything to Nicole's parents he met an old friend for lunch. Eddie Simmons was a commercial real estate agent who leased upscale retail space. It was Brian's first step in considering opening a gallery in Dallas. Close to his roots. More importantly, close to Nicole.

At three pm Nicole's parents, her sister and Brian were back in the ICU waiting room, struggling to pass the time as people do in these situations. It was a boring, sterile place to be at best and the sounds and smells of the hospital were constant reminders that the person Brian loved was fifty feet away fighting for her life. Brian checked mail while her father catnapped. Her sister and mom read books.

Suddenly a nurse opened the door and said, "She's awake! Come in, all of you!"

The nurse warned that she was under a lot of medication and wouldn't likely know them. She also said they could stay only a couple of minutes. "Don't do anything sudden," the nurse cautioned. "Make every move slow and easy. She's been through a terrible ordeal and it's not over by a long shot."

Her eyelids fluttered as Nicole's mother ushered Brian up front to her side. Her family stood on the other. She looked at Brian and the glimmer of a smile appeared. It was faint – just a little turn of her lips, actually – but Brian knew it was there.

"Hey, baby. How are you feeling?"

Her lips opened slightly but no sounds came out. She looked at him quizzically, not understand what was happening. She tried again with the same result. Then she gave up and very slowly turned her eyes toward her parents.

Her mother squeezed her hand a little but got nothing back. "We love you, honey," she said as they all cried.

Her eyes squinted as she struggled to talk. "Wh . . . where . . ." she whispered.

Her mom talked quietly, soothingly. "You're in the hospital. You had an accident in your car. You were pretty banged up and now you're recovering. You've been here three days so far."

Her eyes opened wide in surprise. Although she couldn't communicate they knew she didn't realize she'd been here that long. Her ability to comprehend that statement is a positive thing right now, Brian thought.

As they left she gave Brian a very light tap on the hand and opened her lips again. But nothing came out. A tear rolled down her cheek and she mouthed the word "love."

There wasn't a dry eye in the ICU waiting room after that visit.

CHAPTER THIRTY-NINE

Vatican City/Beaulieu-sur-Mer, France

The incredible pressure of his work at the Vatican had allowed the Cardinal no time for decrypting the document. As days passed he spent an hour here, an hour there, making excruciatingly slow progress. Finally he had had enough. The information in the ancient book could be phenomenal. What secrets did the Templars protect? He was certain he would find out if he had the time to decode it.

He received and destroyed the copy of the manuscript that had been in the Monument Club's library in London. That tied up one loose end; he doubted any other copies existed. And not a word had been heard from Officer Messina since he had so rudely parked himself outside Conti's office. Perhaps the man had learned just how influential the cleric was and decided he was heading down the wrong path. Perhaps he had wisely made the choice not to cross such a powerful man as I, Conti thought smugly.

Oddly, Brian Sadler hadn't called back to arrange to get the original manuscript. Conti thought the man would have been right on this project. Perhaps the family emergency that his assistant mentioned in the call last week was ongoing. No matter. Conti had the coded pages he'd removed – the manuscript was just a diary without them. Interesting but of no real value.

It was time to finish the decryption. Dominic requested a couple of weeks off, called an old friend who was one of Italy's wealthiest shipping magnates and arranged to use his house in quaint Beaulieu-sur-Mer on the French Riviera not far from Nice. No one would be there but him and a staff of five so it was guaranteed to be quiet enough to finish his work.

He sat on the patio of the palatial residence, the azure blue of the Mediterranean Sea stretching in front of him as far as the eye could see. A massive infinity pool lay to his left; it appeared to drop directly off the end of the patio into thin air. He had spent the morning out here, decoding.

Today we find ourselves challenged. As stewards of the secrets we, the sixteen leaders of our Order, no longer can guarantee the safety of the Most Holy Relics. Since we were entrusted with their care in the year of

*our Lord 1129 it has been our privilege and
duty to protect the location and integrity of
these sacred items. And we have done so
without fail. Today unrest in the land where
they lie creates fear and mistrust in the hearts
of the people. They now see us as their
enemies and loathe us, the very ones they
should trust the most.*

*The future of our mission is at risk. The relics
themselves are at risk.*

*We the sixteen have voted to solicit the help of
our Venetian friend the Voyager. Although not
a member of our Order, he has been of
assistance before. More importantly, he now
has the blessing of England's monarch. We
must engage him quickly. We must move the
relics. Time is short and the Voyager is our
only answer. An envoy is being dispatched to
Bristol tomorrow to seek his help.*

Let us pray for success.

According to the diary entries preceding
this encoded page, the year was 1496.
Dominic Conti read the paragraphs twice,
then again. On a notepad he wrote bullet
points listing what he now knew.

- The year is 1496.
- The Templars protect something
  they call the Most Holy Relics.
- They have been doing this since
  1129.
- There is unrest in the land where
  the relics are hidden and those

people no longer trust the Templars.

- The men believe their mission is in danger and want to move the relics.
- They are going to enlist the help of a man from Venice they call the Voyager.
- He is in Bristol.
- He is a friend but not a Templar himself.
- He has the blessing of England's monarch.

He set the manuscript aside. The bullet points would require research. One was easy to deal with – Conti picked up his phone and quickly found out that Henry VII was King of England in 1496. The Venetian Voyager had Henry's blessing – presumably for a journey.

Lunchtime was approaching. Soon someone would come around with wine. The staff maintained the house impeccably but they were like ghosts – around exactly when you needed something but invisible otherwise. He had no idea where they stayed on the property; all he knew was that he had full run of an eighteen-room mansion hanging on a cliff overlooking the sea. To some it would have been lonely – a place more for sharing with a loved one – but Conti was a priest, after all. He was accustomed to being alone and he loved the solitude.

This trip was especially nice – he'd been here four days and the decryption project was moving ahead well. Barring interruption he would finish all thirteen coded pages before he returned to Rome next week. And what things he was seeing as the code was translated! Like a best-selling novel, this was a real page-turner. He just wished he could work faster. It was a laborious, meticulous project and one had to be careful in order to get everything right the first time. He'd incorrectly translated a few symbols earlier and it cost him a lot of time. He couldn't afford more mistakes. He had to concentrate on every symbol.

Conti glanced at his watch; it was almost 11:30 am and he knew soon one of the staff would appear with a cold glass of that wonderful French white he'd enjoyed last night at the casino in Monte Carlo. Dominic wore street clothes this entire trip to remain anonymous. He wasn't identifiable as a pillar of the Roman Catholic Church any longer. Last night he had been just another Italian tourist in slacks and a sport coat having a nice meal and a brief run at the craps table before his driver returned him to the villa.

He had mentioned to the butler this morning at breakfast how much he enjoyed the wine at the casino. The man asked what particular one it was. Dominic told him and the butler said, "We will serve it today before lunch."

Four days ago Conti would have doubted the man's ability to make good on that promise but now he knew it would happen. Not maybe. Absolutely. Somehow these people could do about anything. If you wanted a piece of sea bass grilled exactly as in that particular five-star restaurant in Paris, they made it happen. He knew the wealthy had ways of pulling strings. Obviously they taught their staff the magic as well.

The way of life of the very rich is a good one. For me, a poor man of the cloth, I am just humbled and honored to be here.

He laughed out loud at his thought. Truth be told, he believed just the opposite. *I deserve this kind of life. I could get used to this.* With the help of some four hundred-year-old knights it might just happen.

The server arrived with a chilled glass of the wine he had enjoyed last night in Monaco. Dominic came out of his reverie and returned to the present - a magnificent day on the French Riviera, a glass of perfect wine and a book of secrets to decode. Life was good.

CHAPTER FORTY

Dallas

Every day brought changes for Nicole, some more pronounced than others. She opened her eyes often and glanced around the room, apparently processing where she was and who was there.

On the morning of the fourth day she had looked at Brian and whispered, "Why?"

"Why did this happen? Is that what you're asking?"

She didn't move her head but her eyes locked expectantly on his. Brian couched his answer carefully; the doctor had told them not to say anything that could upset her.

"The brakes failed on your car, baby. That's all we know. It wasn't your fault."

Nicole seemed to be thinking for a moment, then her eyes closed and she was gone again.

Brian worked on business matters and translation of the manuscript from Nicole's apartment each morning. It helped that he was an early riser. Every morning at five, eleven am in London, he spoke with Cory Spencer. Things were going well at Bijan Rarities and Cory handled most routine matters himself.

Brian had missed Arthur Borland's funeral and he regretted he couldn't have been there for Carissa but she completely understood. As long as Nicole was in critical condition it was senseless to fly to London for an hour-long memorial. He had spoken to Carissa several times since he'd been in Dallas. There was no further information from the police about Arthur's death but she was hopeful Brian's continuing look into his activities might provide an answer.

Each morning following his call to London Brian fixed an egg and toast, grabbed a second cup of coffee and worked on the manuscript until nine am when he drove to the hospital. His materials were strewn about Nicole's computer table and he used her Mac for translation and research.

The first morning he'd started by going through the pages to determine exactly how to begin. Unbeknownst to him, Brian was at a decided disadvantage to Dominic Cardinal

Conti.   The journal entries were sometimes
written in Latin, sometimes in French or even
in English.   The latter was medieval – it
looked to Brian like Chaucer's *Canterbury
Tales* – and from his single-semester attempt
at French in high school he thought those
words looked ancient as well.   Conti, on the
other hand, was fluent in Latin and had a
good working knowledge of medieval French
and English.   It took Brian a frustratingly
long time to read even one entry.   The dates
themselves seemed the only things easy to
read.   The first entry was in 1475 and the last
was in 1699.

Brian saw that every so often there
appeared a page with nothing but tiny
symbols.   He passed quickly over those – his
goal now was to get an overview of the entire
project.   The last few pages were entries like a
diary, followed by a final group of symbol-
covered pages.   Last of all was a sheet that
looked different from the others.   In a way it
was like them, in other ways not.   He
examined it closely and then flipped back to
one of the pages of symbols. This last page
appeared to be an answer sheet – a decoder.
It was covered with symbols that also
appeared throughout the book. Next to each
symbol was either a letter of the alphabet or a
medieval French word.   If the symbol pages
were in code maybe this page was the
solution.

He had started on page one but the
process was far more difficult than he had
anticipated.   He was working from a scanned

copy and some of the script was faded. Compounding the problem were the three ancient languages - a few Latin words, then an abrupt switch to medieval French or English. After an hour and half a page of translation he got a gist of what he had before him. This was a journal with chronological entries – a diary. It was interesting but there had to be more than this.

He flipped over until he came to the first full page of symbols. He used the sheet he hoped would break the code, applying it to each symbol. After he'd done a few words he stopped and translated what he had written. He saw a familiar name - Jesus. Strange, he thought. The words were part of the New Testament account of Jesus' crucifixion and resurrection.

He stopped. What's this all about? Who went to this much trouble to encode bible verses? And why am I suffering through decoding them? Suddenly Brian had an idea that might simplify this project a thousand-fold.

Brian quit working on the manuscript and composed an email to Jeffrey Montfort. The man had proven remarkably resourceful at researching the Internet - Brian had a complicated request that he hoped the bookish librarian could fulfill. He wanted a computer program that allowed a person to enter random series of words in one of three old languages and get an English translation back. Brian explained that absent such a program it might take a year to translate the book. He wasn't sure what it said but someone had killed to get it. He might not have a lot of time.

Brian sat in the ICU waiting room in the afternoon and checked his mail. He was pleased to see that Jeffrey was hot on the chase to solve Brian's dilemma. The librarian would contact a friend, one of the Monument Club's members who ran the computer sciences department at Cambridge University.

At seven the next morning Brian had finished his call to London and was seated at Nicole's desk, the manuscript copy in front of him. He skipped the journal entries for now, hoping Jeffrey could alleviate the slow progress of translating. Instead he was working his way down the page of coded symbols, one by one. He compared every single symbol with the decoder sheet and then wrote the letter or word on a notepad. His phone rang – it was a call from London.

"Good early morning to you!" The librarian sounded exuberant and Brian hoped it was because he had good news.

"And to you. What have you learned?"

"First let me say the man I contacted has impeccable credentials and has helped the British Government with some extremely sensitive computer issues. He won't tell me specifics but I know he's highly regarded by MI6 – you know, our version of the CIA? So secrets are old hat to this chap. I said all that to say this. I took the liberty of emailing a copy of the manuscript to him. Listen to this, Brian. Cambridge's computers not only can do the translating for us, he took a look at the symbol pages and the decoder sheet at the end. His computer can decode those too!"

"Incredible! Great job!" Brian said. He meant it. This was too good to be true. He had only a tiny spark of concern that yet another person might be privy to the manuscript's secrets, but the man sounded legit and the time tradeoff was definitely worth the risk.

"And listen to this. The programs to make this happen already exist. He just has to tweak a couple and bam! This project will be done before you know it. Day after tomorrow, in fact!"

Nicole's condition was improving. It was slow, but it was progress. For the first time her primary physician gave the family an optimistic forecast – he said Nicole was on the way to recovery and upgraded her condition from critical to fair. Up to this point each of the doctor's updates had been carefully phrased. He had used terms like "she has a long way to go" and "she's not out of the woods yet." Today was a major shift and cause for relief among Nicole's family and Brian.

If things continued to improve with Nicole he needed to go back to London for a few days soon. There were several routine issues that required his attention and would be better handled in person than by email or phone. He also wanted to meet the Cardinal and get the manuscript that had suddenly changed from a throwaway piece of junk to a mysterious document that was the cause of a bombing.

Brian called the Vatican number and reached Cardinal Conti's secretary who advised the Cardinal was vacationing in the south of France but was scheduled to return next week. He left a message for the cleric to call at his convenience.

On the sixth day of Nicole's hospitalization the primary doctor removed her ventilator. Although her breathing was still labored, prolonged use of a vent can cause pneumonia or other complications, the physician advised. ICU nurses would monitor her vital signs closely. Without the help of the ventilator she took very shallow breaths, hardly enough to move her chest. Watching as she slept Brian thought several times her breathing had stopped. Each time that happened he frantically looked at a monitor by her bed to confirm things were all right.

The internist reported that Nicole's chest and abdomen appeared bruised but otherwise good. No surgery was necessary. Her progress would be slow but she should have a full recovery in time.

Two days later she was awake for several minutes in the afternoon. Sitting by her side Brian said, "I'm going to Europe for a few days, sweetie. I need to take care of some things and then I'll come right back. Your mom and dad will be here just like they have been. Do you understand?"

She slowly mouthed, "Going." And she cried. So did he. He kissed her forehead gently and stayed beside her until she fell asleep. Then he walked out, feeling as though he'd just beaten a puppy.

In the waiting room Brian talked to Nicole's mother. He'd mentioned earlier that he needed to go to London soon but wasn't leaving until it was a good time. "I'm sorry to take off right now but I have a few critical things to handle. Then I promise I'll be right back here to help."

"Go on and go. She's improving – that's good news for everyone. There's not much you can do here but offer moral support. You have a company to run. Her father and I can handle it. One or the other of us will be with her every day. Take whatever time you need."

CHAPTER FORTY-ONE

His vacation on the Riviera drawing to a close, Cardinal Conti was almost finished decoding the mysterious pages of symbols. He had steadfastly resisted reading bits and pieces as he went along. Dominic wanted to read the entire thing at one time, to digest what these Templars had considered so secret.

Conti owed Brian Sadler a phone call. The cleric saw nothing to be gained by delaying the handoff of the original manuscript, so Conti returned his call. He and Brian agreed that Brian would be in Rome the day after tomorrow. They would meet in Conti's office in the Vatican Bank where Brian would take possession of the Crane brothers' manuscript minus, thanks to the Cardinal, the encoded pages.

The appointment fit perfectly into Brian's schedule; he could go to Rome first, pick up the volume then return to London to spend several days at the gallery. He called Jeffrey Montfort to let him know he was coming back.

"Good afternoon!" Jeffrey said enthusiastically. "I'm sure you're calling to inquire where the translated document is. Well, I'm pleased to report it's being sent to me by email this afternoon. It will be in your hands before I leave the Club tonight. Good news, don't you think?"

"That's wonderful. I can't wait to see it. And I was also calling to let you know I'm coming back to London in a couple of days. I have to go to Rome first. I'm going to pick up the original manuscript from the Cardinal who has it now."

"Oh really? What's the Cardinal's name?"

"It's Dominic Conti. He's head of the Vatican Bank. That's where he and I are going to meet in a couple of days."

"Dominic Conti. I saw something about him recently during my research. At the moment I can't recall what it was. If I locate something I'll call before your meeting. It's day after tomorrow, you said?"

"Right. Then hopefully I can see you on Friday. I'll fly to London Thursday after I get the book. I need to go to the gallery Friday morning. Can we get together around 1:30?"

That meeting was set and Brian finalized his travel plans.

He stayed close to Nicole's bedside until Wednesday. She was awake more and more. Although she spoke only a word or two they all thought she could comprehend what they said to her. That afternoon he kissed her goodbye and went to DFW Airport. He made a connection in Chicago and arrived in Rome on Thursday, the day of his meeting.

He had received a voicemail from Jeffrey Montfort while he was on the plane. In a cab from the airport to central Rome he listened to it. "Brian, I remembered what I'd seen about Dominic Conti. You probably think the Knights Templars Order is part of the Masonic Lodge. But there's a different set of Templars. These are directly descended from the ancient and original ones. They're part of the Catholic Church and Conti's head of the secret order. I was looking online at some routine notes handed from Pope Benedict to the new pontiff. They were appointments to this board and that committee within the Church. Dominic Cardinal Conti's name showed up as being appointed head of the 'Order.' I thought that was a bit cryptic – I googled it and found out that's the name the Church uses for the Knights Templars. Pretty simple detective work!" Brian had to smile at the librarian's delight in having known what Brian needed.

Jeffrey ended the voicemail by saying, "Few people are aware of the Catholic Templars. Feel free to use the information I've given you if you need it. See you Friday!"

BOOK TWO

THE THIRTEEN CODED PAGES OF THE KNIGHTS TEMPLARS DIARY

"Now there stood by the cross of Jesus his mother, and his mother's sister, Mary the wife of Cleophas, and Mary Magdelene. When Jesus therefore saw his mother, and the disciple standing by, whom he loved, he saith unto his mother, Woman, behold thy son! Then saith he to the disciple, Behold thy mother! And from that hour that disciple took her unto his own home.

The first day of the week cometh Mary Magdelene early, when it was yet dark, unto the sepulchre, and seeth the stone taken away from the sepulchre. Then she runneth and cometh to Simon Peter and to the other disciple, whom Jesus loved, and saith unto them, They have taken away the Lord out of the sepulchre, and we know not where they have laid him. Peter therefore went forth, and that other disciple, and came to the sepulchre. So they ran both together; and the other disciple did outrun Peter and came first to the sepulchre.

And he stooping down and looking in, saw the linen clothes lying, yet he went not in. Then cometh Simon Peter following him, and went into the sepulchre, and seeth the linen clothes lie, and the napkin, that was about his head, not lying with the linen clothes but wrapped together in a place by itself.

O Lord, hear our prayer. By the grace of God our Father and his Son Jesus the Christ our Lord we have been appointed defenders and guardians of the faith. Let our words and deeds be pleasing to Him and through His holy guidance may we steadfastly continue our mission, guarding the secret with which we have been entrusted for these three hundred sixty-seven years.

Carrying on the tradition of our forefathers, Pauvres Chevaliers du Temple, we the Templars risen from the ashes of our brethren like the Phoenix, do pledge to uphold the secrets given to us, to be faithful stewards of the wealth and treasure amassed and hidden by our forebears and to continue the good works of the Order.

We have willingly assumed the responsibility to maintain the precious objects, religious artifacts, silver and gold we have been given through the grace of God our Father. As the ancients have written in the Bible, "Through wisdom is an house builded; and by understanding it is established. And by knowledge shall the chambers be filled with all precious and pleasant riches." We the sixteen who lead the Templars are humbled by the mighty weight of the responsibility God has laid upon us.

Today we find ourselves challenged. As stewards of the secrets we, the sixteen leaders of our Order, no longer can guarantee the safety of the Most Holy Relics. Since we were entrusted with their care in the year of our Lord 1129 it has been our privilege and duty to protect the location and integrity of these sacred items. And we have done so without fail. Today unrest in the land where they lie creates fear and mistrust in the hearts of the people. They now see us as their enemies and loathe us, the very ones they should trust the most.

The future of our mission is at risk. The relics themselves are at risk.

We the sixteen have voted to solicit the help of our Venetian friend the Voyager. Although not a member of our Order, he has been of assistance before. More importantly, he now has the blessing of England's monarch. We must engage him quickly. We must move the relics. Time is short and the Voyager is our only answer. An envoy is being dispatched to Bristol tomorrow to seek his help.

Let us pray for success.

The Most Holy Relics have rested in their vault far to the East for more than one thousand four hundred years. It is after much prayer and deliberation that the leaders make the difficult decision to move them from their sacred vault. We shall send an envoy of our most trusted Templars to remove the relics and bring them to the West.

The journey will be fraught with difficulty. We are concerned that unrest in the land where they lie could cause harm to the relics themselves or to the trusted Templars who will bear them to safety. We have faced challenges many times in our history. Our founders were burned to death for what they believed. We will not falter; we will not be afraid; we will not waver. For God is with us. And if He is with us, no man can be against us.

We have learned good news from our Templars who traveled to England. The Voyager has agreed to help us. In eight months' time he shall sail, charting a new westward passage to China. And we shall sail with him.

By now the men who went to Ephesus have retrieved the Most Holy Relics and, God willing, they are making their way back to us. They travel under heavy guard. There are more than twenty, strong fighting men all, and we pray fervently for safe travels and a journey free from strife. We know, however, that may not be possible. There are those who would take the relics by force, heathen unbelievers who would delight in their destruction. There are others who want the relics for their own designs. They want to be the owners of these sacred items, to hold them, pray to them, venerate them.

Saint John, the disciple whom Jesus loved, was charged by our Saviour from the cross to care for the Lord's mother as his own. And he did so. John took the Virgin Mary with him to Ephesus. At the appointed time Saint John hid the Most Holy Relics there for eternity. And there they would have stayed if it were not for this unrest in the land.

Our mission comes from God our Father. The mission is not ours, but His. We will not fail.

The men who rode to Ephesus, who now transport the Most Holy Relics, dispatched an advance man, a rider on the fastest horse, to give us news of their progress. The relics are in Italy now, more than halfway to our stronghold here in Bruges. We believe they will arrive here in two months' time. We have arranged a safe hiding place to put the Most Holy Relics until we can determine a final place for them to rest in peace for the remainder of time, until our Lord comes again.

We have engaged the Rook, a small but swift boat, and twenty of our Templars are presently sailing across the waters to join the Voyager in Bristol. They will accompany him as he searches for the route to China. Their mission is to find an area sufficiently remote and uninhabited, to build a suitable vault for God's sacred items, and to await the transport of the Most Holy Relics themselves.

With reliance on God's guidance our engineers have crafted a complex plan, a means to construct a hiding place that will withstand not only the ravages of nature and time, but the schemes of man as well. The men who travel with the Voyager will build this vault. With God's grace it will hide the Most Holy Relics forever more.

We received word from Bristol that our ship the Rook sailed on the eighth day of May in the year of our Lord Fourteen Hundred Ninety Seven. The Rook accompanied the Voyager's small ship Matthew and a crew of eighteen. It is fitting that the lead ship is named for one of our Lord's most trusted and devoted Apostles. We the Knights Templars likewise have been entrusted with the Most Holy Relics. We expect the arrival of our men from Ephesus any day and are ready to accept the burden of caring for the relics until they can be moved to their final resting place.

We wish the Voyager, his crew of eighteen brave souls and our own twenty strong Templars God speed and safe travels to China, if that be where God leads them, or to another place God reveals to our men. We all offer much prayer that they will easily recognize the place God has chosen for His relics. We further pray that the construction of the hiding place will be accomplished with speed and accuracy.

A day of great celebration here in Bruges! The entourage arrived from Ephesus after five long months of journey across southern Europe and northwards to us. We welcomed them with open arms but no fanfare otherwise. The load they carry contains the Most Holy Relics. Our primary motive now is to move them to the safe place that we have arranged for their temporary safekeeping.

The Bishop is aware only that some items of importance to the Church are being secreted in the crypts below the nave of the cathedral. He has no knowledge what they are and we have deliberately misled him about the exact whereabouts they will be laid. It is for his own good, as well as the safety of the items themselves, and we ask God's forgiveness for the lies we have told this man of the church.

There have been rumors in this city that our Order is bringing important items of the Church here for safekeeping. Despite our efforts we have been unable to stop word from being spread. It is unfortunate that we cannot tell the populace what the relics really are. We fear that the people believe we are bringing things of great monetary value – gold and silver, precious stones and ancient cups, perhaps even the Holy Grail. These are things people will steal and even kill for. But this is not what we protect.

If they could only know the Most Holy Relics are far, far more valuable than mere silver or gold. They are the most precious things on Earth and we, the Knights Templars who are entrusted with their perpetual care, will not shirk in our duty to defend and protect them to the death.

Those of our Order will guard the relics at all times while they rest here in Bruges. We pray to God for their safety and thank Him for their successful journey from Ephesus.

For these past four months we have ensured the safety of the Most Holy Relics. As far as the populace knows they lie safely beneath the nave of the cathedral, protected at every moment by one or another of our Templars.

The truth about their whereabouts is the most closely guarded secret in our history. People in Ephesus think the relics are still there; our Templar brethren removed them and whisked them out of the city gates under cover of darkness. The citizenry here in Bruges believe we put something valuable in the cathedral crypt, now closely guarded by our own soldiers. How surprised the people, even the Bishop himself, would be to know the Most Holy Relics lie hidden in plain sight. At times the best hiding place is no hiding place at all.

There has of course been no word from our hearty travelers on the Rook for these four months. We pray they found a suitable place to build the final resting place and today are hard at work constructing it according to the plans of the Templar engineers.

By God's grace we received news today of our brethren and the Rook. One of our own was assigned to wait in Bristol until the Voyager's ship Matthew returned from its trip to China. At last the Voyager has returned to Bristol. Our brother received news from the Voyager along with a letter embossed with a Templars seal. Our brother rode day and night to the coast of England. He boarded a ship and today arrived in Bruges carrying the letter from our brothers on the Rook.

The two ships bearing the Voyager's crew and our twenty brave men reached land after almost fifty days at sea. It did not appear to be China, the Voyager said. Perhaps it was a previously unknown land. While the Voyager

*explored the apparently uninhabited shoreline,
several of our men took our small boat a few
miles north and found a perfect place for the
relics. It was as though God led them directly
to an island not far from the mainland, with a
small, protected bay. The location is remote
but tranquil. It will meet our needs completely.
Thanks be to God.*

*Our brothers advised the Voyager they would
create a Knights Templars settlement in this
land and sailed the Rook north to the island.
They commenced building rude shelters to
house themselves during construction of the
hiding place. Within a week they had begun
to excavate a shaft, felling mighty oak trees as
they needed the wood to shore up the sides of
the pit they were creating.*

*It was unfortunate that the Voyager chose to
involve himself in things best left to our
brothers. He and his men sailed the Matthew
north to see where our brethren had gone.
They saw our settlement, the construction of
the pit and its location. Going there was an
unfortunate decision by this seafaring man.
He has been of immense help to us. Now
what he has seen is a liability. When the time
is right we must deal with him.*

*The secrets we protect are the most important
things on Earth and we are charged by God to
use any means to ensure their safety. For
now the Voyager knows only that we are
building a settlement. If he ever returns to this
place we have settled, he must be dealt with
in the harshest way. The secrets will be*

maintained and the hiding place secured forever.

I am Marco Cabreto, elected by my brothers to lead the Templars. Today, God willing, I along with six others of our Order shall sail with the Voyager back to the land where our men are constructing the secret place.

A day ago we took the box containing the Most Holy Relics from its hiding place, the bookcase of my villa on the coast. It sat on the shelf in plain sight and not a person gave it so much as a glance while the relics rested there.

It is the twelfth of May in the year of our Lord Fourteen Hundred Ninety Eight. We have the box containing the relics and will transport them on the Voyager's lead ship. For this trip he has a fleet of five sturdy ships and a crew of three hundred.

On this voyage we have no need of our own ship, the Rook being already in the unknown land to which we sail, along with twenty of our brethren.

We pray the grace and favor of God for smooth sailing and favorable winds as we transverse the great ocean. Protect our precious cargo and our brave men.

We have safely returned from our journey. For fourteen months we have aided our brothers as they finished the hiding place, created elaborate safeguards as our engineers instructed, and carefully laid the Most Holy Relics in their new home. Once they were in place it took us several weeks to test the traps. Everything worked as it was intended and we departed for Bruges, confident the relics are now safe for eternity.

Because of his decision to learn where our Templar brethren were building their settlement, the Voyager was dealt with. One of his five ships had taken on water early into the voyage and returned to Ireland. The other four carried on to the new land with a crew of around two hundred.

Almost all of the two hundred crew perished from pestilence or an outbreak of food poisoning that was created by our own efforts. The rest of them, including the Voyager himself, were so ill as to be rendered helpless. The twenty-six of us swiftly and easily dispatched them to their eternal fates.

The taking of human life is an unfortunate but necessary burden we guardians face during our journey. The safety and secrecy of our mission is paramount, entrusted to us by God Himself.

CHAPTER FORTY-TWO

French Riviera/Dallas

After the laborious job of decoding the symbol-covered pages Dominic Cardinal Conti read the finished product. It was the last day of his glorious vacation in France and he sat outdoors where he'd spent most of his time. Tomorrow he would fly from Nice to Rome and back to the grind of life inside the Vatican. Today he was engrossed in the translation he had written over many days. He could almost feel the adventure in the words of the Knights Templars as they prepared to move the mysterious "Most Holy Relics" from Ephesus to Bristol, then to unknown points westward across the Atlantic Ocean.

As Dominic sat reading on the expansive patio overlooking the Mediterranean Sea, Brian Sadler was in Dallas reading the same set of decoded pages. He had printed the computer-generated translation from Jeffrey Montfort's friend at Cambridge. This time he skipped the diary entries and read only the pages that had been covered with symbols. Those coded entries had to be the most important ones. As he read he was fascinated by what these men had done and unsure what the Most Holy Relics might be.

One thing kept popping up in Brian's mind: North America. Specifically, Oak Island, Nova Scotia. Whoever the Voyager was, he was seeking a passage to China and a monarch had financed him. Brian's first thought was Christopher Columbus, who believed he'd discovered a shortcut to India but instead arrived in the Americas. Was the Voyager Columbus himself? He stopped to google the phrase "where was Christopher Columbus in 1498?" The answer wasn't surprising but it removed Columbus from contention as the Voyager.

First problem: wrong monarch. Although an Italian, Columbus was sailing under the Spanish flag. He would have had no reason to be in Bristol; his departures were from various ports in Spain. Second problem: wrong place. On May 30, 1498, Columbus sailed from Sanlucar, Spain to the New World, specifically the Caribbean islands he had previously visited. He didn't return until 1500. He couldn't have sailed from Bristol, England with five ships and three hundred men on May 12 of the same year.

Setting aside further speculation, Brian continued his scrutiny of the Templars pages. He'd do research later. There were plenty of clues and enough dates in the decoded pages to likely learn the identity of the Voyager. For now he wanted to read the entire story.

Cardinal Conti had his bullet point notes from the earlier diary entry close at hand. Finding the identity of the Voyager was a snap – it had taken ten seconds to enter the keywords "Matthew," "ship" and "1497". He knew the name of the Voyager and that the ship sailed from Bristol to North America, "presumably Newfoundland," according to the article, in 1497. The Voyager was Giovanni Caboto. When he moved to England and became a sailor for Henry VII he changed his name to John Cabot, a man whom most historians believe claimed the lands of Nova Scotia, Newfoundland, Labrador and perhaps Maine for the King of England.

The information on Cabot fit perfectly. He made his first voyage in May, 1497, just as the manuscript said. His second trip was in May 1498, sailing from Bristol with five ships and a crew of three hundred. The historical facts fit the Templars' account precisely. The only omission from history was that a small ship called the Rook manned by Knights Templars sailed with Cabot on his first voyage, and that six more of the Order joined Cabot's second voyage.

And what of Cabot's demise? Could the Templars in a faraway land actually have killed him and his men as the coded symbols alleged? Cardinal Conti read the rest of the article. Every fact fit perfectly so far. Did this fit too?

Historically there is an element of mystery about the fate of John Cabot. An Internet article told the story of Cabot's five ships, one of which turned back to Ireland after becoming disabled, just as the Templars described. Nothing was ever heard from the rest. Some historians believe the other ships may have been lost at sea. Others think Cabot and his men made it to North America and subsequently disappeared, perhaps killed by natives. A few believe Cabot turned up in Bristol years later after claiming North America for England.

So, Conti thought, the story told by the Templars could be correct. No one knows for sure what happened to Cabot and his men. There is no proof of the sailor's whereabouts after his departure from Bristol in May of 1498. A wave of sadness come over the cleric as he came to grips with what he now knew.

The Cardinal sat back in his chair. *So it's true. Everything fits. Oak Island, Nova Scotia. We Templars have heard for years that our brothers in the fifteenth century buried something valuable there. Relics they termed "most holy." But those stories were distorted as the centuries progressed, fact blending with fiction until the truth was lost. Apparently there had no longer been a need to have men there to guard the relics. They were hidden well and "forever more" according to the men who buried them. Over the years people forgot exactly what, and where and who. Until now. The coded pages revealed the secret.*

He was deeply disturbed as he pondered the implication of the Templars manuscript. "Most holy relics," he said out loud. "Bones. There are bones in the pit." What a sobering, shattering realization. Given the coded Bible verses, that was the only reasonable conclusion. This was horrifying. Everything would change for the Church if this information became public.

Dominic Conti had no idea Brian Sadler was reading the same translation at the same time, thousands of miles away. The Cardinal believed he was the only man on earth privy to a mysterious, obscure secret that should remain veiled forever. Otherwise it would change the entire world.

The Cardinal considered himself a religious man, of course. But he had human frailties - even though he was a leader in the Church he prayed less often than he should. But now he fell to his knees, asking God to help him decide what to do with the secret he had discovered. He never expected an exciting search for hidden treasure to have this outcome. This situation couldn't be worse. He felt the burden of an entire religion on his shoulders. He felt genuine contrition for his sins, especially the one he now faced. He had opened Pandora's box. He had unleashed a monster. Tears flowed as he prayed for guidance for himself but more importantly for the Church.

Brian finished the translated pages of symbols. Within minutes he had retrieved the same online information about John Cabot that the Cardinal had seen. It was becoming obvious that Oak Island could be the place the Knights Templars took the relics for burial.

One other thing piqued Brian's interest. Maybe it was coincidence, maybe not. John Cabot was an Italian whose birth name was Giovanni Caboto. The man who gave the Templars manuscripts to the Vatican in 1875 was named Marco Caboto. It took less than twenty minutes to review the extensive online biography of John Cabot, and the less expansive but also sufficient profile of the wealthy Marco Caboto. Giovanni Caboto, who became John Cabot, was Marco's grandfather many generations back. Marco Caboto had somehow obtained the Templars manuscripts because his ancestor ferried the guardians and the Most Holy Relics to Nova Scotia. Incredible.

Unlike Cardinal Conti who knelt in tearful prayer, Brian was excited, invigorated - feelings he hadn't known since Nicole's accident. She came first, of course. But she was improving steadily, thank God. Now Brian had a mission. Now an adventure awaited him!

CHAPTER FORTY-THREE

Vatican City

As he sat in an expansive waiting area Brian glanced into his satchel where he had put the copy of the manuscript. Since the Cardinal had had the original book for a couple of weeks Brian presumed he had spent time looking at it. Brian had questions and looked forward to discussing the ancient book with the cleric. Hopefully he would find more information about the other volumes in the set as well.

Brian was brought to the beautiful office of the Cardinal and offered tea. Dominic Cardinal Conti introduced himself and welcomed Brian to the Vatican.

"Are you Catholic, Mr. Sadler?" The Cardinal's English was cultured, tinged by only a slight Italian accent.

"I'm not but like everyone else I'm overwhelmed by the sheer beauty of everything here in the Vatican. It's such a magnificent place. I always enjoy coming to Rome. It's one of my favorite places to visit."

The tea arrived and the talk turned to the manuscript. The ancient volume sat on the desk between the Cardinal and Brian. Dominic opened it up to a random page and said, "It's my pleasure to return this book to you. You may not know that the papal archives hold the other four volumes of the set to which this one also belonged. If you and your client decide to sell this book we would appreciate being notified. Of course, we could also offer a generous tax deduction for the owner if he chose to donate it." The cleric smiled.

"I'll pass the information along, Eminence. May I ask how you came into possession of this manuscript? You know, I'm sure, that it was stolen from my gallery in New York during a bombing."

"I do know that and I offer my condolences at the losses you suffered. An anonymous person donated the book to the Church. I wasn't involved in obtaining it. I apologize that I don't know anything about that. I was assured the book itself couldn't have been the cause of the tragedy in New York. After all, it turned up here not long afterwards."

Although he thought the cleric's response somewhat naïve, Brian took it at face value. It was unlikely a man as senior in the affairs of the Catholic Church as Conti would have had direct knowledge of a crime such as this. He moved on.

"On a related subject, may I ask your opinion about something?"

"Of course. Anything."

Brian rose and turned to the front of the manuscript. He leafed through a few pages then looked puzzled. "May I?" he said, turning the book around so he could read the pages.

Brian flipped one page, then another, then went back again. The Cardinal watched him closely.

"Are you looking for something in particular?" Conti asked, knowing what the man was looking for.

"This is strange. Let me show you something." Brian opened his briefcase and took out the thick sheaf of papers that was the scanned copy of the manuscript. He flipped a few pages and came to the first page of coded symbols. Pulling it out, he laid it in front of Cardinal Conti.

The cleric's face turned ashen. He tried to conceal his shock. Where had this man gotten a copy of the manuscript? The man in the Monument Club library assured him the only copy had been taken. Conti had destroyed that copy. Where did Brian Sadler get another?

"What do you have here?" Conti tried to appear nonchalant.

"Have you spent much time looking at the manuscript, Eminence?"

"A bit. I've read some diary entries here and there. It makes for interesting reading but frankly it's a bit dull in my opinion. I had hoped for a little adventure!" The Cardinal talked more freely than normal; he was hoping to find out what Brian Sadler knew.

"This page is different from the others. There are thirteen of them in the manuscript. But this is strange. The original book doesn't have this page. Look, Eminence." Brian leaned over the desk and examined the book's binding closely. "Someone's removed this page."

The Cardinal feigned surprise as Brian carefully turned the ancient pages one by one until he came to the place where the next sheet of symbols belonged.

"This one's gone too. And do you see, sir? It's been removed too."

"All right. I understand what you're saying. Pardon me if I don't see the significance of some missing pages. The manuscript is very old, after all. Could they have been lost along the way? Couldn't they even have just fallen out?"

"Unlikely. From what I've seen here, I think the only missing pages are the ones with symbols. That seems strange, don't you think?"

Conti was wary, cautious. He hoped the response to his next question wouldn't create a problem.

"And what do the . . . what did you call them, 'symbol pages,' . . . contain, exactly?

Brian had no reason to hide the truth. He believed this Cardinal, head of both a national bank and the Knights Templars, would be an ally in finding the truth about the Templars manuscript.

"Eminence, I need to tell you that I'm aware of your secret work."

Dear God in Heaven. What does this man mean? Dominic felt a wave of heat sweep over his body. Beads of sweat formed on his forehead. He strove to maintain his composure.

"I'm not sure what you're saying. What do you believe is my 'secret work'?"

"You're head of the organization known as the Knights Templars. I wanted to let you know I am aware of that fact so perhaps you can help me."

Conti relaxed and forced what he hoped looked like a genuine smile. "I'm afraid you're mistaken. The Knights Templars were eradicated in the fourteenth century."

"I mean no disrespect, sir, but we both know the Knights Templars exist today. I know that you are head of that secret Order within the Church. I want to share some potentially important information with you. I have no idea why the original doesn't have these particular pages, but I located a copy in the archives at a library in London. Luckily my copy did have those missing pages. I've had them translated and I've read the story. It's a fascinating tale, Cardinal."

Conti forced himself to be calm. More concerned than ever, the Cardinal waited for Brian to continue. He must find out whom Sadler had told about the translation. Here was a new set of problems and at least one more person to deal with.

It took ten minutes for Brian to relate the mysterious story embedded in thirteen coded pages. The cleric seemed interested but Conti didn't have the anticipatory excitement Brian had expected. It was almost as though the Cardinal already knew what Brian was revealing. But maybe he was reading the cleric wrong. Maybe this man knew about the Most Holy Relics from other sources. As head of the Templars that was likely. Brian also noticed that the Cardinal looked really upset. He was nervous. Maybe this was normal - maybe it was some sort of health issue the cleric had.

Brian told about how the librarian at the Monument Club helped him find materials Lord Borland had been working on. He briefly related the attack at the club's library and how the intruder had stolen a copy of the manuscript but not before a scan could be made.

"How fortuitous that was," Brian said enthusiastically.

"Indeed," the Cardinal replied warily. "So this librarian has been helping you. Please continue." Conti made a mental note to himself.

"It's a long story," Brian replied. "I'll try to make it brief."

"I have some time. Please tell me everything. I think it's very interesting."

Brian told Cardinal Conti about the Fifth Avenue bombing, the death of Arthur Borland and the sabotage of Nicole's car. He said the FBI was hard at work to see if there was a connection between all this and an Italian Mafia boss named John Spedino.

"Have you heard of John Spedino, Eminence?"

Now Conti became *really* nervous. This American appeared to be fitting all the puzzle pieces into place. Presumably the FBI agent had not again broken his promise – the promise not to reveal Conti's connection to Spedino. If Brian didn't know that, he also couldn't know how the Cardinal got the manuscript. The cleric wasn't certain how to respond to Sadler's question. If the FBI Agent had told Brian about Conti's tie to Spedino, he'd know Dominic was lying. The cleric made a choice. He'd answer with a question.

"An Italian Mafioso named John Spedino? Should I know him?"

"Not necessarily. I just thought you might have run across his name. He was very big in the Mafia in New York at one point – the godfather, in fact."

Conti parried. "Do you believe the Mafia was involved in the crime against your gallery? If so, what would its motive have been?"

"I've thought about that a lot. I'm beginning to think it may be personal – a vendetta against the three of us. Since you have the *original* manuscript, I'm starting to think the attack on the gallery and my assistant was aimed at me personally and the book theft was a diversion. I have a past with John Spedino. The three of us - Lord Borland, my friend Nicole Farber and I - were instrumental in putting him in prison in

Guatemala. We learned he escaped and I'm certain he's involved in the violence against all of us. Since you have the book it seems pretty obvious Spedino didn't care about it. It took him almost no time at all to turn it over to the Church. Atonement for his sins, I guess." Brian looked at the cleric.

Cardinal Conti wasn't smiling. He wanted to end this meeting. Now. He was feeling sick to his stomach; his involvement with John Spedino and the manuscript was becoming more and more difficult to manage. He had told a plethora of lies to Officer Messina of the Gendarmerie Corps, in front of the Holy Father, no less. Now this American Brian Sadler shows up, obviously aware of the meaning of the thirteen pages of coded symbols and with far too many things figured out.

As expeditiously as possible Cardinal Conti finished their discussion. Feigning a sudden lack of time, he thanked Brian for coming and offered to arrange a private tour of the Vatican for him. Brian declined, saying he was flying to London in a few hours, and then he would be going to Nova Scotia to personally find out what the Most Holy Relics were. He wrapped the manuscript in a heavy cloth, put it into his briefcase and left Vatican City.

Dominic Conti pulled out the scotch immediately after Brian Sadler left his office. He poured a stiff one and contemplated the problems that now faced him. He had to stop

Brian Sadler.   That would be his prime mission; solving that problem would alleviate most of the others.

CHAPTER FORTY-FOUR

Dallas – two weeks ago

In a seedy lounge not far from downtown Dallas two men sat at the bar. It was four in the afternoon and only two other customers were in the place. Sammy Freeland was a punk, a decent mechanic and a lousy sports bettor. He wasn't the brightest guy on earth but he fancied himself a winner. His drinking companion was Joey "the Barber" Barberi, a small-time hoodlum who had adopted a swagger and line of bullshit he thought made him seem Mafia. Which he wasn't. What he was, was Sammy Freeland's bookie.

Like many people addicted to gambling, Sammy thought he was pretty good at picking the teams. Next week – it was always next week that was going to make him whole again. Meanwhile his meager salary at the repair shop in East Dallas couldn't match his voracious appetite for the next bet. At the moment he owed the Barber over five thousand dollars. The bookie had let Sammy ride once, then again, as ever-larger bets put Sammy deeper and deeper into the pile of shit he'd created for himself. Sammy couldn't pick a winner if it looked him in the face, Joey Barberi thought. But he had gotten a phone call. There was a job that was perfect for this loser. Joey stood to make fifty grand for this little project. He'd keep almost all the money and not even get his hands dirty. Sammy'd do it for him.

When he was losing, which was almost always nowadays, Sammy Freeland hated having to meet his bookie face-to-face. But there was no way around it. You had to own up to your losses and recently the Barber had allowed Sammy to coast a little. He didn't know exactly how much he was down right now – he didn't like to think about that because it scared him. The interest was twenty percent a week and it mounted up so fast Sammy could only dig out now by picking a winner.

When the bookie came in the bartender had greeted him by name. Joey Barberi was a regular here – every Tuesday around five he sat at the bar and settled bets made the previous weekend. Men in suits, men in shorts, men in dirty work pants – a steady stream of people from all walks of life settled up with the Barber. Each week the bartender silently observed the transactions - the bookie took in a lot more cash than he paid out to other people. From what the man behind the bar saw, bookmaking was a money-making proposition. Illegal, but who cares? Everybody's got an angle and in this one nobody gets hurt. At least not until they can't pay up! That made him smile. These stupid chumps – betting everything they have and more on one game after another. Crazy.

When the bookie sat down next to him Sammy had started things cordially. "Hey, Joey, how about those Cowboys? I think they're on a roll. Man, a couple of points the other way the past two weeks and you'd be handing me a wad of dough! I think this weekend's the deal, man. I'm going all the way."

Joey took a swig of beer and said, "You think this weekend's the deal? Is this the one that's going to dig you out? You owe me five grand, buddy. How much do you want this time?"

"Five Gs more. I'll take five Gs and put it all on Jerry Jones and the Boys. They're going to beat the Redskins straight up, and they're six point underdogs. Romo's playing Monday night and they'll win by a touchdown. This one's a sure thing."

"Little news for ya. The fun and games are over. I've personally covered you with the guys I deal with. Know what that means? *I* don't owe five grand to anybody. I already paid your bet to my guys. *You* owe *me* five grand. You. Owe. Me. You get it?" There was no smile, no friendly banter. This was different. Sammy had never heard the Barber get serious with him before. It was a little scary, frankly.

Sammy took a big drink of beer and signaled the bartender for another. He figured his bookie would pay the tab; Joey always did and Sammy had the sum total of three bucks in his pocket right now. That had to last him till payday.

"I got it, Joey. I know this weekend is gonna work . . ."

"Bullshit!" Joey slammed his hand on the bar so hard two customers across the room looked up. Joey's voice was loud – those guys had been here since lunch and were drunk as hell, and even they heard it. The bartender didn't miss a beat but he stayed put behind the bar, cleaning glasses with a rag like he hadn't heard a thing. He kept his eyes averted and his ears wide open.

The bookie lowered his voice. "Bullshit. You're a loser. You can't pay me five grand, much less the five more you'll owe me Monday night when your damned Cowboys lose another game. You're in deep. You're in really deep and all I have to do is make one phone call. Your life could change forever. You can't work with your damned legs broken. You get what I'm sayin', smart guy? You get it?"

Shit. This was getting bad. Sammy needed to take a leak but now didn't seem like the time to leave. He hoped he didn't pee in his pants. That would be embarrassing.

"Yeah. Yeah, I get it. But I can't pay you what I owe you now. Like you said. You gotta let me try . . ."

"No, Sammy. I *don't* gotta let you try. I have another idea. I have a job for you. Something right up your alley. And you know what? You do this for me and you'll be back to even. That five grand you owe me? It'll be wiped away like the wind-driven snow. Whadda you think about that?"

"Sure. I'm your guy. Anything you say. But I'm a mechanic. I don't know much about jobs. Who do I gotta kill?" He laughed nervously, hoping that wasn't what the job really was about.

"Come on. You been watchin' too many movies. You're a good mechanic. For you this is a piece of cake. Fixin' a car that belongs to some scum-sucking lawyer. A little night job that'll take ten minutes. You don't like lawyers, do you Sammy? Nobody likes lawyers."

"Hell no," Sammy responded, perking up as the Barber lightened up on him. All he had to do was work on some lawyer's car at night? Piece of cake, like Joey said. "Hell no, I don't like lawyers. But if nobody likes 'em, why do you want me to fix his car?"

"It's not a he, it's a she. And you're not really *fixin'* her car. You're kind of *unfixin'* it." He smiled and spoke even more quietly. "All you gotta do is a little brake job on a Mercedes. Simple, huh?"

"Sure, Joey. I'm in! Hey, can I do the job fast and then you front me five more for this weekend?"

Unbelievable, the bookie thought. *This guy's got it bad. But no worse than most of the others. This one just doesn't have enough income to pay his debts.*

"Sure thing. You can do it tomorrow night. And five Gs more for a solid player like you? Piece of cake! You're close to a big payoff. I can feel it." They both laughed.

When Joey talked like that it made Sammy feel important. He smiled from ear to ear. "Me too. I'm gonna win Monday! I can feel it too!"

From ten feet away the bartender heard the whole thing.

CHAPTER FORTY-FIVE

The bartender pulled drafts of beer for the patrons crowding the bar. Monday Night Football would be on right after the news. Tonight was a big game – the Dallas Cowboys hosted their old rivals the Redskins. Although it was here at home the Cowboys' season hadn't been so great and they were six-point underdogs tonight.

The bar was busy, filled with working-class guys and a few women. Most were regulars who stopped by several afternoons a week after they got off work. This part of Dallas was home to junkyards, paint and repair shops and other places where workers got their hands dirty. No problem. In this bar they were welcome. And tonight they'd yell together, hoping to bring the Cowboys a much-needed victory.

The local news was wrapping up as the bartender got a short break in the action. He glanced at the screen – a story was being reported about a serious car wreck in downtown a few days ago. A car careened into a busy intersection after running a red light. The gal driving it was in critical condition. Big story, the bartender thought idly, but why give it so much press? Bad car wrecks happened all the time in a major city.

The next thing he saw captured his undivided attention. The victim's picture flashed on the screen. Man, she's good-looking, he thought. Then it showed her name and the place she worked. Carter and Wells. He'd heard of it. Carter and Wells was a huge law firm. She was a lawyer. A lady lawyer. *Holy shit.*

He turned up the volume as one of the guys yelled for another round. "One sec," he responded, his eyes glued to the screen.

The reporter said that the brake lines on her late-model Mercedes convertible had been cut. Police called it an attempted homicide and Crime Stoppers was offering a $20,000 reward. A number flashed on the screen with a promise that callers would remain anonymous.

I'll be damned. Twenty thousand bucks. And you can remain anonymous. I'll be damned.

He jotted the Crime Stoppers number on a napkin and stuck it in his pocket. His disposition improved dramatically over the rest of the evening, even though the Cowboys lost by two touchdowns. He wondered if that loser at the bar the other day had actually bet five thousand dollars on the Cowboys tonight. But it really didn't matter, the bartender figured. Once he called Crime Stoppers a sports bet would be that guy's least problem.

CHAPTER FORTY-SIX

London/Dallas/Lunenburg, Nova Scotia

In London Brian received updates on Nicole twice a day from her mother, once by phone when Brian awoke and an email around five pm when Nicole's mother went to bed at eleven in Dallas. She was making steady improvement, had been moved from ICU to a regular hospital room and was staying awake most of each day.

The severe concussion she had suffered was an issue. Her neurologist had performed some tests and spoken with her. As far as he could ascertain, she had no memory of the day of the accident or for several days afterwards. She spoke only single words but her comprehension seemed good. Her physician scheduled a visit with a speech pathologist. He and the neurological team believed she might need to relearn some of her mental functions.

Around two pm Dallas time Brian called Nicole's room. Her mother answered and Brian asked if she thought Nicole would be able to listen to him. Her mom held the phone to Nicole's ear and Brian talked slowly to her.

"I miss you, sweetie. I'm coming back to see you in a couple of days. Will you be glad to see me?" Nicole said nothing. She appeared puzzled hearing the sound of his voice on the phone. Her mother suggested they not try it again for a few days, as it seemed to confuse her.

Brian took the day flight from London to Dallas. Her mother and father went back to their homes in Houston and Fort Worth, respectively, for a much-needed break from the hospital routine. He stayed with her during the day and was heartened by her physical improvement. She seemed to know who he was although she said almost nothing. He talked to her about London, the gallery and what was going on with the Templars project. She looked at him when he talked but he doubted she understood much.

The middle of the next week Nicole's sister took over duties and Brian made a quick trip to Halifax, Nova Scotia. He wanted to see Oak Island for himself and had researched online to identify its owners. There were two – Brian was most interested in Harold Mulhaney, who owned roughly the eastern half of the island that contained the original Money Pit and various boreholes dug around it over the centuries. Mulhaney bought his land from one of the men who had spent a lifetime searching for clues to the complex set of traps that protected the secrets of the pit. He had agreed to meet Brian but would offer no information whatsoever on the phone, saying merely that he would think about a proposition only when someone took the time and effort to come there in person and talk about it.

Lunenburg, Nova Scotia is nine miles from Oak Island. Brian sat with Harold Mulhaney at an outdoor coffee shop overlooking the bay. Mulhaney had grown up in the area - he was quiet and somber, as many people in the region prefer to be among strangers. He was a portly man in his seventies who slowly tamped, then lit his battered pipe, pulling contentedly on it as they sat on the patio. He let Brian do the talking and occasionally grunted what might have been responses. Brian wanted information but also he wanted to find out whether this reclusive man would let him make yet another attempt to retrieve what was in the Money Pit.

It had taken Brian a full day to get from Dallas to Boston then Halifax by plane. He drove the rest of the way to Lunenburg and spent the night in a pleasant bed and breakfast. When Brian phoned to say he was in town, Mulhaney had grunted an agreement to meet for coffee the next day.

Harold Mulhaney had started the conversation by asking Brian where he was from. That was about the only positive thing from the entire meeting, Brian later recalled. And Mulhaney's communicative skills hadn't been out for long.

"I was born in Texas, went to university in Oklahoma and now I live in New York City." Brian thought the southwestern references might help the man connect with him. But they didn't.

"New York City, eh? Never been there. Hear it's a pretty big place. So you're a city boy, eh?"

Of course Brian was a city boy. He smiled his best grin and said, "Nope. I'm just a country boy from Texas, sir." The old man harrumphed at that, obviously in disbelief.

"So talk, boy. I didn't plan to spend all day here. Whadda you want?"

Brian talked about himself, his background in the antiquities business and his interest in finding out what was on Oak Island. At one point Brian asked, "I was on a documentary aired by History Channel a month or so ago. Did you happen to see it?"

"Don't know what that is," the old man replied. "If it's some kind of TV show I don't have one anyway."

Brian struggled to keep the man's attention. After ten minutes of listening while he messed with his pipe, the man said, "If you don't tell me exactly what you think you know about my property you're outta luck, city boy."

If this was ever going to work Brian could hold back no longer. He explained about the Templars manuscript and the coded pages. He told Mulhaney he believed the Knights Templars had built the pit in 1497 or 1498 and put something there, something they called the "Most Holy Relics."

"I've been fascinated with the story of Oak Island my whole life," he said. "I love adventure and I'm fortunate enough to be able to afford to indulge my passion for ancient things. If I were the one who cracked the mystery of Oak Island it'd be an incredible accomplishment. And you as the landowner would obviously profit from whatever I found there."

Mulhaney said nothing for a couple of minutes. He just looked at Brian while he smoked his pipe, aromatic clouds wafting into the air. Finally he spoke.

"I want ninety percent."

Brian's astonishment must have shown on his face. "How much money do you want to contribute to the project?"

"Not a dime," Mulhaney replied, sitting back and folding his arms across his chest. "You're putting up the money, son."

"Uh, I want to be fair about this . . ."

"Fair don't really matter. What matters is what I want. I want ninety percent. We got a deal or not?"

"Well frankly I don't see how that would work, sir."

"OK then. Around here we do things a little differently than you guys in the city. Here it's pretty clear if you've got a deal or not. Appears to me we haven't got one." He stood, walked to his pickup fifty feet away and drove off, a cloud of dust replacing the pipe smoke that lingered.

That went well, Brian thought sarcastically as he paid for the coffee.

Lunenburg was a beautiful coastal fishing town with very little to do, especially for someone like Brian. Driven by his ambitions, he couldn't sit and wait for Harold Mulhaney. Frankly he wasn't sure if the guy was bluffing. He might come back to Brian with another offer and he might not. The man was inscrutable.

Brian gave it two hours then drove his rental car to the seven hundred foot causeway connecting Oak Island to the mainland. It had been built in 1965 by one of the treasure syndicates to make it easier to get equipment to the Money Pit. He parked on the shore, got out and looked across at the enigmatic island, so near yet so elusive. He shot a few pictures with his phone even though none of the famous excavations could be seen from this side of the island.

After a few minutes he heard the sound of a car engine and was surprised to see Mulhaney's pickup approaching the causeway from the other side. It would have been too much to hope the old man had been watching for him so he put it down to coincidence. Bryan walked over to the road and waited. Mulhaney would have to drive right past him.

The man stopped his pickup and turned off the ignition. His faithful pipe still clenched in his teeth, he said, "Taking in the scenery?"

"It's beautiful," Brian replied.

"No, it ain't beautiful. It's a scraggly little island that people have fought over for hundreds of years. It's got nothing to say for itself except the secret a bunch of folks think is here. Well, Mr. New York City, I got a deal for you. A take it or leave it deal. No discussions, no negotiating. I'll take five million US and sell you my half of Oak Island plus I get ten percent of the value of anything you find. I'll even help you find it." He started the truck, put it in gear and drove away.

When he had arrived in Nova Scotia Brian had no idea how long discussions with Mr. Mulhaney would take. Last night he'd stayed at the Oak Island Inn nearby and paid for two nights. At four pm he sat on the Inn's patio at the edge of Mahone Bay and emailed Jeffrey Montfort in London. He needed some information on Mulhaney and the librarian was the perfect man to find it.

After a night spent mostly awake thinking about Oak Island, Brian got up around six, checked his phone and saw a response from Jeffrey. He'd look at it soon; first he went to the patio for a morning coffee. It was crisp and cold; the sweater and jeans he wore felt good.

Jeffrey's online searches had turned up everything Brian needed. Two years ago Harold Watson Mulhaney purchased sixty-five acres of Oak Island, roughly half of it, for US$1.7 million. The half he now owned included the Money Pit and the shoreline of Smith's Cove, from where many believed water gushed into the pit through elaborate booby-traps constructed when the structure was built.

Online information about the reclusive man came from only one source - his wife's obituary. The Mulhaneys had lived on a farm near Halifax, fifty miles away. His wife died five years ago; she was the daughter of a wealthy paper baron and apparently left her husband of forty years a significant amount of money. He used some of it to purchase half of Oak Island and built a small cabin there. Nothing else had been written about this man since he moved to the island. There was no indication as to why Mulhaney wanted the important half of Oak Island – the part with the Money Pit. He certainly didn't seem like a treasure hunter. Just the opposite. He was maybe the most blunt, stolid man Brian had ever encountered.

Brian made a decision. He was going to take the man's offer, even though it meant a profit for Mulhaney of over three million dollars in only two years. Money wasn't an issue for Brian; he'd made millions in the time since he took over Bijan Rarities. The thrill of the hunt and the chance to own an enigma still unsolved after centuries intrigued him immensely. He wasn't about to let this go.

Brian called Harold Mulhaney and agreed to the deal. "Do you want me to get an attorney to draw up a contract?"

"Nope. I'll write it. No need to spend any more of your hard-earned money. You're gonna need it for the treasure hunt." Brian detected a hint of humor in the comment. *I haven't seen that before in Mr. Mulhaney,* he thought to himself.

They agreed to meet that afternoon at Mulhaney's house so Brian could see the property he was paying five million dollars for. They took a half-hour tour in the old man's pickup. Brian was fascinated to see the boreholes he had read so much about. He knew the whereabouts of the actual Money Pit itself had been obscured over the centuries by the work of others. But he believed ground-penetrating radar could find it.

Back at Mulhaney's cozy three-room cabin Brian looked over the handwritten contract and surprisingly he felt it would work just fine. He hadn't expected it to be this easy but it was. Obviously a real estate agent would have to draw the final closing documents and prepare a deed, but Mulhaney had done a decent job of drawing up a contract for the sale of Oak Island's Money Pit.

The agreement called for a deposit of $100,000, upon payment of which Brian was free to begin work on the Money Pit. They drove across the causeway to town, made a photocopy of the contract at a drugstore and signed both copies. Brian retrieved his checkbook from his backpack and the deal was done.

"The folks who own the other half of the island aren't as friendly as I am," Mulhaney told him when they had finished. Another bit of caustic humor, Brian noted. "The road from the causeway is on their land but you have a right of entry through their property to get to yours. Other than that, I'd stay off their side. They don't like me much and I'm a local. I don't have a clue how they'll take to a city boy."

The agreement allowed Mulhaney to live in his cabin rent-free for six more months. The cabin was far removed from the boreholes themselves so it wasn't a problem. He'd also offered to help with the project - Brian figured the man might have information he could use and he needed someone on the scene.

CHAPTER FORTY-SEVEN
Dallas

Arriving back in Dallas, Brian was buoyed by Nicole's progress. She was released from Baylor Hospital four weeks to the day after her wreck. Her mother enlisted twenty-four hour care at Nicole's condo. That gave the family a break now and then and ensured someone could care for her every minute, day and night. Her physical improvement was excellent but she still had major problems related to the concussion. Her speech was slowly improving thanks to daily lessons with a professional and a physical therapist came three times a week to help her build back the strength and balance in her hands and legs.

The neurologist had explained that portions of her brain dealing with memory, speech and cognitive skills suffered severe shock from impact. They would likely continue to improve, perhaps even regain a semblance of normalcy, but it would take time. In the meantime she would think, speak and react slowly, remembering some things from the distant and recent past, but forgetting others completely.

The project on Oak Island began in earnest. Brian worked from Nicole's home office as he had previously done. Harold Mulhaney had proven to be an asset and Brian spoke with him every day. He willingly offered to be Brian's eyes and ears on the ground. Having a local on site would be very helpful, Brian figured, and Mulhaney freely gave his time in return for his ten percent stake of the spoils.

Within a week a radar crew had been flown in from Portland, Maine. Brian knew the penetrating ability of the radar depended completely on the makeup of the materials in and around the hole. Wood and concrete would be more difficult than water, limestone and dirt. He hoped they could shoot at least 150 feet – most of the tales of the Money Pit put the bottom a little further down from there.

Harold Mulhaney had advised Brian how best to go about the shoot. He took the radar crew first to a hole about 150 feet from the Money Pit. This shaft, called Borehole 10X, was created in 1970 by another Oak Island syndicate, the Triton Alliance. The shaft was created by a rotary drill and then lined with steel casing. Its total depth was about 230 feet. Metal and some wire were retrieved along with, according to some stories, indications of a treasure chest. But no treasure had ever been brought up.

Since the location of Borehole 10X was known, Mulhaney advised Brian to let the crew work this hole first to see how the radar worked at depth. Sadler agreed.

In the hole the crew collected data for later review, then moved southwest to an indented area most locals believed was the Money Pit itself. A few others claimed it was a natural sinkhole and the original pit was lost. Wherever it was, repeated invasions of the shaft over the centuries had collapsed it. Flooding from the booby-traps installed by the builders took a toll as well. Today the area looked like a wide, shallow crater. There was no visible "hole in the ground."

The crew shot radar at various sites in and around the crater. Finishing up, they told Mulhaney they believed they had gotten more than a hundred feet deep in one of their shots. The crew went home to Maine with a promise to deliver test results in two days.

Harold Mulhaney didn't have a computer so Brian got the radar test results via email and called the old man. Although Mulhaney seemed dry and rough, Brian could sense his anticipation.

"Let me tell you about Borehole 10X first," Brian began. "They went down a hundred and eighty feet to bedrock. The radar indicated some type of metal at the bottom, maybe the same metal and wire the Triton Alliance found in 1970. The crew got a good shot of the entire shaft but found nothing special."

He continued. "Now let's talk about the crater where the Money Pit's supposed to be. They made a total of six shots into the ground, one of which seems to bear out the existence of a deep shaft. The radar worked perfectly for about a hundred feet. They picked up some wood here and there but I'm hoping that was the platforms made of logs that exist every ten feet all the way down. Those platforms should have been mostly demolished over the years of digging but I'm sure parts of them remain. At a hundred feet they ran into wood and possibly metal."

"Hold on right there. You recall what's supposed to be at a hundred feet in the Money Pit?" The old man sounded excited.

"That's where they found some kind of chest - right?"

"Sure is. In 1849 a syndicate called the Truro Company found oak and metal. They thought it was a chest with a top and a bottom, filled with some kind of metal, maybe jewelry."

"OK. That's encouraging because it tells us maybe the crew was shooting the actual Money Pit. So the radar gets weaker after penetrating wood and metal but it hit something at 155 feet that was stone. The shot was so deep and the signal so weak by then that they could go no further, but there does appear to be some kind of stone there. What have you heard about that?"

Harold paused a moment. "Sorry. Had to find a book I needed. Hold on a sec." Another pause. "OK. The book says at 154 feet a cement vault was found. That was discovered sometime before 1900. That sounds like what your radar men ran into."

"Maybe so. At least it's consistent with the old stories. We need some excavating equipment. Can you round it up and get them started as quickly as possible?" That was the first time Brian had ever called Mulhaney by his first name. He didn't seem to object – in fact, Mr. Sadler also became Brian from that point forward.

Two days later they set a timetable in place. A crew from Halifax would be on site the first of the next week to begin removing dirt and debris from the crater. Once they located the shaft they'd start excavating it. The closing date for Brian's purchase of the property was that week as well, so he would fly to Halifax on Sunday and stay a couple of weeks while the crew excavated.

Sitting on Nicole's bed that evening, he told her everything he was doing as Shelia, her caregiver watched TV in the living room. Nicole listened intently and said nothing while he told stories of Oak Island, the

Templar relics, Harold Mulhaney and his plans to find what was there. After nearly ten minutes he realized he had talked too much. She wasn't listening any more so he stopped.

"Do you understand what I told you about the new project in Nova Scotia?"

With a big smile on her face she shook her head. Tears came into Brian's eyes – that was the most positive reaction she'd offered since the accident. She was getting better, even if she didn't comprehend a lot.

"Eat now?" she said.

"I'll fix it," Shelia called from the living room.

He looked into Nicole's eyes. "I'm so sorry, baby. Of course we can eat now. I've worn you out with a bunch of talk. I love you and I love how much better you're getting."

That brought another smile.

CHAPTER FORTY-EIGHT

The arrests of Sammy Freeland and Joey Barberi made front-page headlines in Dallas. Both got their fifteen minutes of fame although each probably hoped for different fame than this.

Nicole's boss Randall Carter called Brian and told him the men had been arrested. At the inn Brian read the news article online and let Agent Underwood know. The FBI man promised to personally investigate the possible connection to the Fifth Avenue bombing.

The anonymous tip from the bartender was exactly what Dallas police had needed to determine who sabotaged Nicole Farber's car. Facing charges of attempted capital murder, the two men were jailed in downtown Dallas. The police detective working the case was surprised when a senior FBI agent in New York called and requested information.

Sabotaging brake lines on a Dallas lawyer's convertible didn't sound like an FBI matter to him and these two losers who were apparently involved didn't look like major criminals. But who knew?

Sammy sang like a bird but he wasn't the one the cops wanted to hear. His court-appointed lawyer sat next to him as he admitted doing the "brake job" on the Mercedes. He confirmed the bartender's story word for word. Joey Barberi hired him with a promise to erase five thousand dollars in gambling debts and give him a new five grand line of credit. Which, coincidentally, Sammy had lost on the Cowboys game Monday night. That was the only good thing out of all this, Sammy figured. He might be in jail but at least Joey the Barber couldn't break his legs when Sammy didn't pay.

Thanks to the bartender and Sammy, the police knew Barberi ordered the job. Now they wanted to interview Joey the Barber to find out why he wanted to hurt Nicole Farber. Usually these attacks against lawyers were retaliatory, aiming to hurt an attorney who'd been on the other side of a case, but Nicole didn't do that kind of legal work. There was nothing on the surface to indicate Joey Barberi should have had a vendetta against her but nobody could find out for sure. At the moment Joey wasn't talking.

Barberi hired a high-profile local attorney who specialized in criminal defense, ironically the same area of law that Nicole practiced. Joey entered a plea of not guilty and conferred with his lawyer. An offer was made to the Assistant District Attorney assigned to the case. Joey's lawyer told the ADA his client merely facilitated the job, acting on instructions from a person whom he feared.

The representative from the DA's office refused to negotiate, pointing out that they had Barberi dead to rights with the testimony of the bartender, who saw and heard the entire thing, and Sammy Freeland, the perpetrator, himself. Things were at a standstill for ten days until Special Agent-in-Charge Jack Underwood called Brian.

"If we can link these guys to Spedino we can figure out what happened," the agent said. "I know you've got friends in high places. Are you willing to use a favor?"

Brian said he'd do anything to help Nicole and made a phone call.

Three days later the Dallas County District Attorney was at his desk when his secretary buzzed him. "Sir, the White House is on line one."

He laughed, thinking his assistant had been taken in by a prank caller. "I'm busy, Margie. I've never had a call from the White House in my life. How do you know it's actually them? Tell them to put the President himself on the line right now. That should take care of it."

In a moment she opened his office door. She was white as a sheet.

"He's . . . he's, uh, on line one, sir."

"Who?"

"The President. He's waiting to talk to you."

"You've got to be kidding. What the hell's this all about . . ." He picked up the line and curtly said, "OK, whoever you are. Start talking."

He heard the voice so familiar to Americans everywhere. "I'm sorry to interrupt your day, Mr. District Attorney, but I need your assistance."

Needless to say, the apologetic District Attorney jumped at the chance to help the President. Once he realized the potential magnitude of this case he pulled it away from his assistant. This would be very high profile. He wanted this exciting case and he needed the attendant publicity it was going to generate. Politics never stopped – DAs were always running for office.

The police were surprised when they learned the Assistant District Attorney who had been handling the case had been removed. The boss himself would be running things from now on. That was so unusual at this early stage of a case no one in Dallas could remember it ever happening. It made the news.

Joey Barberi's attorney presented his demands - a reduced charge from attempted capital murder and no prosecution for unrelated non-capital crimes that might come out during questioning. As an enticement to agree, the lawyer revealed to the DA that Joey's boss in Kansas City had told Joey about a guy who had a job he wanted done. That second person had paid Joey $50,000. Barberi had never met that man. He had done a couple of previous jobs for him in the past, also arranged by phone. If the District Attorney approved the plea bargain Barberi would tell everything – what the job was, what he knew about the man who paid him, what bank the fifty grand came from, everything. They would turn over Joey's phone and bank records and cooperate fully with authorities.

When President Harrison had spoken to the District Attorney he requested the DA involve FBI Agent Jack Underwood in discussions about the plea bargain. Joey Barberi wasn't the most important cog in this wheel – they were after the people at the top.

Agent Underwood and the DA talked about Kansas City, a known Mafia town, and how the bookie's testimony might link this case to Spedino. The DA called Joey the Barber's lawyer and agreed to the terms he had offered.

Special Agent-in-Charge Underwood flew in from New York to join the interview process. When he arrived the senior Dallas police detective who was leading the questioning asked why the FBI was involved. Underwood explained that this case involved a top Mafia figure they'd been trying to take down for years. And confidentially, he told the detective, the President of the United States is involved.

Underwood concluded by saying, "I can't tell you more than that, but trust me that we want to handle this interrogation by the books. This is a critically important case."

The local cops didn't know exactly how to take this but they cooperated fully with Agent Underwood. Especially when the District Attorney himself did something he'd never done before. He personally attended Joey Barberi's deposition.

"I'm a bookmaker," Barberi explained, immune from prosecution for that crime due to the agreement with the DA. "I work for some guys in Kansas City." He named them. Underwood later ran them through the system - they were small-time criminals who ultimately worked for the mob although they weren't Mafia themselves.

Joey's boss in Kansas City had called a year or more ago. Joey would be hearing from a man who needed a job done, the boss told him. Given a promise it would be worth his while, Joey accepted.

"This man called me and used a series of numbers to identify himself. That's what my boss told me was going to happen. He asked me to do something; I did it and he wired me ten thousand bucks. Done deal."

Joey said he'd done one additional task for the man, netting him twenty thousand more, and finally there was the brake job on Nicole Farber's car, for which he was paid fifty thousand dollars. When Sammy Freeland later learned that information it pissed him off. He'd done the dirty work and netted a lousy five grand out of the fifty Joey had made.

Armed with the information Joey Barberi provided, Agent Underwood took over the investigation. Joey had authorized access to his telephone and bank records and in short order the FBI determined that the caller who had set up the brake job on Nicole's car was in Italy using a throwaway cell phone. The wire transfer had come from UcretsizBank in Ankara, Turkey. Citing Turkish law, the bank would say only that a Turkish corporation owned it. It turned out that Turkish company was owned by a Liechtenstein trust. The trail stopped there; Liechtenstein was a tax haven - ownership information was difficult or impossible to get. The tiny country prided itself on secrecy and this case would be no exception.

UcretsizBank refused to provide any information on activity in the account because of Turkey's secrecy laws. If money laundering were alleged the financial institution could be more forthcoming, but that wasn't the situation here.

Jack Underwood took a different route. He called a law school classmate of his at the CIA in Langley, Virginia. He explained the case he was working on and that it might involve the Mafia at high levels. His friend agreed to check with the CIA Station Chief in Istanbul to see if he had any connections at UcretsizBank. Forty-eight hours later he called Underwood with some news.

"This may or may not help, and it's not much," the CIA man said. "This is all I know. The Turkish bank account received a $5 million deposit a week before the car sabotage in Dallas. The fifty thousand was wired out to a Dallas account and the rest is still there. I don't know if the five million is related to your case but it's a hell of a lot of money regardless."

"That may be helpful . . ."

"I'm not quite through. I have one more odd bit of information to give you. That five million deposit I mentioned. It was a wire transfer from the Institute for the Works of Religion."

"What the hell's that? Sounds like a church."

"It's the bank that the Catholic Church owns. It's also called the Vatican Bank."

CHAPTER FORTY-NINE

Vatican City

Work on John Spedino's extradition to the USA had commenced the moment he was arrested in Italy. As a condition to handing over the Mafia don, the US had to agree that he would not face capital punishment for his crimes. This was a standard requirement for extradition from almost all western European countries. Spedino was immediately flown to New York City accompanied by FBI agents. He was transferred to the Metropolitan Correctional Center in downtown Manhattan where he would remain until his arraignment. At the moment he was charged with unlawful flight to avoid prosecution and drug trafficking, the latter charge pending from over a year ago, before his incarceration in Guatemala. The US Attorney hoped to add murder charges shortly.

A few days later as Dominic Cardinal Conti worked at his desk his cellphone rang.

The screen showed, "Blocked," so Conti declined the call. In a moment a voicemail was left. As Dominic listened to it he first was surprised, then a little fearful but also angry.

He heard a recorded voice. "This is a collect call from the Metropolitan Correctional Center in New York. This call is from . . ." The message paused for the insertion of a name and Conti heard a familiar voice. "John Spedino." Then the recording continued. "To accept all calls from this number press *13. To decline all calls from this number press *15."

Conti had heard that the godfather was now in New York to face charges relative to the Fifth Avenue bombing. "I have nothing to say to you, John Spedino," the Cardinal muttered as he considered whether he should decline all calls. If Spedino called again maybe he'd accept just to see what the old man wanted. He pressed *13 and hung up.

Five minutes later the same blocked number appeared on his cellphone screen. Conti pressed *13 again and accepted the collect call. Mindful that calls from correctional facilities were recorded, Dominic would be careful what he said.

"I was hoping you wouldn't decline my call, Dominic. It was smart of you to accept it."

"What do you want? I have nothing to say to you."

"Oh, but I have something to say to *you,* Cardinal Conti. Something very interesting happened. The FBI has a recording of a conversation between you and me . . . or part of a conversation, I should say. Someone gave them the part that incriminated me but forgot to include the rest. Remember the rest? The part that shows *your* involvement?"

The cleric chose his words carefully. "I have no idea what you're talking about. I asked you to get a manuscript for the Church and of your own volition you murdered a number of people. That had nothing to do with me."

"I only have a few minutes left. These calls are five minutes maximum – one of the minor inconveniences of being in jail." He laughed. "Here's why I called. I have nothing to lose at this point. The Feds think they have an airtight case against me. I wonder if they know about $5 million that was wired from the Vatican Bank to an account in Turkey? Does that ring any bells? Do you remember wiring money for a job you hired me to do? It must have been a *big* job – five million's a lot of money just to get a manuscript. What if they know about that? You gave the FBI a doctored tape of our conversation, Dominic. I'm going to make sure they know the true story. I'm going to give you up. Your life will soon change forever, just like mine did thanks to you. Best wishes, Eminence. You won't hear from me again."

Spedino hung up.

This is bad. I have to silence him.

In New York the next morning the warden of the Metropolitan Correctional Center called the FBI's office a few blocks away. He told the Special Agent-in-Charge about John Spedino's call to a man he addressed as "Cardinal Conti" and "Dominic." The warden advised the number Spedino dialed was foreign, to country code 39. Underwood looked it up while they talked. It was the code for Italy. It was also that of Vatican City. The agent wasn't surprised. He'd have been more surprised if it hadn't been.

Within an hour Jack Underwood had listened to Spedino's phone call and sent a request to the godfather's attorney. Underwood wanted an interview. If Spedino was ready to give up Conti, Jack Underwood was ready to listen.

CHAPTER FIFTY

New York/Vatican City

It took a couple of days for John Spedino's attorney to respond to the FBI's request for interrogation. The US Attorney's office got involved since the godfather's lawyer asked for a number of concessions in return. By now every agency working on Spedino's case was aware the President himself had an interest in it. The US Attorney was careful to ask his bosses in Washington what they wanted him to do.

From the conversation between Spedino and Cardinal Conti, the FBI believed Spedino truly did have nothing to lose at this point. Spedino was already immune from the death penalty as part of his extradition agreement. He was going to spend the rest of his life in prison one way or another and from the call it looked like he was willing to take a leader of the Church down with him.

So they refused to negotiate with Spedino's attorney. They would play a waiting game to see if John Spedino would talk without a plea agreement.

The next morning Spedino's attorney came back with news that his client, against the advice of counsel, had agreed to tell them what he knew about the Fifth Avenue bombing.

In his Vatican office, Cardinal Conti felt as though his life were spinning out of control. He was losing his grip. He had three murders to plan. His very existence – his life as a revered cleric and senior official of the Church – was in danger of collapsing. He would go to prison! He would be mocked, ridiculed, his name a synonym for scandal and deceit forevermore. He would be the Cardinal who shamed his office, his Pope, his Lord.

Be rational, Dominic. Think through this. He glanced at notes he had made on a pad, laying out his thoughts so he could formulate a plan. John Spedino had to die, but the godfather was safely in a Federal prison in New York. He also had to get rid of Brian Sadler and that librarian in London. Conti didn't even know that man's name. This dilemma would be humorous, Conti briefly thought, if it were a stage play. He was plotting to kill a man whose name he didn't even know. How in God's name had he gotten to this point?   He wasn't used to arranging murders.   Except when he used John Spedino now and then, of course.   That was different.   That extended back to the days when they were young and good friends and Spedino had taken care of business for the politically connected cleric.   But now his so-called friend had betrayed him.   Conti wouldn't allow him to get away with it.   Back to business. *Figure this out, Dominic. Come up with a plan. You always have. You can do it again.*

Prison killings happen every day, at least in the movies.   Surely Conti could get someone inside to do the job.   That would be the easiest and would remove Spedino from the picture.

Brian Sadler had said he was flying to London. *That's where his gallery is,* Conti reflected. *I can get someone to take care of him and the librarian at the same time. Some kind of accident. Of course it'll be suspicious given the Fifth Avenue bombing and Brian's involvement, but they'll never pin it on me.*

He wasn't satisfied yet with his plan, but he pressed ahead to the next step.   He would find someone to pull this off.

CHAPTER FIFTY-ONE

New York

The interrogation of former Mafia chieftain John Spedino was held in a secure room inside the facility where the godfather was incarcerated. The U.S. Attorney for Manhattan attended along with Underwood, Spedino's attorney and the Deputy Director of the FBI in Washington. It was a high-profile cast for an important meeting.

A court reporter created a record of every word spoken in the room. Two tape recorders provided redundancy. No one would miss a word of this testimony.

Spedino's attorney said his client wished to make a statement to begin the proceedings, after which the usual question-and-answer session could occur. The parties agreed and Spedino began to talk.

And talk, and talk. John Spedino was an educated man and an eloquent speaker. In front of him lay a notepad on which he'd made several pages of entries. He referred to it often. He elaborately described his long-time relationship with Dominic Conti, from the days when the Cardinal was a young cleric in Rome until now. The mobster talked about the Templars manuscript and Conti's obsession to have it at any cost. He filled in the missing conversation that occurred just after the bombing, the part Conti had deleted from the recording he gave the FBI.

It was obvious to everyone that John Spedino was coming clean because of his enmity toward his former friend. He had no need to further implicate himself, but he had chosen this path for one reason – revenge. His career as a criminal was finished. The rest of his life would be in a prison cell. And if it was to be, he was going to take his Judas to the cross with him. Regardless, those in the room were surprised at how calmly and quietly he described how he'd masterminded the Fifth Avenue bombing and the deaths of eleven people, the killing of Arthur Borland and the attempted murder of Nicole Farber. Those were personal, the godfather pointed out. They had nothing to do with Dominic Conti. Those were paybacks for previous wrongs against him.

By the end of the day John Spedino had handed Dominic Cardinal Conti to the authorities, wrapped, bow-tied and on a silver plate.   The cleric was in this up to his eyeballs.

The godfather slept well that night in his prison cell.   *Ah, but revenge was a satisfying accomplishment.*

CHAPTER FIFTY-TWO
Vatican City

Dominic Conti was at his desk in the Vatican early. He was close to a solution. On his notepad he outlined points. He would transfer ten million Euros from the bank to a personal account he'd set up in a tax haven country. Then he'd travel to Sicily, birthplace of the Mafia. He'd be incognito – no one would recognize him as a priest. He'd ask around, throw some cash at the right people and come up with a name. He'd hire a hit man who could arrange the whole thing. For enough Euros that man would kill Spedino, Sadler and the nameless librarian.

Cardinal Conti was a desperate man. Thoughts had flown through his mind all night and he'd prudently jotted each one down. Sometimes the best ideas came to you in the middle of the night, he'd thought. He had them all on his notepad. Crazy ideas, ranging from hiring a demolitions man to blow up the Monument Club in London with Brian and the librarian in it, to using his priestly garb to get into the prison in New York City and hire a killer to assault John Spedino. Some of them were easier than others to wrap his mind around, but he wrote them all down.

Around a quarter to nine a knock came on his office door and his secretary entered. Conti glanced up and then went back to work on his idea sheet.

"Get me a cup of coffee when you have a chance, please," Conti said without raising his head.

"Eminence, there are some men here to see you."

What? Why would the secretary allow visitors into Conti's office unannounced? What on earth was he thinking?

The Cardinal glanced up, looked across his massive desk and down the long office to the door where his faithful assistant stood next to three persons – two Swiss Guards with pistols drawn and Frederico Messina, the head of the Gendarmerie Corps of Vatican City. He became lightheaded as bile rose into his throat.

"The Pope wishes to have a word with you, Eminence," Messina said. "Please come with us."

Conti glanced down at his desk. "I'll just clean this up," he muttered as he picked up the notepad full of his plans and ideas.

Messina strode quickly to the desk and pulled the pad from the cleric's hand. "Please leave everything just as it is, Cardinal Conti. We'll take care of your things." Conti's shoulders sank. That little notepad would be the death of him.

The Cardinal walked slowly around his desk, taking in all the personal mementos in the bookshelves of his office. Here was a record of his life – pictures with Popes and world leaders, little keepsakes he'd picked up in his travels, things he'd considered important.

He knew this was the last time he'd ever see them. It made him sad. Given his religious upbringing, he should have been sorry he'd betrayed everything a man of God stood for. That thought crossed his mind but Dominic was sad because he hadn't had time to finish the Templars project. He knew what was in the pit. He just wasn't sure how to let the world know about it. He wanted the fame and glory for revealing it, but he hadn't finished planning how to keep it from hurting the Church.

Dominic Cardinal Conti was deeply saddened, but not because of things he had done. He was sad he'd gotten caught.

CHAPTER FIFTY-THREE
Nova Scotia

Brian met Harold Mulhaney at the Oak Island Inn at six am for breakfast. It was a gorgeous fall morning and they were ready to begin excavating the Money Pit. The crew had moved heavy equipment into place over the weekend and today at eight everything would commence.

The crater on the northeast side of Oak Island looked like a construction site by nine am. Heavy equipment moved earth from the bottom of the indention and a boring truck sat idling nearby, waiting for its chance to move into place and begin excavating. The place was noisy – Brian and Harold watched a dozen men engaged in a variety of tasks.

Brian's cellphone rang. He saw the London number and walked to Harold's pickup. He climbed in, shut the door and answered the call. It was significantly quieter inside the cab.

Jeffrey Montfort's usually cheerful voice was positively bubbly today. "Good afternoon, my good man!" the librarian said.

"You sound chipper!"

"Oh yes. I am chipper. I've found something I overlooked earlier. I don't know if you even knew about this or not, but I've got something that's going to make your life a lot easier!"

"Don't keep me in suspense. What is it?"

"When I first met you we perused a list of the documents and books Arthur Borland had viewed during his hours at the library. I believe I mentioned there were a few odds and ends he'd requested, but you and I focused on the Templars manuscripts. That was my fault, dear boy. I led you astray, I'm afraid."

Brian could hear the excitement in Jeffrey Montfort's voice. The man wanted to reveal his information to Brian his way, in his own time, so Brian resisted the urge to hurry him up.

"I can't wait to hear what you've found."

"Do you recall Lord Borland mentioning anything about a man named Simeon Lynds? And that we have his diary from the early nineteenth century?"

"Absolutely. He and I discussed it. Arthur said Simeon was either a Templar himself or he was involved with those who were. I think Arthur believed Simeon Lynds found out from the Templars what was in the pit."

"I've read the entire diary in the past twenty-four hours. Didn't get much sleep last night, frankly. I couldn't put it down because I knew you were right there at the Money Pit. I knew today you'd be standing on the very ground where Simeon Lynds searched for the treasure in 1804. And I found something. This is so exciting I couldn't wait to call you, but I had to get my friend from Cambridge University to do one more decoding project. Then I had to bide my time and wait until it was daylight on your side of the pond. Now it's time to reveal my secret!"

Brian was getting caught up in the man's exuberance. Suddenly he was jolted back to reality by a harsh rap on the passenger window of the pickup. Harold Mulhaney was standing just outside the truck.

"Hey Jeffrey – hold on a sec. I have to deal with something. I'll be right back."

He put the phone on mute and opened the car door. Mulhaney told him the bulldozer had scraped the land down about three feet and they had uncovered a much smaller circular crater. "OK with you if we pull the dozer back and let the boring start there?"

Brian gave his approval and returned to Jeffrey. "OK, I'm back. Ready to hear your secret!"

CHAPTER FIFTY-FOUR

Vatican City

Dominic Cardinal Conti sat in the same chair at the Pope's desk where Frederico Messina had interrogated him a few weeks ago. His life was crumbling before his very eyes. He had even vomited in the hallway a few minutes ago as he was being brought here. Some young priests had seen the whole thing – policemen surrounding him, the indignity of throwing up and soiling one's priestly garb, and the shame of what these young priests would ultimately learn about him. It was all over. Dominic knew that. He just didn't know what was next.

After the usual formalities of greeting the pontiff, Conti was told to sit. The three policemen stood at the back of the Pope's office. The pontiff spoke softly. "Dominic, I feel certain you know why you're here. I'm willing to hear your confession if you feel the need."

"I do, Holiness. I have grievously sinned."

The Pope asked the officers to wait outside his office. He came around his desk and sat in a chair by the disgraced Cardinal. He held Conti's hands in his own and the man told him everything. It took almost half an hour, long enough that Officer Messina had quietly peeked in the door twice just to be sure everything was all right. Conti had cried real tears, not tears of contrition but tears of remorse . . . that his life of finery, wealth and stature was over.

When the confession was finished the officers returned.

"You're going to be arrested now, Dominic," the Pope said gently. "I'm removing you from all your duties in the Church and with the bank. I'm greatly disappointed in you. You've disgraced the priesthood and shamed yourself. You've cast a stain on the Church. Is there anything else you'd like to say before these men take you away?"

"There is, Holiness. It's for your ears only. May I approach you?"

The officers instantly became alert, fearful that the deranged man might harm the Pope. But the gentle pontiff waved them away and walked around his desk. He spoke soothingly to the obviously agitated, mentally fragile cleric.

"Come, Dominic. Speak, my child."

Conti whispered in the pontiff's ear. The Pope's eyes opened wide. He was clearly startled at what Conti had said. "How can you be sure?" he stammered. "Are you sure?"

The disgraced Cardinal whispered, "It's true, Holiness. A man named Brian Sadler is going to find what the Templars hid in the pit. The relics. I've finally figured out what they are. What they must be. There's no other answer, given the information passed down for centuries in code."

Conti looked in the Pope's eyes and said again, "The relics in the pit are the bones of Jesus Christ."

CHAPTER FIFTY-FIVE

London

The diary of Simeon Lynds had given Arthur Borland information on his work at Oak Island and his possible ties to the Knights Templars. But Borland apparently hadn't read the entire volume. It was excruciatingly detailed and tended to be repetitive – the librarian stayed with it to the end only because he felt it might provide a clue.

And what a clue he had found.

A dozen pages from the end of the diary was a loose piece of parchment that had been inserted into the diary, presumably by Lynds himself. It was full of symbols – the very same ones that appeared throughout the Knights Templars manuscripts.

"I can't tell you how excited I was when I came across this page! I laughed, I cried, I jumped up and down! Thank God no one was here to see me – I was acting like a schoolboy.

"I immediately went back to the Templars manuscript and confirmed the symbols were identical. To me that means that Simeon Lynds was a Templar for sure. He was there when the author of the Templars diaries wrote some of the entries and he definitely knew how to read the encoded pages. He knew the Most Holy Relics were in the pit because he had decoded the same pages you and I did!"

"You've definitely got my attention. When do I get to find out what Simeon Lynds' page of code said?"

"Soon, very soon. I'm just so excited to tell you about this. Let me give you just a bit more background then I'll reveal the secret!"

Montfort said he immediately scanned and emailed the page of code to his professor friend at Cambridge for decrypting. Since there was only one page the decoding went very quickly and Jeffrey had his answer within two hours.

"While you slept I read about something you need. Something critical to the project you're working on at this very moment!"

Brian waited. Jeffrey's penchant for the dramatic, especially coupled with his unbridled enthusiasm, could be frustrating at times. But Brian didn't want to stifle his excitement. The man probably hadn't had this much fun in years.

"All right, Jeffrey. Shall we have a drum roll?"

"Ah, if only we could. I wish I were there with you to see your face . . . but enough! I know you're ready to hear what I learned. You of course know that the Money Pit has booby-traps – two tunnels that bring seawater from Smith's Cove to the pit itself. Whenever a dig gets to a certain level, the pit always floods. It always happens and no syndicate, no matter how much money they spent, ever learned how to stop it. That single thing is the reason no one has ever gotten to the bottom of the pit . . . and the bottom of the mystery, for that matter." He laughed.

"Simeon Lynds was a Templar, and he had secret knowledge about the Money Pit. Why, you say? Because on that one sheet of coded symbols, the sheet he stuck in his diary, he revealed the way to turn off the tunnels that flood the pit."

Brian was stunned. This was monumental. With this information they would succeed in finding what was in the bottom of the pit. The Most Holy Relics of the Knights Templars. Whatever they were.

CHAPTER FIFTY-SIX

Vatican City

A brief press release from the Vatican made world news. The two-paragraph statement stated that Dominic Cardinal Conti, head of the Institute for the Works of Religion, had been relieved of all duties by the Pope effective immediately. The Gendarmerie Corps of Vatican City had arrested Cardinal Conti that day. He was charged with misappropriation of funds from the Vatican Bank for the purpose of engaging in criminal activity. An investigation was underway to determine possible links to other crimes, including the Fifth Avenue bombing.

Back in the Gendarmerie office, Frederico Messina summarized the information he had gathered on the Cardinal's crimes, including his complicity in the bombing of Bijan Rarities in New York. The notepad Conti had been holding when he was arrested was particularly damning. It showed his future plan to arrange the murders of Brian Sadler, the librarian from London and the Mafia godfather John Spedino. Conti was in serious trouble.

In addition to removing Conti from his duties with the Bank, the Vatican issued two papal edicts. The first was a decree from the Pope removing Dominic Cardinal Conti from his office as head of the secretive Knights Templars. Secondly, in a sweeping move the Pope directed the Knights Templars be disbanded. Henceforth it would be a crime to assemble in the name of the Order. Interestingly, it was the second time in history a Pope had disbanded the Templars. The last time this happened the Pope had burned them all. This time it was a bit more civilized although the penalty for anyone caught disobeying the pontiff's order was severe – excommunication from the Church.

The Vatican has only rudimentary cells for the temporary detention of prisoners. The holding area is usually reserved for unruly visitors who break the rules or fail to respect the property of the Holy See. At the Pope's order, Dominic Conti sat in one of these cells. Ordinarily he would have been immediately transferred to the City of Rome's jail to await arraignment but the pontiff wanted to know more about this thing with Jesus' bones. He wanted to find out what Dominic knew and how he'd found it. So the disgraced Cardinal sat in a tiny cell while his bored guard read a newspaper in the next room.

The Pope prayed. It was the same prayer he had offered perhaps a hundred times since this distasteful episode with Dominic Conti had reared its ugly head. It was a prayer for guidance.

The matter of the bones of Jesus was monumental. It would impact Christianity like nothing else ever had. The very basis of this religion was that Jesus Christ was immortal – the actual Son of God. Although he became a man, all Christians believe he died, was resurrected and ascended to heaven to live with his Father.

There could be no bones of Jesus.

If there were bones then he wasn't the Son of God. He was just a man who wasn't immortal at all.

Atheists, Muslims, Jews and Christians alike would be interested in this little dilemma, for strikingly different reasons. As leader of the Catholic Church the pontiff had to bear responsibility for handling this affair. No Pope in history had ever faced such a problem. This one prayed once more for guidance. Then he ordered Dominic Cardinal Conti to be brought to his office.

The men conferred in private for over an hour. Conti told the Pope what he read on the Templars' encoded pages. He said the American Brian Sadler had read them too and he was going to Nova Scotia to find what was in the Money Pit.

When they finished Conti asked the Pope what charges the pontiff expected would be filed against him.

The Pope's expression changed to one of sadness. "You have committed grievous sins, my child. The blood of many people is on your hands. You have lied, stolen and disgraced yourself and the office with which you were entrusted. Any speculation on my part as to what charges you will face would be just that – speculation. I urge you to pray for forgiveness. And if you are a good man somewhere in your heart, you will pray for Christianity itself. You will pray that the bones of Jesus are not in the pit."

The Pope had to find out what this man Brian Sadler was doing in Nova Scotia. Something must be done quickly to stop him. Finding the bones would topple the world's largest organized religion. The pontiff firmly believed this to be true. Brian Sadler could not find the bones of Jesus. He knelt and prayed.

CHAPTER FIFTY-SEVEN

Oak Island

Sending a rotary drill down the shaft of the Money Pit was easy. A few obstructions were encountered but by noon they had drilled nearly eighty feet. A core sample of the material they removed was laid out on the surface near the pit. Brian and Harold would go through it after lunch.

Brian hoped to find something at around a hundred feet then again at the bottom of the shaft. At the higher level early boring had indicated wood, perhaps a chest, and bits of metal. At the base of the Money Pit, over 150 feet down, he hoped to find a concrete bunker of some type with the Most Holy Relics secreted inside.

The radio in Harold Mulhaney's pickup was on as he and Brian drove back to the cabin for a sandwich and a beer. The noon news was being broadcast from Halifax.

Brian caught the end of a story and the words, "charges against the Vatican-based Cardinal include using Church funds to perpetrate a crime."

He turned up the radio but that segment was over. Brian grabbed his phone – on CNN's site he read the story of the removal of Dominic Conti from his duties and the charges against him. The article stated that other charges were being considered, including a possible link to the Fifth Avenue bombing in New York City a few weeks ago.

Over lunch Brian told Harold how Conti had been connected to the Knights Templars manuscripts and the Money Pit. He had met the cleric only a few days ago in the Vatican to take possession of the manuscript. The volume was missing thirteen coded pages – now Brian figured the Cardinal had deliberately removed them to keep them secret.

Brian's mind raced. "And what if Conti was behind the assault on the librarian and me in London? What if it was all about getting that copy of the Templars manuscript so we couldn't break the code? And if that's true, go back one more step. What if he was involved in Arthur Borland's death?"

The more he thought about it, the more complex this all became.

"Hold on there a minute, son," Harold said in his practical way. "I ain't a churchgoing man but you're talking about a man who's high up in the Catholic Church. Don't you think you're gettin' a little farfetched accusing him of assault and murder? He's a preacher or something. I think you're barkin' up the wrong tree, myself."

Brian had felt that way too but things were looking more and more as though the cleric was right in the big middle of all this. Why a man of the cloth, especially a man of his standing in the Church, would go to these extremes was a mystery.

Brian amended his settings so he'd get notified if any more news became available about Dominic Conti.

CHAPTER FIFTY-EIGHT

Jeffrey Montfort emailed Brian the decoded sheet from Simeon Lynds' diary. Brian sat in Harold Mulhaney's truck and read the entire document. Not only were there detailed instructions showing exactly how to stop the seawater tunnels from flooding the Money Pit, there was a bitter explanation why Lynds himself couldn't follow his own directions.

The sheet revealed that Lynds was not only a member of the Knights Templars, he was their appointed leader in the early 1800s. He was a wealthy man from a nearby town who formed the Onslow Syndicate. Lynds used his influence to raise money from other men of means in order to search for the treasure in the Money Pit. He never told his partners he was privy to two Templars secrets. He knew how to stop the pit from flooding and he knew that something called the Most Holy Relics rested at the bottom. He didn't know what the relics were – he just knew that the Order had guarded them for a thousand years.

The oath of secrecy Lynds had taken as head of the Templars prevented him from revealing how to turn off the flooding. His partners would have asked questions he had taken a vow not to answer. Instead, according to the sheet in his diary, he planned to let the Onslow Syndicate's money pay for the excavation of the pit. Once it flooded, as it invariably would, the group would eventually give up. Lynds would retain ownership of the site, return on his own and retrieve the treasured relics by using the secret he'd learned.

Brian looked at an Internet site showing a timeline of the Money Pit from 1795 to the 1950s. The Onslow Syndicate did in fact disband in 1805 and Lynds remained involved with Oak Island. In fact forty years later a "Dr. Lynds," probably a relative of Simeon's, was a major investor in the next treasure-hunting syndicate, the Truro Company.

The end of Simeon Lynds' sheet revealed why he didn't find the relics himself. He had put so much of his personal wealth into the Onslow Syndicate he couldn't fund the next step – he ran out of money before he could implement the secret of turning off the floodwaters.

In an unfortunate end to his chapter of the Oak Island mystery, Simeon Lynds died destitute, his dream unfulfilled.

Two brief paragraphs at the end explained exactly how to block the floodwater tunnels. Brian got cold chills as he thought about men who had passed down these instructions from generation to generation - guidelines from the Templars engineers who built the pit in 1497, written down in code by Simeon Lynds in 1805. The directions were fairly simple; the hardest part would be finding two landmarks that were mentioned. They existed hundreds of years ago - Brian hoped they were still there today.

At two am while Brian slept a quiet ding on his phone signaled a CNN news alert. Brian slept through it. He didn't learn until the next morning that a crazed Dominic Cardinal Conti, muttering to himself in a Vatican holding cell, calmly removed the sash from around his clerical robe, knotted it around an overhead pipe, tested it for strength and prayed for forgiveness. Then he hanged himself.

CHAPTER FIFTY-NINE

In 1850 members of the Truro Company syndicate discovered the reason the Money Pit flooded. In Smith's Cove Truro workers built a rock seawall, a cofferdam, to hold back the tides. They wanted to see the floor of the cove and they found something incredible.

Simultaneously with construction of the Money Pit someone dammed the cove, drained it and removed a portion of the bed of the cove and the beach adjoining it. In an unbelievable engineering feat a solid layer of river stones covered with coconut fibers was placed on the sea floor. Where the area was above sea level the builders put sand over the French drain they had constructed.

Water flowed easily via gravity to the shoreline. But these early builders weren't finished. They built two water tunnels, each five hundred feet long, connecting to the

French drain at the shoreline. These two tunnels intersected the Money Pit itself at around 100 and 150 feet, respectively.

The result of this huge project was a simple booby-trap. When anyone attempted to excavate the Money Pit, things went fine until they removed dirt and rock at the hundred-foot level. When that happened a small portion of the wall would collapse into the shaft, driven by pressure from the seawater in the flood tunnel. If they somehow beat this trap another awaited them fifty feet down.

Since the boys had discovered the pit in 1795 none of the well-financed syndicates had managed to beat the ingenious, unbelievable obstacles created by the builders and engineers centuries earlier. Everyone wondered what group had the capability and the willingness to build this amazing storage pit on an uninhabited island in what is now Canada. And everyone wondered how long ago it was built.

Simeon Lynds had known the answers to both questions. The Templars had passed it down to him. Now Brian Sadler and Harold Mulhaney knew the answers too. In May 1497 the Knights Templars built the pit to hide the Most Holy Relics. They used complex engineering techniques and created a hiding place that held its secrets to this day.

Brian and Harold read the instructions from Simeon Lynds' diary a half dozen times. Leaving the crew to continue excavation of the Money Pit, they walked five hundred feet to the shore of Smith's Cove.

In the 1800s two large triangular stones were found between the Money Pit and the shoreline. No one knew if they were part of the puzzle or if they were merely natural rocks. Too large to move and with no known purpose, they fortunately remained in place. It took an hour to locate them in the tall grass and scrub, but Harold and Brian were successful. They knew from Simeon Lynds what had to happen next. It would be easier today than in 1497 when the flood tunnels were built.

Brian moved ten men and the bulldozer to the area where the triangular stones rested. The machine moved one of them and the workers dug underneath it. They found a narrow shaft about two feet wide, lined with timbers. Brian lowered a rope until he heard it hit water. He pulled it up - ten feet below one of the flood tunnels ran underground to the Money Pit.

The other triangular rock yielded identical results and another flood tunnel. They now knew exactly where the tunnels were located. Brian referred to the instructions Simeon Lynds had encoded. The workers felled small trees, removed their branches and crammed them tightly into each shaft like toothpicks in a holder. When the tree trunks rested on the floor of each flood tunnel and filled the vertical shafts the men added dirt and rock. The result was a plug that should stop the flow of water from Smith's Cove to the Money Pit. Shortly they'd find out if the Knights Templars instructions given to Simeon Lynds were true or false.

The Money Pit itself was over twelve feet in diameter. Brian's new plan was to remove enough fill to lower a man 150 feet into the pit to retrieve whatever was at the bottom. Up to now he hadn't started that part of the project because he was afraid of flooding at the hundred-foot level. Now he was confident that problem had been solved. They could be mere days away from discovering what the Most Holy Relics really were.

CHAPTER SIXTY

A young man in a Cooper Mini drove across the causeway from the mainland onto Oak Island. As soon as he was on the other side he encountered a burly guard with a holstered pistol and a leashed Rottweiler. The man stood in the middle of the narrow rutted road, blocking it. He held up his hand.

"What's your business, mister?"

"Good morning. I'm traveling in the area. I've read about Oak Island and wondered if I could look around. It seems a fascinating place."

The man guarding the road noticed the stranger spoke English with a distinct accent. But then half of Canada did that.

"You used to coming on people's private property without asking?"

The man in the Cooper responded pleasantly. "No sir, I'm not. I wasn't aware this is private property."

"You didn't happen to see the sign on the mainland, right before you drive across the causeway? It says 'No Trespassing.' Do you read English?" The man's demeanor was curt and tough but the traveler in the Cooper remained upbeat.

"I do, in fact. I saw the sign but hoped I would find someone like you with whom I could talk about seeing Oak Island."

"Well, we've had our talk. Turn your car around and get off the place."

The man did exactly that. He'd learned what he needed. The causeway was guarded, either by the owners of this half of the island or by Brian Sadler's crew. It didn't matter which.

At the Money Pit, excavation by hand was underway in earnest. By now the pit had been cleared out so deeply that heavy equipment couldn't be used any more. Brian's crew chief put every man to work digging in the hole, removing bucketsful of dirt or pumping air down the shaft. By the end of the day they were down nearly a hundred feet and the shaft was twelve feet in diameter. The work stopped here because a few feet further they should come to the place where boring indicated wooden chests and metal would be found. Brian had a hunch where this stuff came from; if they found anything he'd be able to see if he was right.

Tomorrow morning would tell the tale. Every other time in history someone had gotten to the hundred-foot level, the Money Pit had flooded. Brian hoped Simeon Lynds' instructions worked.

At two am a rowboat negotiated around the cofferdam Brian Sadler's crew had built and landed on the shore of Smith's Cove. Its occupant crept quietly toward the Money Pit, aided by a nearly full moon. He watched and listened closely for signs of a watchman.

Close to the pit itself a guard sat in a chair next to a dying fire. He was drinking coffee from a mug and the Rottweiler that had been at the causeway that afternoon lay next to him. A shotgun was leaned against a tree close by

The intruder stopped as he heard the dog's low growl. He retreated softly before the animal could announce his presence and rowed slowly back to shore. He had the information he needed. By day there was a guard at the causeway. At night the guard and the Rottweiler moved to the Money Pit.

CHAPTER SIXTY-ONE

There was jubilation at the site the next morning. The Money Pit was as dry as it had been the afternoon before. There had been no flooding – Lynds' directions to stop the flood tunnels had worked perfectly.

Brian was eager to discover the secret of Oak Island. He was pleased to see that Harold Mulhaney seemed excited too, at least as animated as the stodgy farmer could be.

Last evening at the Oak Island Inn Brian had made his nightly call to Nicole. He'd told her his hopes that the pit wouldn't flood and she said she hoped so too. She was fully comprehending now, asking questions and offering comments. She wasn't her old self yet, but she was a world better than she had been only a week ago when he had last seen her. After his ten-minute conversation with her Brian called Nicole's mother in Houston. They discussed Nicole's encouraging progress. They kept in touch every day by email and she promised to let Brian know if she learned anything new about Nicole.

This morning the crew was anxious to get started and work progressed well. Brian estimated they had two days of digging left before reaching the 150-foot level and what they assumed would be the bottom of the Money Pit. Today the crew in the shaft dug carefully until they came to an unusual platform – this one made of spruce instead of oak like all the others. They carefully removed the old logs and saw a deteriorated wooden chest below. Its lid had disintegrated and a thick layer of dirt caked everything. As the tunnels flooded long ago, mud had flowed upward, oozing over everything it touched. Once it dried anything there became encased in hard soil.

The workers used short picks to flake off the encrusted mud. Finally one of them gave a shout. "I've found gold!"

A bucket went down the hole on a rope and everyone heard a clunk as the man deposited what he'd found in it. Back at the surface Brian reached in the bucket and brought out a bracelet. It was filthy but there was no doubt it was made of gold.

"There's a hundred dollar bonus for each of you tonight!" Brian yelled. The enthused workers cheered. Down in the shaft two men knelt side-by-side and continued digging with bare hands and small picks.

"Coins! We've got gold coins!"

The workers on the surface went wild.

This was the most encouraging thing of all. Coins were dated and dates would help determine the earliest time the gold could have been buried.

The workers in the pit sent up a handful of mud-encrusted coins in the bucket. Brian and Harold dipped one or two in water and rubbed off the dirt. The gold coins had Spanish writing and were dated in the 1690s.

Although this wasn't the prize Brian Sadler sought, this discovery was significant even if nothing else was found. A horde of old Spanish coins would be worth a fortune to numismatists. More investigation would have to be done but Brian figured one of the pirate stories about Oak Island was true. His theory was that a privateer, quite possibly Blackbeard, came to Oak Island and used the Money Pit to hide his booty. Historians knew the pirate frequented this remote area in the early 1700s so the dates on the coins fit well.

As is the case for all archaeological activity in Nova Scotia, Brian's project had required a permit. He placed a call to the Office of Culture and Heritage Development and advised they had found treasure in the

Money Pit. He was told he could continue excavating. A governmental representative would arrive tomorrow from Halifax. An official called later with instructions on where to temporarily store the items from the pit for safekeeping.

By the end of the day the workmen had removed nearly two hundred gold coins and more than fifty pounds of various gold chains and bracelets. It was a small cache by comparison to other hordes discovered in the past, but Brian knew there were dozens of places along the remote coastline that pirates likely hid their loot. Whoever this pirate was, he hadn't put all his eggs in one basket.

When the workmen left the island at five, word spread quickly throughout the area that treasure had been found today. That evening Brian and Harold Mulhaney sat at the Oak Island Inn's busy bar having a celebratory drink. A crowd of locals packed the tavern, re-telling stories of the pirates who had roamed this area. Brian and Harold were instant celebrities; as new townspeople showed up the pair was pointed out at the bar.

The barkeep was as excited as the others about the treasure horde. He asked several questions and Brian gave him a summary of the day's events.

"How do you keep people from stealing the gold tonight?" the bartender asked. "Is it locked up somewhere? Or shouldn't I ask?"

Brian told him what they had done with the things they brought up from the Money Pit. He wanted to spread the word that the treasure wasn't on Oak Island any longer. They didn't need unauthorized visitors.

"The Cultural Office gave us instructions. We left a guard at the site tonight for security but there's no treasure left there. The sentinel's there just in case somebody gets nosy. The treasure itself was moved this afternoon to a bank in Lunenburg. It'll be safe there until the people from the government in Halifax arrive."

A young man sat at the bar near Brian and Harold, listening to the conversation like most of the other patrons in the tavern. He heard the bartender ask, "So are you through looking? Was gold what you came here to find?"

Brian's answer was cautious. "We don't know what's at the bottom of the Money Pit. We think something is, but no one knows what. So far we're the first to even reach the hundred-foot level without the shaft flooding. This find is a bonus – I would bet money it's pirate treasure – but I also bet whoever buried it didn't dig the Money Pit. He just borrowed the top half of it. I hope there's more to come. We're going all the way down."

"Is there more gold down there, you think?"

"Who knows? Everyone here's heard the tales about Shakespeare, aliens, crown jewels from fallen monarchies – all that stuff. After all this time nobody has a clue if anything's down there or what it might be. Maybe we can find out. By day after tomorrow if all goes well we may know a lot more."

The patron at the bar hadn't participated in the conversation. He hadn't even glanced toward Brian and Harold. He just nursed his beer. After the two left the tavern a half hour later the stranger paid his tab, walked to his Cooper Mini in the parking lot and drove away.

CHAPTER SIXTY-TWO

At eight pm Brian was in his room preparing for a shower. It had been an exciting, exhausting day. His cellphone rang and he was thrilled to see the caller's name displayed. Nicole. It was the first time she had called him since her wreck.

"Hey," he answered. "Is it you?"

"It's me," came the familiar voice. "This is the first phone call I've dialed myself. I remembered how to do everything, Brian." She started crying. Tears rolled down Brian's face too as he thought how far she'd come, but how difficult even the simplest tasks were to someone who was struggling to regain their cognitive skills.

"I'm proud of you, baby. You're really getting better fast."

"I miss you. I hope you come back soon. And I saw your picture on the news tonight."

That was a surprise. "You did? Are you sure?"

"Yep. You found a bunch of pirate treasure today. It made the national news."

With the entire area abuzz about Blackbeard's gold he wasn't surprised the networks had picked up the story. But no locals had contacted him for a comment. That was a little surprising.

"Did they interview anybody about the treasure?"

"There was a man on the newscast. I don't remember his name. He had on overalls and was older than you are. Some man from the government also talked."

Most likely they had spoken to Harold. That old guy was reclusive but he was getting his time in the spotlight tonight. He'd take a look at the Internet later and see what Harold had said.

"I'm hoping we can reach the bottom of the pit in the next two days. Then I can take a few days off and come to Dallas. I can't wait to see you."

After ending the call Brian watched the news story. He saw Harold Mulhaney expound on subjects from Edward Teach aka Blackbeard the pirate to what lay at the bottom of the pit. Brian held his breath as the interview continued. Harold was privy to most of the information Brian had learned about the Knights Templars and he hoped the old man hadn't given away anything that should be kept confidential.

And thankfully he hadn't. Mulhaney had a mysterious look on his face and a gleam in his eye as he responded to the reporter's questions. "Us locals have heard for years about what might be at the bottom of the Money Pit. Just today Mr. Sadler and I proved there's something valuable there, and we ain't even at the bottom yet. I think I know what's down there. It's old, it's rarer than anything on earth and it's priceless. That's all I'll tell ya." And he shut up, refusing to answer anything more.

Good for you, Harold.

CHAPTER SIXTY-THREE

The representative from the Cultural Office in Halifax was at the Money Pit by nine am. Brian gave him a tour and let him speak with the men who had discovered the gold in the shaft. His visit ate up ninety minutes of valuable time but it was unavoidable. The government of Nova Scotia had been extremely helpful throughout the entire process and today was no exception. The man thanked Brian for his cooperation and left to visit the bank in nearby Lunenburg, where the gold was stored.

Brian took Harold aside and congratulated him on a good interview. "You made national news in the States," he said.

Mulhaney just smiled. Brian almost laughed out loud. He had never seen Harold smile.

"And thanks for keeping the Templar information confidential."

"No problem, son. My daddy used to say you gotta learn when to talk and when to shut your mouth. That was one time I had talked enough."

With renewed vigor the crew went back to work in the pit. Excavation continued and by one pm they were at a hundred and fifty-four feet, stopped by a piece of concrete blocking the pit. This was the best sign yet. It was exactly what Brian had hoped for – the early syndicates reported a cement vault with some type of wood inside at this level. Up until now the excavators had run across nothing more than the platforms of logs every ten feet that were described by earlier diggers, but suddenly they were excited.

Brian stopped the work for the remainder of today. He explained to his men that there was a second flood tunnel just above the level where they were now. If that tunnel held during the night they could break through the concrete tomorrow and see what lay below. But if the Money Pit flooded it would be best not to have opened the concrete vault. If for some reason they couldn't easily remove the contents this afternoon, flooding tonight could destroy whatever was there. Better to wait for a new day and ensure the flood tunnel was properly dammed up.

Brian gave his men a pep talk, thanking them for their hard effort and encouraging them to be ready to achieve their goal tomorrow. He asked them to get a good night's sleep and meet him at the site at seven am, just after sunrise. If their luck held and the pit was dry, they would learn the secret tomorrow.

Brian told his crew chief and two other men to stay so they could plan the strategy for tomorrow. As they sat with cups of coffee ten feet from the fabled Money Pit, they discussed what lay ahead.

After a long afternoon when he returned to the Oak Island Inn he called Nicole and told her everything that had happened today. The excitement in his words was palpable as he explained the wonderful things that might be the Most Holy Relics. And she understood. She asked probing questions and mentioned things they'd discussed days earlier. He was more encouraged tonight than ever. She was on the way back. Not quite there yet, but definitely on the mend. He went to sleep a happy man in every way.

CHAPTER SIXTY-FOUR

The same rowboat landed on the beach at Smith's Cove at 3:30 am. The man from the tavern was dressed completely in black, his face covered by a ski mask. He carried a dart gun and on his belt was a silenced pistol in a holster. He had a small backpack. He walked toward the Money Pit, staying in the shadows and listening for any sound of the guard's presence.

Thirty feet from the excavation point he saw the guard smoking a cigarette. The man was sitting in a lawn chair facing the intruder. He held an iPad in his hands and was staring intently at its screen. The dog was nowhere to be seen.

The stranger moved quietly through the trees and brush until he was behind the sentry. He could hear the iPad now; the man was watching a movie. He moved to within five feet of the guard, raised his dart gun and fired. The guard toppled forward out of his chair onto the ground. The trespasser had ten minutes before the man would awake from the light anesthetic the dart had contained. That was more than enough time. He tied the guard securely to a tree and gagged him.

Confirming no one else was around, the stranger opened his pack and removed two sticks of dynamite and a cap. With precision learned from years of practice he prepared everything and dropped the sticks into the Money Pit. A timer would detonate the dynamite in half an hour. The explosives were now lying a hundred and fifty feet down the shaft, on top of the concrete vault below. The guard would be safe from the detonation. But the bottom of the pit would be ruined.

The water was calm as he rowed slowly back to the mainland, docked the boat right back where he had stolen it, got in his Cooper Mini and drove to Halifax.

CHAPTER SIXTY-FIVE

At six am Harold Mulhaney sat in his pickup outside the Oak Island Inn. The sun would rise in twenty minutes – he and Brian wanted to be at the pit ahead of the work crew who were coming at seven.

They crossed the causeway onto the island and drove to the Money Pit. As he got out of Harold's truck Brian called out to the guard but got no response. The men looked around and heard a noise. The guard struggled against his ropes and gag, still securely bound to a large oak tree.

They cut him loose. "This is exactly what I was afraid was going to happen," Brian said after the man told him what had transpired during the night.

"When I woke up from being drugged I was tied to this tree. In a few minutes I heard a loud 'whump' and saw smoke come out of the Money Pit. I never knew what hit me, but I think someone sabotaged the project. I let you down. I've let the whole crew down, and everybody in this area who thought they'd find out today what's in the pit."

Brian comforted the man. "Things are never as bad as they seem," he said, more optimistically than the guard would have expected for having lost the prize he came for.

The guard asked, "Do you think we still can go down into the shaft and open the concrete vault?"

Brian and Harold walked over to the Money Pit. Seawater stood just thirty feet below them. One or both of the flood tunnels had burst and the pit had filled with water up to sea level, just like every time before. There would be no searching down in the pit.

CHAPTER SIXTY-SIX

Oak Island/Dallas

By seven the entire crew had assembled at the site. Brian explained to them what had happened. Word had obviously gotten around the area the afternoon before. Plenty of people knew they had reached the bottom of the Money Pit and were preparing to open the concrete vault the next morning.

Someone had other plans – he either wanted to sabotage the entire project or he intended to open the vault and steal its contents. If it were the latter he would have needed more help. Brian was inclined to believe someone had decided to stop his search for the Most Holy Relics. The perpetrator of this act had put explosives in the shaft. Now the pit was flooded and there was no way to know how much damage had been done at the bottom.

To say the men were disappointed would be a vast understatement. They talked quietly among themselves, their eagerness to begin this exciting day quashed by the grim news of defeat.

The work crew was sent home. Brian and Harold went back to his cabin near the Money Pit, loaded a small crate into the back seat of the pickup and drove to the Oak Island Inn. Brian's suitcase was packed and ready to go. He threw it and his backpack into the truck bed and they drove to Halifax.

At the Office of Culture and Heritage Development they met with the representative who had come to the pit two days earlier. They told him everything that had occurred since his visit to the site and handed over the crate they'd brought. The official was particularly concerned to hear about the assault on their guard and the bombing of the Money Pit. The official promised a governmental inquiry and said he would alert the Royal Canadian Mounted Police. The man assured Harold and Brian the Mounties would be on site immediately to open an investigation. He thanked Brian for his efforts and for the forthright and efficient way he had conducted the entire mission in Nova Scotia.

Brian and Harold Mulhaney had a cup of coffee at a Starbucks near the Halifax airport. They talked about the amazing events that had transpired in the last week. They would keep in close touch; there was a lot left to do on the Oak Island project before they were finished. Harold would represent Brian on the scene from now on.

He caught the American flight to Philadelphia, made a connection and was in Dallas that evening. He hadn't told Nicole he was coming and the doorman at her condo agreed to let him go upstairs unannounced.

Brian rang her doorbell and heard Shelia's voice. "Who is it?"

"Pizza delivery for Nicole Farber," he said loudly.

The caregiver responded, "We didn't order a . . ."

Then Brian heard the sound of banging – someone was frantically trying to open the door. Finally the lock turned and the door opened wide. Nicole was standing there sobbing, a huge grin on her face. She jumped into his arms. Neither of them talked for what seemed like forever. Then she said, "You're a bastard for not telling me you were coming back."

"I wanted to surprise you."

"Well, you did. Get in here. Shelia, I'm good for tonight and hopefully longer if I can talk this man into sticking around Dallas for a few days. You're off for now. I'll call you tomorrow about when I'll need you back. Oh, forgive me! Brian, you remember Shelia.

She's the best and she's been a working miracles for me!"

The caregiver laughed at her exuberance. "You're like a little girl, baby. Don't you hurt yourself! Be careful with her, Brian. She's mended well but she's still fragile."

Nicole smiled and hugged Brian tightly. "Don't you worry! I've been waiting for this guy for a long, long time. He's the best medicine for my recovery. He takes good care of me!"

CHAPTER SIXTY-SEVEN

A joint press conference was set for the afternoon after Brian returned to Dallas. Half of the broadcast was from the studios of CTV Halifax where the Minister of Culture and Heritage sat before the camera alongside Harold Mulhaney. The other half featured Brian in the Victory Park studio of the ABC affiliate, Channel 8 in Dallas.

The press conference aired at 5:45 pm Dallas time, coinciding exactly with ABC's national news. A half hour before the conference a release was distributed to the international press. The headline read "Ancient Box Discovered in Nova Scotia; Money Pit Gives Up its Secret At Last." Social media sites like Twitter were going crazy – this broadcast was certain to break records for viewership given its exciting news.

At the appointed time the Canadian reporter welcomed viewers to the show and introduced the Minister and Harold Mulhaney. "Mr. Mulhaney participated in the discovery of an ancient stone box over a hundred and fifty feet below the surface. The box was in a shaft built centuries ago by the Knights Templars," the reporter announced.

The feed switched to Dallas where Brian was introduced and his background as a renowned gallery owner and wealthy amateur archaeologist was explained. Video footage of Oak Island and the Money Pit ran as Brian described the area and the background of what brought him to the fabled place. As the camera came back to him, he used a large poster to explain the Money Pit. It pictured the shaft in cross-section from the surface to its bottom. The flood tunnels were shown, as were the ten-foot platforms of timber and the area where the gold coins and jewelry had been found.

"Mr. Sadler, please explain to our audience how your foresight one afternoon a few days ago thwarted an attempt to sabotage your project."

Brian explained what had happened the afternoon the work crew reached the concrete barrier at 154 feet. He had stopped the work for that day, retaining three senior members of his crew on site to strategize.

One day previously the men had discovered what appeared to be pirate treasure. By dusk word had spread like wildfire among the people living nearby. With a crew of twenty men it was impossible to keep a secret and Brian knew the townspeople would quickly hear that today they'd reached the bottom. Tomorrow Brian's crew would open the concrete vault. This would be major news and everyone would be eager to learn what was up on Oak Island.

By 1:30 pm Brian and Harold had made a decision. Instead of waiting to ensure the shaft didn't flood during the night, they would take a major chance. Clandestinely the three workers would descend into the shaft and cut open the concrete vault. They had several hours of daylight left, hopefully enough to remove whatever was in the vault itself. If they couldn't remove it the five of them would personally guard the site all night and pray to God the shaft didn/t flood before they could extricate whatever was there.

While Brian and Harold waited at the surface the three crewmen labored in the shaft. The concrete had held remarkably well for hundreds of years, withstanding flooding of the shaft numerous times. A tiny hole was the only evidence of test boring in the early 1800s, and it had long ago plugged itself up with mud. The men used picks and at 2:40 pm they broke through the top of the concrete.

Brian explained for the television audience that the vault itself was a cube four feet on each side. Tightly fitting inside it was a wooden box, the top of which came off easily. Nestled inside the box, protected on all side by cedar shavings, was a stone chest with ancient inscriptions and carvings of a fish on it. It was roughly a foot long, eight inches deep and ten inches tall.

The three men who had opened the vault were sent home with hefty bonuses and a promise of secrecy until the government could be informed of the discovery.

A picture of the box flashed on the screen. It was an ossuary with two parts: a lid and a base. It would have held the bones of a deceased person. In ancient times ossuaries were used by many cultures; they would usually be placed in niches inside caves.

Before the news broadcast Brian Sadler had asked an expert to examine the ossuary. He said it was Jewish, made during the period known as the Second Temple, its style placing it roughly between 100 BC and 100 AD. The carvings on the box were faint and difficult to make out. Further tests would determine if the marks were words like those found on other Jewish ossuaries.

Switching back to the Canadian studio, the Minister of Culture explained what happened late that evening. Brian Sadler and Harold Mulhaney had placed a guard at the site. A police investigation revealed that an intruder landed a boat in Smith's Cove, walked to the Money Pit and tranquilized the guard. He was tied up and gagged and the man dynamited the shaft, causing the flood tunnels to flow thousands of gallons of seawater into it.

For the sake of archaeology, the Minister continued, it was fortunate that Brian Sadler had decided to remove the artifact in secret. The ossuary was now in an undisclosed location monitored by the government of Nova Scotia, awaiting further examination both in Canada and the United States.

The press conference ended with the Minister's assurance of cooperation going forward. "We will engage in a close working relationship with Mr. Sadler and Mr. Mulhaney as we learn more about this incredible discovery."

CHAPTER SIXTY-EIGHT

Dallas

The day after the press conference Brian received a call from the Archdiocese of New York. He knew the Archbishop; they had met several times as a result of Brian's involvement in high-profile antiquities and the Church's interest in many of his discoveries. The Church was important to Brian's work and played a major part in some of the important pieces he handled.

The Archbishop told Brian that the Pope was interested in the ossuary that had been found, especially in the ancient inscription that appeared on it. He asked if the pontiff could be informed ahead of the general public once Brian knew more about it.

"Excellency, although I want to be cooperative I can't promise that. The decision's not just mine to make. I have a partner, Harold Mulhaney, and the Minister of Culture in Halifax has a voice in this project too. But I'll see what I can do; shall I let you know what I find out?"

The Archbishop responded affirmatively and Brian asked, "If I may ask, why is the Pope personally interested in the box and its inscription?"

The answer was sprinkled with a little humor. "Sometimes his Holiness doesn't let me in on his thinking. I'd speculate that he's interested in whose bones are in the ossuary, assuming you ultimately find there are bones at all."

Brian said he would try to let the Archbishop have advance notice of any discovery but couldn't promise anything.

The ossuary hadn't been opened. The piece was so old and potentially so fragile that it had to be handled extremely carefully, and only by experts. Brian had conferred with the Minister of Culture and reached an agreement to bring it to New York where experts at the American Museum of Natural History could perform a close examination in every respect. It would be flown from Halifax the following week and Brian would be at the Museum when it arrived.

It could take several days, maybe even weeks, before definitive information was known about the box. No one knew if this ossuary held bones, as one might expect, or if something else was in it. Brian knew the Templars called this the Most Holy *Relics* – plural. So it wasn't just the box itself. It was what was inside. And the Pope undoubtedly knew about the Most Holy Relics from the research of Cardinal Conti.

He thought about what scenario would make the Pope the most concerned. If the ossuary was being used for its original purpose, then it held bones.

Brian was well aware of the furor that had arisen in the academic community a decade ago about another ossuary. A prominent Israeli collector turned up a first century bone box with the inscription "James, son of Joseph, brother of Jesus." A tremendous battle had occurred between the Israeli Antiquities Authority and the collector, including a seven-year court battle to determine if the inscription was forged much later than the first century.

The collector ultimately was found not guilty of forgery but the judge's acquittal was accompanied by a caveat that he was not ruling on the authenticity of the inscription or that it was two thousand years old. To this day many scholars believed that ossuary proved the historical existence of Jesus for the first time ever. Many others labeled it a complete hoax.

Brian considered what he had learned. Taking the Knights Templars manuscripts at face value, this latest ossuary was the repository for the Most Holy Relics. They had been in the care of the Templars since 1129, they were in Ephesus and in the late 1400s Templars moved them overland to Bruges, Belgium, then by boat to Bristol and across the sea to a new place where a hiding place was constructed.

Giovanni Caboto, or John Cabot, was the Voyager who carried the Templars and the Most Holy Relics. The latter built a pit and Cabot "involved himself in things best left to our brothers." Much of his crew died of disease or food poisoning at the hands of the Templars. The rest, including Cabot, were "dispatched to their eternal fates" and the Cabot expedition of 1498 was never heard from again.

One coded Templars sheet was nothing but Bible verses – the story of Jesus on the cross entrusting his mother to his disciple John, and the verses about Jesus' burial and resurrection.

Could the bones be those of Jesus himself? How could that be possible? Brian had been a regular churchgoer since he was a baby and he knew that Jesus Christ had risen from the dead and ascended into Heaven. No bones. No reburial. Period. End of story.

Brian was certain this was what concerned the Pope. He was afraid the ossuary contained the bones of Jesus along with an inscription describing them. If Jesus hadn't in fact risen from the dead, John, the self-proclaimed "disciple whom Jesus loved," would have been the natural choice to gather his bones. It was generally accepted by Bible scholars that John and the Virgin Mary went to Ephesus, where John continued his preaching and evangelizing, and Mary eventually died. There was even a shrine to her in Ephesus.

What if John had carried Jesus' bones along when he and Mary went to Ephesus? Had he buried the bones there and did Knights Templars protect them over the centuries, keeping the secret from the world?

If all that were true, Brian couldn't imagine the earth-shattering consequences. Non-believers would have a field day. If you couldn't believe that part of the Bible, what parts could you believe? It would be catastrophic in its impact on religion.

CHAPTER SIXTY-NINE

Toronto

"This is a collect call from the Metropolitan Correctional Center in New York. This call is from . . ." - there was a pause - "John Spedino." The recording continued. "To accept all calls from this number press *13. To decline all calls from this number press *15."

The man in Toronto who had destroyed the Money Pit pressed *13 on his single-use cellphone and immediately heard the godfather launch into a rage.

"Good job you did for me," Spedino said sarcastically. "I guess you've seen the news. Brian Sadler found an ossuary in the Money Pit. Wasn't that pit exactly what I paid you to take care of?"

"I did the job exactly as you directed. It was done as expeditiously as possible. If the timing was off that's out of my hands."

"Out of your hands?" the mobster exploded. "You idiot. You were supposed to make sure . . ."

The man disconnected. He wasn't interested in the ravings of a has-been who couldn't even hurt him with those incriminating words. He'd been paid in advance so he and the former mobster were square. And Spedino didn't know where he lived, so that made things even better.

He tossed the phone in a trash bin as he walked down the street. John Spedino had been a powerful man once, the Canadian knew. But his upcoming trial and the massive evidence against him made Spedino completely powerless to retaliate. The godfather had no way to find the man, much less hurt him.

CHAPTER SEVENTY
New York

Two weeks later the examination of the ossuary was complete. Antiquities experts at the museum in New York opened the box, found decaying bones and immediately moved to preserve them from the air they hadn't known in two thousand years. They would ultimately be carbon-dated to the first century AD.

Working alongside the museum staff were two linguists from the Hebrew University in Jerusalem. They took rubbings of the faint inscriptions on the outside of the ossuary and made them legible using computer-generated enhancements. Some words were missing a few strokes here and there due to the extreme age of the box itself.

The Minister of Culture and Harold Mulhaney agreed to allow Brian a courtesy call to the Archbishop in New York.

The cleric took Brian's call immediately. "What did you find out?"

"Excellency, I hate to be flippant about something the Pope considers so serious, but I think this is the proverbial good news-bad news call. I believe the good news for the pontiff is going to be this. If the inscription can be believed, the bones in the box aren't those of Jesus Christ."

There was a faint sigh of relief on the other end of the conversation. "And . . .?"

"I did a bit of research on the Catholic faith before I made this call, Excellency. I know you believe in Mary's assumption to Heaven - God took the Virgin Mary's body to Heaven after her death. So I think the inscription on the ossuary may be the bad news. The inscription says

Mary, blessed Virgin, mother of Jesus, wife of Joseph

"Archbishop, the Most Holy Relics guarded by the Templars for centuries are the bones of the Virgin Mary."

CHAPTER SEVENTY-ONE

Dallas – Six months later

The opening of Bijan Rarities' new gallery in Dallas was a major event. The beautiful store in the Crescent Court was just blocks away from Nicole's condo in the Ritz-Carlton. High-profile clients and celebrities joined news crews from Texas and the nation to toast Brian Sadler's glitzy showroom in his home state of Texas.

The Government of Nova Scotia had quickly reached an agreement with Brian and Harold Mulhaney on the division of the gold coins and jewelry. There were a number of laws on the books governing antiquities and treasure, given discoveries in the past and the province's history as a hangout for pirates. In the gallery a side room was dedicated solely to the gold and it was the must-see highlight of the evening. The room was named the Collette Conning Hall in memory of Brian's valued assistant in the

New York. The area had displays of the exquisite Spanish coins and jewelry they'd found, all of which certainly had been buried by pirates. A diorama with thrilling tales of the buccaneers' exploits entertained the visitors.

The disposition of the bones and ossuary were more challenging. The artifacts obviously couldn't be divided three ways so attorneys for Brian and Harold were negotiating with the provincial government toward a solution. Brian had offered to donate the half of Oak Island he had purchased from Harold Mulhaney to the government for a national park. Local and provincial officials already were planning a museum surrounding the Money Pit itself. It was sure to be a major tourist draw for this otherwise quiet locale. For now the bones and ossuary remained in the American Museum of Natural History's sealed chamber for protection.

Since he couldn't show the ossuary itself Brian did the next best thing – there were videos and slideshows showing the excavation and the discovery. These ran on huge screens hanging from the ceiling along the main showroom walls. Photos of the artifacts also lined the walls. Everyone loved the presentation, especially the press who bombarded Brian with interviews as much as he'd allow. He gave them time but he had to circulate among his guests – in this crowd were people who frequented the top social scenes of New York, London or Dubai.

Along with the celebrities and clients were two people who had become very close to Brian Sadler – Carissa Borland and Harold Mulhaney. He and Nicole would meet them tomorrow for lunch once things settled down after tonight's gala event.

This was Nicole's first appearance in public since her accident. Outwardly she looked as beautiful and poised as she had always been. Inside she was still mending both mentally and physically, but her physician assured Brian she'd be fine for an hour or so. She sat in a chair and greeted dozens of friends she knew through her legal practice and social activities in this metropolitan city. Shelia stood close by and took her home once she began to tire.

The party wrapped up and by eleven Brian was with Nicole. Back at her condo he changed into sweats and met her on the patio for a nightcap. He told her how he'd missed the glittering skyline of downtown Dallas. He sipped Pyrat Rum with a cube of ice; she drank Perrier from a bottle.

Nicole held his hand. "I'm glad we agreed on our future. I'm so glad you're willing to be here with me, even if I'm not the person I once was. I promise I'll try. I'll try so hard to get back to normal."

Brian smiled and held her hand. "You're great, sweetie. If nothing ever changes you're just perfect right now. I want you just the way you are, and I'll take care of you."

There were a number of things that still weren't right for her. Nicole couldn't drive – her reaction time was slow and her intuition and concentration were lacking. But she was wealthy – she could hire a driver if she needed. The best news was that her doctors said she'd likely improve over time.

She also wasn't ready to go back to work. Randall Carter offered to hold a place for her at the law firm indefinitely, but after a long discussion with Brian she decided what would come next. She resigned her high-stress, long-hours job and would eventually open a solo practice. It would be totally opposite from the crazy world of Randall and Carter, but at this point it sounded wonderful. And there was no hurry. She could take her time, get better and spend valuable moments with Brian right here.

He had agreed to relocate to Dallas and move in with Nicole. The gallery here would be the flagship and they would split their time between Texas and London. As he traveled making acquisitions and seeing clients she would be free to go with him. Shelia would travel with them as long as Nicole required assistance. She'd made it clear that was fine with her.

Nicole yawned and stretched. Brian smiled at her. "I know you're tired, baby. Let's go to bed."

She turned out the light and snuggled with him. He reached to the nightstand then turned to her and took her hand in the darkness.

"Oh yeah, something I forgot," he said as he placed a small box into her palm.

"Will you marry me?"

Made in the USA
San Bernardino, CA
16 November 2015